Twice in

Twice in a Lifetime

Helga Jensen

hera

First published in the United Kingdom in 2021 by Hera Books

This edition published in the United Kingdom in 2022 by

Hera Books
Unit 9 (Canelo), 5th Floor
Cargo Works, 1–2 Hatfields
London, SE1 9PG
United Kingdom

A CIP catalogue record for this book is available from the British Library.

Print ISBN 978 1 80032 782 5
Ebook ISBN 978 1 912973 59 0

This book is a work of fiction. Names, characters, businesses, organizations, places and events are either the product of the author's imagination or are used fictitiously. Any resemblance to actual persons, living or dead, events or locales is entirely coincidental.

Look for more great books at www.herabooks.com

Printed and bound in Great Britain by Clays Ltd, Elcograf S.p.A.

To James
Dream Big

Prologue

When I discovered that my husband had been having an affair for the past year with Tanja Tart (she only added the 'J' in there for effect, by the way), there were three options:

1. I could cut holes in every pair of Richard's designer jeans, and pull Tanja Tart's hair extensions out one by one whilst hoping that the glue was firmly attached to her scalp.

2. Sell any of Richard's leftover belongings on eBay, along with a story detailing his indiscretions, in the hope that people would feel sorry for me. Who knows, someone might bid millions for his sheer and utter crap, including the racing bike and those stupid Lycra cycling shorts that he started wearing on his forty-fifth birthday.

3. Or, move on graciously, even if it means gobbling enough Nutella to bring on a nut allergy, drinking Pinot Grigio through an eco-friendly straw and a teeny dabble with Botox. There is also a rather handsome New Yorker in there somewhere too.

Naturally, I chose number 3. After all, you should always choose the route in which Pinot Grigio and Nutella are involved.

Chapter 1

A cottage in Laugharne, west Wales – D-Day

It's a beautiful, warm summer's morning outside, but inside my heart feels bitterly cold.

As I look at the decree absolute that has just landed on my doormat, I realise that my life has fallen apart. Not even a soothing cup of tea can make things better; vodka would be so much more appropriate right now. In fact, I believe you should be sent a complimentary bottle of Absolut with every decree absolute.

> *Free bottle of wine/vodka/gin (state your preference) with every decree absolute.*

I would definitely use that as a marketing technique if I were a lawyer; after all, they charge enough.

Even this envelope that I am staring at most probably cost enough to save part of the rainforest. Then there's the stamp and the piece of paper inside. I am pretty sure they were all invoiced at an enormous profit, one that presumably bought the partner's wife a new Jaguar.

Of course, I would have preferred a new Jaguar, or to spend the £250 an hour in Dolce & Gabbana on their latest collection and not at the law firm Thomas and Smith, but life doesn't always turn out the way you planned. If it had, then I would be lounging in a villa in Mustique beside a sizzling hot Red Arrows pilot, with big strong arms, drinking Cristal and chatting to some celebrity or other. No, forget the celebrities, all I need are those big strong arms. A hug would make things so much better right now.

Sadly, there is no hug, or *cwtch* as we like to say in Wales, and I am not in Mustique, not even close. I am, instead, sat in my rather bijou kitchen, eyeing up the dish cloth that needs to be thrown out and wondering how many germs are currently breeding on it. Apparently, it is 200,000 times dirtier than my toilet seat – I googled.

Funny what you do to procrastinate when there are divorce papers in front of you. Today feels so final and, even though I knew this day would come, I still feel unprepared.

The envelope won't wait for me much longer, though, and I have no choice but to tear it open. I place it to one side where it lies discarded and of no importance. Ironic, as that is actually how I would describe the way I feel about myself right now.

My eyes scan across the official letter with its angry-looking big red stamp.

Between Amelia Simpson and Richard Simpson

Between the petitioner and the respondent be dissolved by reason that since the celebration thereof said respondent had been guilty of adultery...

I don't read the rest of it. There really is no need. I know what happened. Tanja Tart looked my husband up on Facebook and the rest, as they say, is history.

You see, Tanja Tart was in university with Dick. I try not to call him Richard any longer. There is only one word for him and I feel that sums it up. Not that I am bitter, or anything.

It all started out innocently enough.

> OMG! Richard, I found you on Facebook

or something like that.

This was promptly followed by some photos that she 'conveniently' found of the two of them. I should have known then that it wouldn't take long before he got carried away. Dick was always on Friends Reunited when it was launched all those years ago. He would spend hours being nostalgic about his past. What is it about middle-aged men and reminiscing? They look back at the past with rose-tinted spectacles – that are probably bifocal by now – and it takes them right back to their twenties. Suddenly they don't have kids and revert to a time when they had a girlfriend with perky boobs and no cellulite.

Over the past few months, I have found it difficult to believe that a midlife crisis and a woman who puts a silent J in her name, just to be pretentious, could result in the end of a fifteen-year marriage and all the history that we shared. Sadly, however, a couple of messages on Facebook and Dick was right back in university, although he seemed to forget the bit about his student accommodation and the fact that he had to live on noodles for four years. Instead, he was taken back to a time when he was there with Tanja, perusing art galleries and drinking pints in the Student Union bar while she supped on Babycham.

Even though it cannot be denied that Dick could be a cantankerous little shit on many occasions, my heart died a little when I read the messages one year, seven months, thirteen days and twenty-one hours ago. I wasn't snooping when I discovered them; he had left his messages on the desktop for all to see. I had only popped on the computer to check the weather for our day out in Tenby the next day. I assume he wanted to be found out, and naturally that was the end of the Tenby trip that the boys and I had been so excited about.

The knot in my stomach grew bigger as I read the exchange in front of me and the shock began to sink in. Yet I also couldn't stop myself from reading further.

> Awww, Richard, it's so amazeballs chatting to you after all this time! XXXX

Who says amazeballs over the age of twenty-one?

> Remember that night in Savannah's and you spilt red wine all down your shirt. The moment you took it off and... LOL X

I most certainly wasn't laughing out loud when I came across Dick's reply.

> How can I ever forget? Want to meet up and you can tell me whether I still have abs or a dad bod?

It was even followed with a winking bloody emoji.

As their relationship grew closer, the emojis developed into hearts! I even spotted an eggplant and can only presume Dick was considering the commitment of an allotment with Tanja at that point.

I confronted him as soon as he returned from the golf course and a look of relief washed over his face. It was as though it was all my fault that he had to lead a double life. There was no question of reconciliation. He packed his bags and left for Tanja's immediately, whilst the life I knew came tumbling down in an instant. It seems harder for the one left behind who was oblivious to it all; I suppose he had more time to prepare.

On a positive note, though, I don't ever have to look at Dick's unforgiving, far too clingy, cycling shorts ever again. Those are now Tanja's problem.

With that thought in mind, I sign the paperwork that I have dreaded so much.

'There, you're welcome to him, Tanja Tart,' I say a little too loudly.

'What's that, Mummy?' shouts Jasper.

'Oh, sorry, munchkins, Mummy's talking to herself.'

I'm giving Jasper the hug I need so badly when Rupert appears from his room.

'Stop being so loud. I'm trying to build a castle on *Minecraft*. It's very important.' He gives me a scornful look and walks back inside.

It is hard to believe they are twins sometimes; they are both so different. Jasper has mousy brown hair and Rupert is fairer. Jasper loves to wear crocs and collects little flags to pop into the holes, whilst Rupert prefers his smart trainers. They might share a love of computer games and the same eating habits, but that is about all. When we went to the local bonfire event last year, their differences were obvious, even to strangers. Jasper became upset that a little girl was crying as she wanted his candy-floss. He is such a sweetie that he handed her the candy-floss that he was about to tuck into. The toddler's mum looked at me in horror when Rupert shouted, 'Oi, give that back. That cost £2!' and grabbed it back from her. He is so similar to his dad it can be scary.

And now, apart from some dust-layered crystal wine glasses, these gorgeous boys, with their funny little personalities, are the only thing left to remind me of my marriage. I am so thankful for them. I squeeze Jasper a little tighter than normal once again and give him a proper *cwtch*, while mentally thanking Dick for the wonderful boys we have. I might hate him right now, but there were good moments sometimes. He also helped create the most utterly precious boys in the world too, and they miss having him at home. I must remember that the boys still love their dad, even though their mother feels like punching him.

Yes, I am feeling positive. I therefore promise that I will never punch Dick in the face or pull Tanja Tart's hair extensions out. Maybe I will even stop calling her that. No, that is going a bit far – she shall always remain as Tanja Tart.

Despite the name-calling (after all, everyone needs a bit of fun in their life), I have decided there shall be no more tears, not even a hint of bitterness. I will handle this divorce with dignity, but only if I can find that Nutella jar at the back of the cupboard.

Chapter 2

'Right, let's log on to *Plenty of Sharks Out There*,' says Sian enthusiastically.

She glances over at me from the laptop with the same mischievous look she has given me ever since we were in the first year of the comprehensive together, when we bonded over the heinous PE teacher, Mrs Jones. We still swear it was all her fault the school made us wear those humiliating navy nylon shorts. I am beginning to wonder if this is where my fear of cycling shorts stems from.

'Wait, let me google something first, Sian,' I insist.

'No, I won't waste a moment longer. I'm finding you a date. It'll take your mind off Dick. It must be at least six months since Tanja moved in with him. Yet here you are still pining. Come on, you must realise it's time to move on,' says Sian sternly.

Her words take me back. I really don't need reminding that Tanja Tart sold her house in Cardiff six months ago to move in with my husband. Apparently, she made a huge profit, just to add to the insult.

'Look, Sian, I don't want to join a dating site; it's the last thing on my mind. My heart is irretrievably broken. I have my boys, my wine and my chocolate. It's much

8

safer to stick to those. Anyway, what more does a woman possibly need?'

Speaking of chocolate, I wonder if there are any Creme Eggs left in the shops. I think the Spar down the road usually has them at strange times of year. I could totally devour a Creme Egg right now.

'Amelia, anyone can see how lonely you are. You do realise you're substituting chocolate for a man, don't you?'

'I don't want a man in my life. Not everyone needs a man. You don't have one.' I immediately regret the last bit. I should never have said that.

'Look, what I mean is plenty of women are single and are happy on their own. Besides, the ink isn't even dry on my divorce papers. I only signed them yesterday,' I argue. 'Anyway, give me the laptop, I've been thinking. I want to google something. I want to see if a phobia of cycling shorts exists.'

Sian looks at me incredulously and bursts out laughing.

As I key in 'fear of cycling', immediately the search engine finishes the sentence off for me. 'Fear of cycling... shorts.' Ha, I knew I wasn't the only one who had ever googled such a thing.

Okay, so it doesn't say there is a common fear of cycling shorts, as such, but there is vestiphobia, which is a fear of clothing. No, I definitely do not have a fear of clothing. I love Mango too much. There is cyclophobia, which is a fear of bicycles. I suppose I am somewhere in between.

Sian snatches the laptop off me and types something in.

'There, that's what you have. Sarmassophobia!'

'What? Am I going to die?'

'No, but you may die a lonely old woman surrounded by chocolate wrappers if you don't do something about it.'

'Don't be so silly,' I respond.

I unwrap my chocolate mini roll as Sian turns the screen towards me. 'Read it!' she demands.

I read the first line, wondering if sarmassophobia has anything to do with the liver; my alcohol intake has been rather bad since I found out about Tanja Tart.

'A fear of dating is a very real phobia,' it succinctly explains.

'Oh my god, so it's nothing to do with my liver then?'

'Amelia! Stop being such a hypochondriac. Shall we add that to your list of phobias?'

'Oh, Sian. You said so yourself, being scared of dating is a real phobia. It's hardly surprising after being with one person for so long, surely you get that? You know I always had a fear of heights, squirrels, cyclists… clowns. This just means I now have one more phobia,' I say.

'Well, then you have to face your fears. I'm going to find you a date. I'll deal with your squirrel phobia another time. Now, let's get back to *Plenty of Sharks Out There*.'

Her familiar happy face has been replaced by a look that tells me she is on a serious mission and I will not be getting out of this.

Sian begins my registration, entering my name, which is followed by my age. I will admit, we agreed to take a few years off. I am sure guys lie all the time on there. One of the men I saw lurking on Sian's account most definitely wasn't 5 foot 10, and he did not look remotely like a hedge fund manager. Not that you can really tell, of course, and I don't mean to stereotype, or anything, but there is usually a Hermès tie involved somewhere.

Unfortunately, Sian is no stranger to dating sites. She has been single for the past three years, ever since her husband, Jack, was killed in a freak accident involving an inflatable sumo wrestling costume. It was such a shock when it happened, and Sian still refuses to discuss it. Instead, she makes a joke about everything and, if you didn't know her, you would never know about the horrific accident involving the love of her life. It broke her heart, and I often wonder if she will ever truly get over it. I stayed with her for the first three nights after the accident to make sure that she at least had sips of water. Dick was very good at the time and happily looked after the boys. He told me to stay with Sian as long as it took to get her eating properly. I was so relieved to have such an understanding husband, but now I wonder if he just wanted me out of the house.

Sian and I no longer discuss Jack's accident. She would occasionally mention it after it first happened, but it's not something that she likes to discuss.

Since Jack died, I have noticed that Sian can't talk about anything remotely morbid or sad. She can't even watch *Springwatch* in case a weasel gets stuck in a log or a baby wood mouse gets captured by a murderous cat.

Although she is familiar with *Plenty of Sharks Out There*, Sian hasn't been on that many dates, but I think she secretly enjoys perusing the site and looks through it in much the same way that she used to look at her mother's Freemans catalogue when we were teenagers. I don't remind her, but I know full well that she used to turn to the pages of the men in their underpants first.

I try to take my mind off this memory by reading Sian's description of me. I am intrigued and slightly excited to see how she will describe me.

> Undersexed mum is looking for hot passionate man for steamy sex sessions.
>
> Don't be shy, please apply.

'Get that off, Sian! That's horrible,' I say as I almost choke on my cold cup of tea.

'JOKE. Okay, how's this?'

She quickly types away, and I watch the screen in front of me, still finding it hard to digest the fact that I am about to go live on a dating site. This is not what I ever imagined I would be doing at this point in my life. I am forty-eight years old. I wanted to grow old with my lovely family, not go on dates with strangers making small talk and trying to rebuild a new life. I can't imagine going on a date. Will I be one of those women who talks bitterly about her ex all night? Perhaps.

The screen lights up with the description of the new me. The reluctant divorcee.

> Recently divorced, mum of twins, with brown hair and green eyes is looking for a loving relationship. I am tall and slim. (Okay that bit is a lie.) 42 years old. (Shush). Contact me if you like nice walks, good food and lots of wine.

I am not sure about the 'lots of wine' part. Perhaps it is a little soon to introduce that bit. As I read through my dating profile with my photograph staring straight back at me, I freak out slightly. I hope nobody answers. The thought of a date with a stranger terrifies me. Maybe it would be nice to have someone who could unscrew the lid off my Marks & Spencer's strawberry jam when it is stuck, but that's about all I could use a man for right now. My plumbing is a bit dodgy too, I suppose. I am embarrassed to admit that I am not quite yet a strong, independent woman and am still used to Dick taking charge of such jobs.

'Ooh, I don't know, Sian,' I protest once again. 'I think this is a really bad idea. I mean what if the boys saw my photo?'

'Well, if your boys are looking through *Plenty of Sharks Out There*, then something's wrong somewhere. It'll be fine, I promise. Trust me, my lovely bestie.'

The last time she told me to trust her was when she went through a phase of wanting to be a hairdresser and insisted she use me as a real-life Girl's World. The perm solution burnt my scalp, and I was left with a bald patch for six months. Ryan Smith in Year 4 even dumped me over it.

I get a bad feeling about all of this.

'There, all done.' Sian smirks as she presses the dreaded confirm button. 'Now let's see who's on there at the moment.'

I have to admit this bit is quite funny. I didn't even know sites like this existed before Sian showed me. The internet was hardly around when I met Dick. So I still find it astonishing that, with the flick of a button, there are rows and rows of men in front of me. It feels like some kind of marketplace. There are columns of men in all sorts of different poses. Some are dressed in fancy dress costumes; if I had to guess I would say they are the fun-loving ones. A few guys are with their dogs; I like that. These would be kind, I suspect, as it shows they love animals; although they could have borrowed someone's dog, I suppose, or be some horrible dognapper person.

I look a little harder to try and work out which ones the psychopathic murderers would be. There seem to be lots of those on dating sites nowadays. You only have to read the *Daily Mail* or *Take a Break* to prove my theory.

Some of the men on the page look serious and are unsmiling. However, this look doesn't appeal to me at all – they appear far too moody. I have already had one of those men in my life. I certainly don't need another.

My favourite profiles are the ones of the men who mention their children – some of them sound nice. One man, who has a beautiful photo, stands out from the rest. It has been taken on a beach, and a man in shorts is holding hands with two little ones, a boy and a girl. They all have their backs to the camera. It looks like a very precious moment as the sun sets in front of them.

'Awwww, look, Sian,' I swoon. 'How cute.' I surprise myself with this positive reaction. Perhaps internet dating isn't so bad, after all.

We click on the man's profile for a closer inspection. It says he is David Thompson, who works in accounting and he is 41, widowed with two children and a dog. Widowed, children and a dog! Perfect. He is a bit youthful at seven years younger than me, but he wouldn't know that since we lied about my age.

'Come on. Let's look at his other photos,' says Sian.

I have to admit that I am now very curious and a prickle of excitement rises from within me.

'Oh my god,' Sian screams as we pull up his photos. 'I don't believe it.'

I look at the photo aghast.

'It can't be. It must be a mistake?'

Sian and I look at each other curiously. She quickly pulls up another photo and, yes, there he is. It is definitely him and his name is certainly not David.

'Markus Thomas!' We both scream at the same time.

We stare at each other in disbelief, neither of us able to speak for a while.

Sian is the one who eventually breaks the silence.

'THE Markus Thomas who is always boasting on Facebook about how much he loves his beautiful wife.'

'Perhaps someone has stolen his photos off Facebook, or something,' I say. We have to give him the benefit of the doubt. He can't have done this by himself; he is the most loving, faithful man possible.

'They just renewed their vows in Montego Bay, and he bought Jane that beautiful sapphire ring. Amelia, he is The Perfect Facebook Husband; this can't be happening.'

It has to be a mistake, as Jane is very much alive for a start. I saw her in Tesco on Monday.

Sian quickly stalks Markus's Facebook page and does some investigative work to see if the photos have been taken from there. Sian and I make the best private detectives. I think men underestimate a woman's stalking powers, quite frankly.

'It has to be his own doing, Amelia. Look, it even says, "longest relationship: over ten years". He's been married to Jane for ten years.'

Oh, Markus. Of all people. This can't be happening.

'Let's wind him up,' giggles Sian as she starts to type: *Well, hello, fancy meeting you on here…* 'No, wait,' she adds. 'Let's make up a fake profile and arrange to meet him for a drink, and then we will tell Jane anonymously, and she will turn up and find out the truth about him. We will be like vigilantes for sneaky married men.'

Sian lets out a Machiavellian laugh, like a witch about to cast a spell, as she sets about opening her fake account.

As for me, I can't begin to see the funny side, as I have now lost every single romantic bone in my body. If The Perfect Facebook Husband, Markus Thomas, is on here, saying such an awful thing, then there is absolutely no hope left in this world.

Romance is officially dead, unlike Jane.

Chapter 3

Mum's house – the end of an era

Following a good sleep and the revelations on *Plenty of Sharks Out There*, I have deleted my account and decided that I will never consider dating anyone, even if Sian does accuse me of sarmassophobia. It is time to invest in myself and the boys and certainly not in any relationships. Then, when the boys grow up and no longer need me, I shall go to India and live in a yoga retreat. Do they have wine at yoga retreats? I presume they must, otherwise they wouldn't be so calm about everything.

Yes, I shall become a healthy-living, super-fit, chilled-out yummy mummy. As I keep reminding Sian, I do not need any man in my life, not now, not ever. Seeing Markus on there is further proof that men can't be trusted.

I really don't want to sound like a man hater. I am not really; I mean I still think Robson 'Gorgeous' Green is cute. I know normal women like men such as George Clooney and Tom Hardy, etc, but Robson seems like the perfect man to me, even if he does do boring man things like fishing. I suppose it might be fate that we never meet, though, as even if it was love at first sight, he might come home with a massive trout and expect me to know what to do with it. He would then subsequently dump me when he discovered that I actually have no idea what to do with a fresh fish, except want to try and revive it and throw it back into the river. I do like Tim Peake too. He's lovely, the way he goes around schools and teaches children about space. I wish he'd come to our school and do a talk on being an astronaut, then it might motivate me to help with the reading sessions a bit more.

Aside from 'Ravishing Robson' and 'Terrific Tim', Jamie Lewis is the only other man I have any time for right now. He might not have a massive fishing rod or educate the world about space, but Jamie has the kindest heart I have ever known.

Take today, for example. Jamie is helping me clear out the last remaining things from my mother's attic, as he knows how much I have been dreading it.

The thought that her house has been sold is so difficult to accept, as it is the one thing I have clung onto. I know it is only bricks and mortar, but it was a home. A place we lived throughout my childhood, where she taught me to bake Welsh cakes and bara brith and, when I was older, she would stay up late waiting to make sure I got home okay after a night out. The house has always been a safe place; a cocoon full of memories – happy, cosy memories. The thought of a new family moving in breaks my heart in two.

For weeks I tried the lottery so that I wouldn't have to sell it, but it was futile. I was left with no choice but to sell up, as the salary I earn at the bookshop, along with Dick's small maintenance allowance (when he is forthcoming with payments), doesn't leave me with too much left over each month. There was no money left in the marital pot either, after the timely collapse of Dick's stocks and shares in the middle of the divorce. Then there was the cost of the dementia care home that Mum was in before she died.

I still feel terrible that she had to stay there for the last year of her life, but Dick was adamant that she couldn't live with us. What with the boys' school, his demanding job and me in the bookshop most days, he said we would never be able to cope. I was finally persuaded when he asked me how I would feel if she stepped onto the busy main road outside our front door whilst I was at work. She was getting more and more forgetful and was often found at a bus stop waiting for her 'school bus'. Dick said I wouldn't be able to live with the guilt if something happened to her and so I agreed to move her to the care home. What I didn't know then was that two months after her death he would no longer be living with me either.

-

A sense of dread washes over me as I open the door to the bungalow for the last time. The post has piled up a little, and I step on the latest David Nieper catalogue. Mum used to love ordering her slippers from the catalogue. There are no slippers here now though. Her home is practically empty. Her much-loved possessions removed. Many of them I kept in my house, others were donated to the dementia charity. I wonder if they ever did manage to sell her size 2 shoes. I wish I shared the same petite build that she had been blessed with and not my mammoth size 7 feet.

'Come on, you, let's get this stuff down,' says Jamie as I stand there thinking of Mum.

Quite skilfully, he has managed to lower the attic ladder on his first attempt – something nobody has ever mastered.

'You stay there and I'll pass things along to you, okay?' he shouts.

I gingerly move to the left of the attic entrance as I see a daddy-long-legs heading towards me. He climbs up Mum's pink flowery wallpaper, which has faded with the years of sunlight, and then disappears into a hole in the coving. Lucky thing, he gets to stay here.

'Ready?' shouts Jamie as I'm oblivious to him passing something down.

A picture frame appears through the gap. It is a portrait of Aunt Emily. This picture has been passed down to us through the generations, ever since Victorian times. I always found it so spooky that my mother had to banish it to the attic. I asked her countless times to contact *Antiques Roadshow*, or *Flog It!*, but she said we have a duty to keep it in the family. I have never understood why old-fashioned people look so scary.

I study Aunt Emily and worry about taking it home. The family obligation has now been passed to me, but it will completely freak the boys out. It still scares me and I am grown-up. For once, though, I can see the family resemblance and realise that I am getting the same saggy jowls. Unfortunately, it wasn't just the portrait that was handed down through the generations.

Two large boxes appear next, the contents of which I have no idea about. However, one of the boxes is not quite sealed properly, and I notice that poking out from some loose masking tape is Lippy, my favourite childhood stuffed lion. The little lion I took everywhere with me. My mother had kept him all these years. The tears start to form now. The realisation that I have lost Mum forever and that she had kept Lippy and oh… It's just too much. I break down and start to sob.

'Hey, are you okay?'

Jamie clambers down the ladder and puts his arm around me.

'Come on, let's get out of here as quickly as we can. It's bound to be emotional. There's only one thing left… Let me grab it and take you back to the car.'

I wipe the tears against my faded black T-shirt, leaving it stained and crumpled and resembling my inner emotions.

'Can you grab this for me?'

I look up at the attic hatch to discover a bright pink suitcase being lowered and am immediately transported to 2000. It was the year that I won a 'Spot the Ball' competition in the local newspaper, and the prize was a trip to New York for two. My entry turned out to be the winning one, and I had two weeks' notice until my trip to the Big Apple.

Sian begged to come with me and went out and bought lots of new clothes ready for our trip of a lifetime. However, things didn't go to plan and Sian got a bout of appendicitis right before the flight. It was too late to arrange to take anyone else at that stage and I had to be brave and go alone. Of course, I was apprehensive but, even from her hospital bed, Sian encouraged me. She told me I would be fine and she was right. I must have been a lot braver in those days. Sian begged me to take lots of photos for her, which quite possibly made me do more sightseeing than I would have normally done. She also insisted that I visit Tiffany's, her favourite shop in the world. I was given strict instructions to report back every single detail.

As I think back to New York, the suitcase becomes too tempting. I have to open it. Immediately I see the pink-haired troll my mum gave me, as the plane would have certainly crashed had it not accompanied me. There is also a New York baseball cap, and a dark navy Virgin Atlantic jumper that I bought on my flight. I had wanted that colour, as Princess Diana had one similar and always wore it to the gym before she died a few years earlier.

'And what is this?' asks Jamie, lifting the mood by pulling out a bright red thong from the open suitcase.

I laugh as I quickly try to hide the offending pants in my pocket.

'This thong embarrassed me twenty-odd years ago too, I remember.'

I think back to how I got so carried away in Victoria's Secret all that time ago. It was the most glamourous shop I had ever seen. I was immediately struck by the enormous selection of jewel-coloured matching sets of underwear, which were displayed besides stuff I never knew I needed. It was very different from the items I impulsively bought in British Home Stores; no wonder I splurged. I must have bought a dressing gown, matching nightdress, bras, and this, the red thong. Those were the days when this thing could fit me. I look at the size, XS. Was I ever an XS? Perhaps they never did fit me and I was trying to show off to the skinny girl who was working there. That explains why they are still in the suitcase with the tags on, unlike the other items I bought, which are long worn out.

'So, how did it embarrass you then?' says Jamie. 'Go on, I won't tell anyone and I definitely won't tell Megan, I promise.'

Even the mention of Jamie's girlfriend, Miserable Megan, doesn't stop me smiling as I think back to that strange, yet wonderful day.

'Okay, don't laugh. I was so excited with my shopping that I unwrapped it all in the taxi on the way to Tiffany's,' I start.

'You always have been impatient, Amelia.' Jamie laughs. 'Go on…'

'Well, I was still inspecting it all when the taxi driver said we'd arrived at Tiffany's. He was even more impatient than I am! I had to quickly find the money to pay <u>him</u> and try frantically to put everything back in the shopping bags simultaneously.'

'I don't get it.'

'The thing is that when we pulled up, there was the most handsome man I had ever seen. He had a beautiful suit and thick dark hair. I thought he looked like a movie star. Anyway, he was waiting for a taxi and I opened the door and he went to step in. He smiled at me as he jumped in and then he noticed I had left something. The thong…'

'Oh no.' Jamie laughs.

I blush as I recall what happened next. I seem to remember that I was the same colour as the thong that day too.

'This is where the story gets exciting, Jamie. This gorgeous man got out of the cab and handed me the thong. He said, "Is this yours?" I honestly wanted the ground to open up and swallow me. The cab driver got so irritated that he shouted at the guy to get another cab, and so we're both stood on the sidewalk looking at each other with this thong in his hand. I think I eventually snatched it from him,' I explain.

I try to picture the guy precisely, but it was far too long ago to remember his exact features, only that he was extraordinarily handsome; too handsome perhaps.

He was very forward I remember, which was a bit different to the boys back home.

I try to think of his name and recall a piece of paper he gave me with his name and phone number. It was quite unbelievable as the most handsome man I had ever met actually asked me out on a date there and then. I didn't have the courage to call him, like I promised, even though I had never seen anyone like him before. I mean, they say some things are too good to be true and he most definitely was. Why would someone like that be interested in a normal person like me? He could have been a human trafficker targeting Welsh girls, a cannibal, or anything. No wonder I caught him looking at my bum. He was probably working out how many meals he would get.

Beginning to wonder if his telephone number is still in the suitcase, I dig around and find a piece of paper in one of the pockets.

'He gave me his number. This must be it,' I say to Jamie but, as I look closely, I notice that it is a scrunched-up dollar bill. I feel a wave of disappointment, but I guess I am now one dollar richer and he could have been a psychopath anyhow.

I hunt through another pocket and pull out a thin silver chain with a horn of plenty dangling from it. I had totally forgotten that I had worn this around my neck in my twenties. Oh goodness, I thought I was so cool after buying it on our first day in Majorca one summer. Unfortunately, I couldn't wear it from the third day of our holiday. Sian and I hired a boat and I got so sunburnt, after smothering myself in baby oil, that the sensation each time it bumped against my skin felt like torture. However, as soon as the redness subsided and I stopped peeling, it once again had pride of place on my décolletage. I thought I was the bee's knees wearing it on a night out when I got back home, how embarrassing!

'What's that there, is this his number?' Jamie asks, suddenly spotting a yellowing scrap of paper.

I open it up and look at it in disbelief. The writing is faded now, but you can still see the name, Patrick, and a telephone number with what looks like zillions of digits that make up some kind of area code.

My face lights up as I think of our short moment together. Perhaps this is how Dick felt when Tanja Tart reminded him of his student days.

'Maybe you should call him,' says Jamie.

I laugh at Jamie's crazy suggestion and hold the paper in my hand for a moment longer than I should. As I look at it, I instantly feel young again. It was a time when my mum was here and the thought of going through a horrible divorce would never have entered my mind.

I pop the number in my pocket and start picking up the rest of the things. We need to pack everything away and get them back home, even the haunting portrait.

I momentarily forget the New York trip, as this is the last time I will ever be allowed into my mum's house. This time tomorrow the new occupiers will be spending their first night here. The thought of which makes me feel totally crushed once again.

Chapter 4

At home – Aunt Emily

Dick is due to drop the boys off any second, which means I don't have much time to go through the stuff from the attic. In fact, I am thinking about opening one of the boxes when Rupert and Jasper come bounding through the door.

'We had the best time with Dad!' Rupert says, carelessly throwing his overnight bag down on the floor. Jasper can hardly get in as it blocks the front door.

'We played rugby with Dad at the park. He bought us our very own rugby boots. Dad says they're designer,' Jasper explains when he finally manages to get in. 'Look!'

He pokes his hand into his Minions overnight bag and pulls out the muddiest pair of boots I have ever seen. I can't tell what make they are as the mud splashes off them and dirties the carpet. I'm not sure if I am more annoyed with the fact that Dick suddenly seems flush with money, or that there is mud everywhere. I really must think about a new job so that I can treat the boys to nice things too.

I try to appear cheerful to everyone even though my heart still breaks when I think of how Dick and I divide our time with the boys. The way he drops the boys at the door and then drives off quickly stings every time. You would never believe it is the same person who shared such a big part of my life. The fact that we created these boys together and sometimes actually enjoyed each other's company seems quite absurd when he now looks at me with such disdain. I don't know what I did to make him hate me so much. Was it the job I took at the bookshop to give me some independence that made him look else-where? Did he always secretly hanker for a trophy wife who looked perfect all day and night, like Tanja? Whatever the reason, I wasn't enough for him and Tanja is.

There is no time for emotions though; I have two filthy children to sort out.

'Boys, go and get ready for your bath and I'll be up in a minute,' I say.

However, the boys obviously spot the portrait of their great-great-great-great aunt Emily and screams come in unison from the living room.

'Argggggggggggghhhhhhh. What's that? Is it from a haunted house, Mum?' asks Rupert.

'You found the portrait then.' I laugh.

They both come running towards me, each one grabbing a leg.

'I'm scared,' says Rupert.

'Me toooo,' says Jasper.

'Me three,' says a voice.

Where did that come from?

'I'd better be going,' says Jamie. 'Megan wants me to drop her off at Pilates. She's going for a drink with the class after, so needs a lift there.'

Ha, I bet she doesn't post pictures of her drinking wine on her Instagram fitness account, in which she is normally seen slurping on kale or putting her teeny bottom in the air in her tight yoga pants. She forgets that Sian and I were in the same class as her. We all remember her going to the chippy every lunchtime and smoking Regal King Size with the boys. Jamie might not remember because he went to the Welsh language school in the next town, but Sian and I do. That's the problem when people stay in the same village all their lives: they never forget anything.

'Oh, well, thanks for today,' I say, giving him a hug. 'You really are the best.'

I close the front door behind him, and the boys and I enter the living room to inspect Aunt Emily.

'I don't want it in here,' screams Rupert. 'I'm going to stay with Daddy until you get rid of it.'

'Yeah, it is scary, Mum,' adds Jasper.

I look at the portrait that has frightened me for many years. I don't know what to do with it. She is, in fact, a beautiful lady, apart from the jowls, but she is very stern looking. I think that is why she scares everyone.

'I know, I know,' says Jasper, wriggling about, as if he has the answer to a difficult math's question at school.

'What, my darling?' I ask.

'You know how we watch *Cash in the Attic*, *Flog It!*, ooh, and *Antiques Road Show*? Let's get rid of it. Let's make some moneeeeeeey!'

I can't help but laugh as they repeat what I begged my mum for so many years. The boys jump around me now getting excited. A blob of dried mud, from Jasper's shorts, disrespectfully splats Aunt Emily's eyebrow.

'Let's make moneeeeeey, let's make moneeeeeey!' they chant together.

I look at the portrait. I do wonder how much it is worth. I am not very good with antiques though. It could be £5 it could be £5 million. I really would have no idea.

'Sell it… Sell it… Sell it!' the boys chant.

'We could go to Disneyland,' Jasper pipes up, giving me an especially cute face that nobody can ever deny.

'Okay, well, let's look at antiques on the internet and see what we can find.' I decide. Even for insurance purposes I need to know roughly how much it is worth, I suppose.

Do I look up Sotheby's or the local car boot sales though?

I am looking for inspiration when I come across a website called *Value My Stuff*.

It asks for details about the item, and we have to measure the length and width of the portrait. I have never seen the boys move so fast as when I asked for the tape measure. They are convinced it is worth millions and that they will now practically be moving to Disneyland full-time and possibly never go to school ever again.

We enter all the details and have to wait for a response. I don't know how the boys are even going to sleep until we get that reply. We have had to pay a nominal fee, so I only hope the picture is worth more than that. A message appears on the screen that it will take 48 hours to get the valuation.

'If it's worth five million pounds, then I promise to kiss the scary face.' Jasper laughs.

'Urgh, you're disgusting,' says Rupert. 'I wouldn't kiss her no matter how much she's worth.'

'Right, boys. Now get ready for that bath,' I order, as there is nothing else to be done now that we have to wait.

The boys groan and head upstairs. While they get ready I peek my head into the big box that I still haven't had time to open.

Lying on the top are some old clothes from the 1980s. Why on earth would I have kept those? I find a jelly bag, bright pink ankle warmers, a hideously bright orange skirt, which must have made me look like a highlighter pen, and a white T-shirt with 'Choose Life' emblazoned across it. I even find Roland Rat and Gordon the Gopher cuddly toys. Finally, I come across dozens of records.

First I pick up 'Kiss Me' by Stephen Tintin Duffy, then records by XTC, Frankie Goes To Hollywood, Scritti Politti, Rick Astley and Nik Kershaw. Oh, how I loved listening to these vinyls.

I delve a little deeper into the box and discover a mix of albums and singles. There are *Chart Attack* albums full of one-hit wonders, along with Paul Young's brilliant album, *No Parlez*. No eighties record collection would be complete without Wham!, and I fortunately find 'Club Tropicana'. Then I discover something quite shocking and disturbing: there in front of me is Keith Harris and Orville's 'I Wish I Could Fly'. I accept that maybe my taste in music wasn't always that good. Still, I can't wait to show them all to Sian.

It will have to wait until tomorrow, though, as I am utterly exhausted and need my bed. Today has been tough and I am drained, both physically and emotionally. It has been a real mix of emotions. I have encountered both happy memories, but also incredibly sad goodbyes. It doesn't stop me picking up the yellow scrap of paper that I put on my bedside table for safekeeping though. I snuggle under the duvet and study the handwriting. I can't help but notice how neat it is. Every letter is perfectly formed and elegantly written. Patrick, so that was his name.

Once again, I think about how breathtakingly handsome he was. Was he really that beautiful? Or has my mind, and the absence of time, played tricks on me? I know that I don't remember every detail, but he was certainly tall, dark and very handsome. I will call him Perfect Patrick. I bet he hasn't aged and is as handsome as ever. I wouldn't think that he would be the type to sport a beer belly. I imagine that he has a full head of soft, dark hair, perhaps peppered with grey at the sides by now. He won't be completely grey, definitely not, and if he is, he will be the type to dye it, so nobody would ever know. He would look even more distinguished and elegant with symmetrical grey streaks in front of his perfect little ears. His eyes, the colour of the Mediterranean Sea, will be encircled by laughter lines which portray the beautiful life he has led since we met.

Of course, he has a Manhattan apartment, probably overlooking Central Park. I wonder if he has a dog and if he takes it for walks there. Does he have adorable little children? Perhaps a demanding ex-wife. I bet he has a high-flying career. He may even have a driver and one of those cars you see in the movies that drive him from meeting to meeting, while he sits in the back making important phone calls. So many thoughts run through my head.

Finally, I am curious: does his phone number still work? What would happen if I called him? I mean, surely, you can't ring someone up and tell them that you are finally ready for that date they asked you on over twenty years ago, can you? Of course not. For a start, anyhow, I am off men for life and I am off to a yoga retreat to drink wine. Plus, I am sure his phone number wouldn't be in service by now. If I was interested in dating and he did answer, what would I say? If his phone number doesn't work, how far would I go to find him? I picture myself on *Good Morning America*, explaining about my dream man, who I only know as Patrick. It would be rather romantic I suppose.

To be reunited with Perfect Patrick, the handsome stranger I met outside Tiffany's. It would be more exciting than anything ever seen on *Surprise Surprise* and the like.

But what if I went on there and he didn't know who I was and millions of people were watching? Imagine the embarrassment. Tanja Tart would love that; she would be laughing so much she might even lose one of her veneers. God forbid, Dick may even think I have lost the plot and insist on custody of the boys.

No, finding Perfect Patrick wouldn't be at all romantic; it would be a disappointment and I would make the biggest fool of myself. Besides, someone like that is certain to have a beautiful wife with toned legs that go on and on. Although, I suppose that he could be completely hideous now and then it would shatter my romantic illusion of him. Perhaps the past is best left there. It is fun to daydream but, whilst I am sworn to singledom for the rest of my life, I am also a firm believer that what is meant to be is meant to be. If he was meant to be in my life then something would have brought us together a long time before now.

Besides, nobody is perfect, so it is better that we never meet. I don't want to know if he has any flaws. What if he has a penchant for stripy pyjamas and velvet slippers? What if he wears tight trunks on the beach? No, definitely best that I never know. Instead, I shall dream of Perfect Patrick and how my life could have been had I taken a different route. This feels excitedly like my favourite movie, *Sliding Doors*. What if it could have been me living in a Manhattan apartment? I bet he would be the type to bring me breakfast in bed, on a perfectly presented tray; he would even add a rose on the side. He would make me proper English tea (because I would have trained him well) and then he would kiss me and put his arms around me. It would be nothing like my marriage to Dick, where he turned his back on me every night. Patrick's arms would be those strong arms I have secretly desired for years, and then he would make love to me. None of this Christian Grey stuff. Oh no. It would be passionate and steamy. He would grab me so tenderly and, oh my god, then he would…

'Muuuuuuum! Muuuuum! I've been calling you for ages.' I suddenly hear Jasper's voice as he bursts into my room. 'Rupert has wet the bed!'

'I have not wet the bed, Mum. Jasper, stop lying. You know it was my glass of water. Muuuuuum! Muuuuum! Where are my clean pyjamas? I'm soaking wet. I'm getting pneumonia.'

I jump from the bed and search in the ironing basket for Rupert's clean pyjamas and think once again how very different my life could have been. Oh yes, for a start I would have probably paid someone to do the ironing.

Chapter 5

The living room – reminiscing

'Bloody hell, that has to be worth something, surely?' says Sian, looking at the portrait.

I have been thinking much the same thing for the past 24 hours. I wonder how much it can be worth.

I suppose in some ways it would be handy if it wasn't anything of great value. That way I can keep it in the attic, without the children knowing, and then I am not the evil family member who parts company with it after so many generations. On the other hand, I can't help but wish it were worth thousands. Okay, maybe millions. Then the boys could have everything they have ever dreamed of, all because of Great-great-great-great Aunt Emily.

'Anyway, there's more. Come and check out the other boxes I have,' I say.

I knew Sian would love this stuff.

'Noooooo! Hazell Dean, Simple Minds, we loved them,' she says, picking up some of the vinyls.

'I know and look what else I have.'

I show her one of our favourite records ever: Sister Sledge, 'Frankie'.

We sing the lyrics together. Still remembering every word faultlessly. It is one of those perfect moments, like when those little iPods came out and you could download all the songs you hadn't heard for years. There is nothing quite like dancing and singing around the lounge with your oldest friend who you have been through so much with.

What I haven't told Sian yet is that I also have my old record player in the other box. I pray it still works.

I present it in front of her, carefully placing a record down on the turntable as she jumps about with excitement. I succumb to the dust and it makes me sneeze, causing the needle to jump as I put it down. The music is a little scratchy sounding and not too great, but it wouldn't have quite the same effect if the sound quality was perfect. This is what you call truly authentic.

'Wait for it,' I say. 'This will bring back memories.'

I put on Samantha Fox, 'Touch Me'.

'Waahhh. Can't believe you have this. Reminds me of the rugby club disco. Do you remember? Wasn't that where we first met Jamie and his gang?' says Sian.

'Those were the days. The awful stamp they used on our hand wouldn't come off until the following Friday,' I say with a laugh. 'Ooh, do you remember one of Jamie's friends had a real thing for you,' I add.

'Oh my god, Geraint. He came and brought me a Coke over and asked me to dance. We must have only been about thirteen. What was he thinking?' says Sian.

'Yeah, he was a bit pushy. Lucky though, as we'd never have made friends with Jamie if it wasn't for Geraint.'

'No, he did have a word with him for me. Never bothered me again. Jamie's always been good at sorting people out. Why he can't see through Miserable Megan, though, I don't know,' says Sian.

'No, that is odd. He's never really had any serious relationships since the divorce. I think he was too busy with his dad before. Maybe he's a bit lonely now his dad has gone. They were so close,' I say.

'Wah! You have Madness. Oh, I love this song.' Distracted, Sian picks up a single.

We find a few other wonderful singles and a Kim Wilde album that I don't remember owning but, without any warning, the needle finally gives up. The arm of the record player screeches along the album, scratching it completely as it does so. Our moment of nostalgia becomes diminished as fast as the Kim Wilde 12-inch. Now I understand why technology moved on from those old hi-fis; hooray for new technology.

'I bet some of these records are worth something, Amelia,' says Sian.

'Oh, I don't know. I doubt it,' I say as I pick up 'Agadoo' by Black Lace.

'Record shops would probably pay me to keep my records away from them if anything,' I joke.

I must have been very young when I started collecting these records. I am so grateful that Mum kept them all. Although there was no need for her to keep everything. I even found a pink shell suit in the box. Must have been from the early 1990s. For a moment, I did wonder whether it should go in a blue refuse bag, or a black one. I doubt it could be recycled, though, as it looks highly flammable. You certainly wouldn't want to be walking past a scented candle wearing it, that's for sure. Therefore, I finally opted for the black bin bag ready for next week's refuse collection. I have also ensured that there is no trace of my address anywhere in the bin, so that I can never be associated with it and it remains untraceable. I am not even going to tell Sian about it or I will never live it down – even though she had one in purple.

'Ooh, there is something else I have too. Another surprise. One from New York.' Sian is going to die when she sees this.

I hand her Perfect Patrick's telephone number.

'Are you serious? Is this the guy you met in New York? You kept his number? How could you control yourself? I thought you threw it out even though I told you not to,' she says.

'I didn't realise that I'd left it in the suitcase. I must have kept it as a souvenir,' I say.

I suddenly feel a tinge of regret that I didn't go out for that drink. But surely even if I had gone on a date with him, we would have had nothing in common. I was used to boys asking if I wanted a snog and a Snowball in the local nightclub, The Moonraker. This guy definitely knew his Sauvignon from his Chardonnay and would never have drunk a Snowball, not even a Malibu. Maybe he would be the type of person who would sneer at the idea of a spritzer and the like and I don't appreciate that kind of snobbery.

Also, I still don't understand his motive. Within two minutes of meeting me he had asked me out. Why me? New York was a big city; he could have asked anyone he wanted out on a date. He wouldn't have had a shortage of dates with his good looks. Why would he try and pick up a tourist he had never met before? It was all a bit strange. Nowadays, I would have assumed that it was some kind of social experiment for YouTube, or something, but there was only Jeremy Beadle about in those days.

'Why don't you call him, Amelia?' says Sian. 'This could be so much fun. Imagine, he might sweep you off your feet. You're not moving to New York though; I'd miss you too much.'

'I'm not going to call him. It's just a bit of fun, that's all. Reminded me of the great time I had in New York.'

'Oh, come on, we have to at least ring the number. Don't be a spoilsport. We can put the phone down if he answers. Let's hear his voice,' begs Sian.

'No, Sian. Don't. It could be the middle of the night there anyhow. Besides, what would you say? You remember the girl you met outside Tiffany's in 2000… Don't be so silly, Sian.'

As usual Sian is being insistent and pulls out her mobile phone and starts dialling the international number.

I try to pull the phone off her.

'No! Don't. Please don't call him. You can't do this to me, Sian. I wish I hadn't told you now. I am never telling you anything ever again,' I threaten.

My head is in my hands as I hear the phone ring on the other side. I could really kill Sian sometimes. I know if he answers she won't keep her mouth shut.

I pray there is no answer.

'Hi, your call cannot be answered right now. Please leave a message.'

Thank goodness it is an automated voicemail. I hit the phone out of Sian's hands before she can think of leaving a message.

'Enough, stop it,' I say. 'I know you'll leave him a message.'

I take the paper with the phone number to ensure she doesn't attempt to ring him again. Although I am a bit concerned that she still has the number stored on her phone.

'Don't ring him again, okay. You'd better promise me,' I beg.

'Say I can organise you a divorce party and I will see what I can do.'

'A divorce party?' I say incredulously. 'Do people actually celebrate getting divorced? It's horrible, not a cause for celebration.'

'Everyone's doing it nowadays,' says Sian. 'All the celebs do it and there's always some divorce party on reality TV programmes. It's fun. Come on. I promise not to call your Perfect Patrick if you let me arrange one.'

'I don't know. Is there cake?'

'Yes, you can definitely have cake, Amelia. I'll order one especially for you.'

'Okay, well, if you promise not to call Patrick and bring cake, it's a deal.'

'You're on. The next weekend the boys are over at Dick's, we'll invite a few of the girls over and have some drinks. We can even put some music on if you can get the needle fixed. It'll be a laugh.'

I still think it strange that anyone would have a divorce party, but the thought of having the girls round and eating cake does sound appealing.

'Right. I'd better go, my sweets; I have a party to plan. I'm so excited.'

I immediately wonder if the party is more for Sian than for me.

'Don't forget to invite Jane. I think she might be in need of a girls' night out,' I say.

Sian has arranged to meet Markus next Tuesday, and I am so worried about Jane. I can't decide if she is better knowing the truth or living a life of oblivion with the best husband in the world. I suppose she deserves to know; I just don't want to be involved in breaking her heart. If I am honest, I wish we had never found out.

Jasper and Rupert have been playing *Minecraft* for an hour when I finally interrupt them. They are quite disappointed when I poke my head around their bedroom door.

'Ohh, Mummmm, I'm in the middle of something very important. Do we have to go to bed now?' groans Rupert.

I don't normally allow them to play on the computer before bed but, as it's almost the weekend, and Sian had popped over, I broke the rules.

'Come on, let me read you a bedtime story,' I say. 'Don't tell me you're too old for one.'

'No, Mummy, we'll never be too old for a bedtime story,' says Jasper kindly.

Rupert, on the other hand, is yet again in a bad mood. I think the divorce has affected him quite badly as he was so close to Dick. His dad never could do any wrong in Rupert's eyes, even when Dick would sometimes let him down and not get home from work in time to take him to the movies, or whatever they had planned. Dick would quickly make up for it with some grand gesture; like coming home with a huge remote-control car, or a giant box of Lego. Everything would soon be forgotten.

'Right, what shall we read?'

'Why don't we read one of the books that we found in the box? Your old books,' says Jasper. 'I'd love to hear one of the stories that Nana used to read to you.'

In the other box, brought down from the attic, were many of my childhood books, including Hans Christian Andersen and Enid Blyton classics.

Despite having such wonderful books beside me, I decide to read *Cinderella* since I am feeling a bit tired and, if

I'm honest, it is a lot shorter than anything else at hand. It is very girly, I know. But I don't often get the opportunity to do things with them that don't involve grisly boy stuff, so I have to indulge in this one-off opportunity.

As the boys snuggle into each of their bunks, I sit on the lower one with Rupert and read the story out loud.

'"How lovely that she found her prince and, not only that, she also got to own such a fabulous pair of shoes."'

Rupert yawns deliberately.

'Okay, Rupert, it's finished now… And they all lived happily ever after,' I conclude.

'Well, why didn't you and Daddy end up like that then?' says Rupert, startling me with his harsh words.

I don't even know what to say for a moment and try to compose my thoughts. I do what I always do when I find myself in a sticky situation and make a joke of it.

'Ah, well, you see, Daddy isn't a prince. It only happens like that when you marry a prince. Daddy is a banker and not a prince. There's a huuuge difference.'

Jasper laughs, and Rupert eyes me seriously.

'I've heard you call her Tanja Tart, you know,' he replies.

'Rupert, don't say that,' I scold him, partly because I am feeling so guilty.

I make a mental note to remember that the boys are always listening, even when I think they are not.

With the stress of the divorce, I am acutely aware that I have not been the best mum over the past few weeks and may have said some naughty things out loud. However, Rupert's words have upset me. I definitely won't call her Tanja Tart anymore. Well, not in earshot of the kids anyway. I can't promise when I am talking to Sian that it won't slip out.

I know divorce affects children in different ways and so I consider how I can make it up to them.

I decide that I will make them a nice meal and I might even try and find a healthy chicken nugget recipe, since that is all they both eat. Then, when they come home from school, I will spend all afternoon helping them with their homework and taking an interest in *Minecraft*, even though no adult I know of understands it. I must first purchase *Minecraft for Dummies*, so that I can pretend I know what I am on about, and I might even be able to throw in a *Minecraft* term every now and then, like creeper or mod. I mean what is a *mod*? They were those guys on mopeds in my day, but I don't think the boys mean that, as I did ask them once if the mods had bikes and they had no idea what I was talking about. Taking up *Minecraft* will be like learning a new skill, a whole new language. Yes, this will be fun, just like when I first went on Club Penguin with them and we built the coolest igloo ever.

For a moment, I feel content. These boys are my life. I am so glad of their company. However, in the back of my mind I have a niggling thought that I can't quite shake off.

When the boys grow up and have partners of their own, what will happen to me? The harsh truth is that I am far too unbendable to run off to a yoga retreat. Is it selfish to worry about life without the boys at home and me being needed? Children grow up so fast, already these years have whizzed by. Without them here, I think I would fall apart. What will I have left when they leave home? The answer frightens me.

Chapter 6

The kitchen – I am officially Supermum

I haven't had the best of starts today. I was so positive about it being a new day and how I would turn over a new Supermum leaf, but then I had a phone call from Dick. It seems that he now wants joint custody of Tammy the tortoise. Not content with stealing only my husband, Dick has informed me that Tanja has always wanted a tortoise and therefore he feels it only fair that he takes ours, since he paid for it many years ago. He says he will come by at 3pm to pick Tammy up, and I can have her/him (we still don't really know the sex after fifteen years) at weekends. This, he says, is what happens when I get custody of the boys all week. I am enraged. I tried to point out that this means the boys won't see Tammy, but he told me that if I disputed his demand it would result in legal action once again.

Dick loves the drama of lawyers, even if he doesn't want to pay for them. It was his choice to go off with Tanja, so I don't know why he makes life difficult for me. I wish I could get him to see me as the mother of his beautiful boys, instead of a major inconvenience in his life. I often wonder if he ever loved me at all. Did he marry me because he wanted a promotion at the bank? His branch manager, Mr Evans, did appear to only promote the staff who were steady and married. Or did Dick marry me because he thought he would have cheap holidays, as I was working in a travel agency when we met? I wanted to be a nurse when I left school, but my mother's friend owned the agency and offered me an immediate job. Had I trained as a nurse I would never have met Dick and would have accomplished my dream job.

I am so sceptical of things now that I don't even look back fondly at the time Dick came in to book a skiing holiday with his friends and our eyes met. Dick is so mercenary that I now believe he only proposed to me so that he could get a discount on his annual boys' golfing holiday to Portugal. Instead of our eyes meeting with a look of love in them, I think he just saw '50 per cent off' holiday signs.

Well, he won't be happy if he gets any invoices from the vet for Tammy. Pets can be expensive. I have to choose my battles carefully. As Tammy will be going into hibernation in a few months, if Tanja Tart wants to look at a box in her shed with a sleeping tortoise for five months, then so be it. Reluctantly, I agree but, as I have been upset about what I shall call 'Tortoise Gate' all morning, I didn't manage to get out of the house and go on the quest for preservative-free chicken nuggets, kale, or not even one grain of quinoa. Instead, I realise that I do have the ingredients for Welsh cakes in the house, and the boys love their Welsh cakes, so I dig out my mum's special Welsh cake recipe. Every Welsh mother has their own special recipe that they pass down.

Mammy's Welsh Cakes

1lb self-raising flour

8oz butter
8oz currants
8oz caster sugar
2 eggs
milk to mix

I haven't had one of my mum's Welsh cakes for years. My mouth is already watering as I mix the flour, sugar and butter to create a breadcrumb-type mixture. Next I add currants and then the eggs. I can't resist stealing a piece of uncooked Welsh cake mix, delicious! My legs ache as I come to the end of cooking the Welsh cakes on the traditional plank my mother used to have. I have now been standing for so long that I am sure I'm starting to get varicose veins. I did sit down once, while I was cooking, as I overheard something on *This Morning* about some man having a midlife crisis and leaving his wife, but then I managed to burn a whole batch of Welsh cakes. So, I didn't find out what happened in the end and had to return to turning over my Welsh cakes.

For the first time in ages the boys come home to the smell of cooking.

'Ooh, something smells nice, Mum,' says Jasper the second we open the door.

'Come and see what I made earlier,' I say, leading them into the kitchen, where the freshly baked Welsh cakes are waiting for them.

'Welsh cakes, nom, nom, nom,' says Jasper.

Rupert, meanwhile, stuffs one straight into his mouth without saying anything.

'Have you got any homework to do?' I ask.

'No, Mrs Jones was off sick today,' says Rupert.

'That means we can play more *Minecraft*,' adds Jasper.

'I'd love to see what you do. Can I come and watch?' I ask.

Rupert rolls his eyes, while Jasper agrees to allow me to observe.

–

I am sat in their bedroom for all of five minutes before I want to fall asleep. I really don't get this. All I see are a lot of blocks piling up. I am struggling with this part of becoming the utopian mum.

'Oh, and is that a mod you are making there?' I ask, feeling so intelligent.

The boys don't answer though; they are too busy with their creepers, or whatever it is. No, I still don't have a clue what is going on. I may as well give up.

'I'm just going to make a cup of tea; anyone want anything?'

'Yeah, a trip to Disneyland,' Rupert answers sarcastically. 'Did you hear back if that horrible painting is worth anything yet?'

'Don't be mean, Rupert. She's one of our ancestors. Don't speak about the painting like that,' I snap.

All we seem to do is bicker.

If only the painting were worth a lot of money, then I could surprise them both with the Disneyland trip. I haven't even told them about Tammy yet. If I could successfully plan a holiday like Disney for them then it might cheer them up a bit.

'The company needs more information,' I say. 'It's starting to get a little complicated. They want me to check if there's a signature on the back and a few other details. I'm scared I'll smash it, so don't want to fiddle with it too much. The frame already looks like it'll fall off.'

'Well, I want to go to Disneyland. Ask Daddy, he'll give us the money,' says Rupert.

I haven't asked Dick for a thing since the divorce. I am too proud and, even if it means I struggle, I refuse to ask him for anything. I don't want to give him the satisfaction.

The Disneyland trip, however, affects the boys and so, for the first time, I have to consider that if the painting isn't worth anything then I may need to go to Dick for the funds. I suppose it is the least he can do for them.

'Ring Daddy and ask him for the money. Pleeeease Mum,' begs Rupert.

Jasper smiles. 'It would be nice to go to Disneyland, Mum.'

My stomach sinks. It is my worst nightmare, having to go cap in hand to Dick, especially after today's run-in with him.

'Ring him now, Mum,' insists Rupert.

He hands me the phone and presses 'Richard' on the contact list. Please let him not notice that it says 'Dick' in brackets.

'Why does it say Dick after his name?' demands Rupert.

'Oh, um, because it's short for Richard, darling,' I say, totally unconvincingly.

'But that's a bad, bad, word,' he says.

'Hello,' answers Dick, right in the nick of time.

'Oh, um, hi. Listen, I'm really sorry to bother you but the boys have this idea in their heads of going to Disneyland. They've asked me to call you to see if you could perhaps loan us the money for us to go.'

'Perhaps loan, or do you mean GIVE you the money? It makes a difference,' he says, his inner banker making an appearance.

'Well, I don't know yet. I have this antique picture that might be worth something—'

Dick cuts me off abruptly.

'You have an antique. What, do you think it's a Picasso? You've been watching too much TV. I take it you mean *give* you the money then. How much?'

This is why I don't want to beg Dick for anything. He can be so condescending. However, one look at the boys' hopeful little faces suddenly gives me the tenacity to deal with Dick.

'I don't know, I'd have to get some brochures and check. Look, it's not for me. It's for the boys. It's the least you can do,' I whisper down the phone.

'The least I can do!'

Oh no, I forgot how careful you have to be when dealing with Dick.

'Tanja wants to go on a skiing holiday and we're planning our wedding… Look, if anything, me and Tanja will take them. You got to keep the house, so if you think I'm paying for you to have a holiday too, you have to be insane. I have a week off soon and it isn't skiing season yet… S'pose it'll be fine. Now is that all? I want to get back to *Escape to the Chateau*.'

The boys look at me excitedly as I put the phone down.

'What did he say, what did he say?' asks Jasper.

They are getting married. I had no idea. I suppose it is obvious that it could happen, but so soon and without even talking about it to me. Although I guess he doesn't have to tell me. He mustn't have told the boys either, or they would have definitely blurted it out. I just about manage to prevent myself from saying this part of the conversation.

'He said yes. You can go to Disneyland.'

The boys are hysterical.

'When will we all go, Mummy?' asks Jasper.

'I don't know, honeybuns. I think it might be soon. Dad is going to have a chat with Tanja and see what they can arrange.'

'Why is he checking with Tanja?'

'I think he wants to take you both with Tanja. Perhaps he wants to have a special holiday. You're home with Mummy almost every night. It would be lovely for you both to go with him,' I say.

The truth is that the thought of the boys going away with Dick and Tanja Tart is killing me. I wanted to take them. Admittedly, Dick is better with rides than I am, but I wanted to be the one to take them on the less frightening boat rides and treat them to hot dogs. Dick has done this to be spiteful. I scold myself and remind the bitterness that burns inside me that what is important is that my two boys have their dream holiday. With or without me.

'We're going to Disneyland; we're going to Disneyland.'

The boys are still dancing around the room five minutes later. I can't quite join in with their enthusiasm. Yet again everything gets too much for me; the news that my boys are going on holiday with a woman who isn't their mum, and that Dick is getting married again, comes as a bombshell to my already fragile emotional state.

Without any warning I begin to sob against the fridge door. It starts with a quiet cry, a teeny squeak of a sob. Then a bigger sob and then they become unstoppable. I feel as though I have broken into tiny pieces and there is nothing anyone can do to put all the pieces back together again. I am a divorced Humpty Dumpty.

I slide down the fridge door, taking the holiday magnets with me. I continue sliding down, until I reach the floor. I want to smash every magnet against the wall. I pick up a ceramic magnet in the shape of an island and examine it. Did we really have a good time when we went to Crete? I certainly remember that Dick had a tantrum in the taverna over the cheap Greek wine and his squid not being to his satisfaction. He stormed off and went for a walk along the beach to cool off. I had to walk the boys back to our villa alone; they were only small; the road was dark and I was terrified a car would come around the winding road and hit us.

Was his tantrum a ploy to rush off somewhere with his mobile phone and call his PA at work? He was always going on about 'Lovely Linda'. Oh goodness, it's not enough that he has made me completely depressed and I've lost my confidence, he's even making me paranoid now.

Divorce is such an emotional rollercoaster; some days I can cope, others I feel like I am going to have some kind of breakdown. I desperately want to feel better, but the grief keeps popping up like a jack-in-the-box when I don't expect it. But then again, it's not every day the man you were with for over fifteen years tells you he is remarrying. Surely, I'm allowed to have a breakdown today.

'Mum, can we watch a Disney DVD?' shouts Jasper.

'Oh, yes, of course. Watch it upstairs. I'll be up in a while,' I say, trying to hide the desperate sadness that I carry in my heart. The last thing I need is for the boys to see me upset yet again.

I really don't know how to cope. If only Mum were here, she would know what to do. How did it all end this way? I was a young girl not so long ago, with a fun job and a husband who I thought loved me. Of course, I don't regret giving up the job at the travel agency, so that I could take extended maternity leave all those years ago, but I do regret trusting a word that Dick ever said.

I get up off the floor to open the fridge door and pull out a bottle of wine to comfort me, but something makes me put it back.

Wine, chocolate, not even carrot cake has the answer. Only I can pull myself out of this once and for all. The only thing I am doing is ruining my health and gaining so much weight that nothing fits me any longer. Even in this state I realise that neither Dick, nor anyone else for that matter, is worth doing this for.

It has to stop once and for all. Tomorrow is a brand-new day and, no matter what happens, Dick is not going to ruin it. I am stronger than this. I have seen my mother not recognise me at the end of her fight with dementia. If I can get through that, I can do anything. Sian lost the love of her life and managed to get back on her feet. Jamie's lovely dad was killed in a dreadful car accident six months ago. Yet Sian and Jamie are managing to carry on with life. Bad things happen to good people. Dick isn't even dead – although maybe that's part of the problem, I laugh to myself. No, I would never wish ill on the father of my children. I simply need to accept my situation. It's over. I need to move forward and not waste another moment of my life hankering after a man who now sees me as worthless. Dick is getting married and I must therefore move on with my life too.

It is time for me to be around people who value me, who care and cherish me. Everyone is worthy of at least that.

It is certainly time for a new beginning, I know that much. I suppose that new beginning could involve one teeny phone call to New York. I mean what harm can it do to see if Perfect Patrick remembers me? I admit that, until I found that paper, I hadn't given him a moment's thought, but I do remember him. I wonder if he recalls giving it to me.

'Stop it, Amelia. He's never going to remember you,' I say out loud to myself. But my brain won't let it rest.

It's like there is a devil on my shoulder telling me, 'Go on, do it.'

'If you don't ring then you never get to find out,' the devil is saying.

It would be fun to find out more about him, for sure. I weigh up the pros and cons. Worst-case scenario he doesn't remember me, thinks I'm a stalker or is married and his wife murders me for contacting him. Best-case scenario I make a lovely new pen pal, or he was my soulmate all along and we will spend the rest of our lives blissfully happy. He will ask me to move into his penthouse apartment and we will walk our chihuahuas (brother and sister from the same litter) in Central Park. The boys have always wanted at least one puppy.

At first glance the benefits certainly seem to outweigh the risks. It's worth one phone call, surely?

Chapter 7

In a cafe – finding Perfect Patrick

My stomach is in knots and I feel sick. This is supposed to be exciting, not nerve-wracking. My heart feels like it is about to explode as I dial the number in front of me. If Perfect Patrick does answer, my voice is going to be all shaky and weird. He probably won't even understand me I will be so jittery. I might need an ambulance in a minute, as I can hardly keep my heart in my chest. Boom, boom, boom. I am sure he will hear this all the way in New York. Take deep breaths, deep breaths.

'Hello.' Oh no, it is a woman's voice. Put the phone down, put the phone down.

Slam. Why, oh why, did I put the phone down? She might have recently bought the home and she will know Patrick's forwarding address. Or she might be his wife, the one with the long legs – you know, the murdering one – my anxiety-ridden brain is screaming at me.

I sip my latte. What do I do? I don't have much time as I have to head back to work soon. Another deep breath calms my heart rate a little.

Okay. I will try again.

'Hellllo.' This time she sounds agitated.

'Oh, um, oh, um, hi. Sorry, I got cut off just now. Um, is this Patrick's home? I mean, like, is umm, Patrick there, please?'

'I don't understand. What?' she says.

'Oh, sorry, I'm um calling from Wales, it's my accent. You know, in the UK?'

'What?'

Okay. 'May... I... speak... to... Patrick... please?' I say very slowly and succinctly.

'Patrick? Who the hell is Patrick?'

'Oh, so you don't know Patrick?'

'No, should I?'

'It's okay, I think he lived there a very long time ago. Thanks.'

With that the phone goes dead. No goodbye, nothing. Do Americans not say goodbye on the phone, or something? So rude. Oh well, I suppose it shaved a few seconds off my phone bill.

Now what should I do?

I pick up the phone to Sian, like we both always do to each other in any crisis. I had decided not to tell her of my plan to call him, as I couldn't cope with her texting me every five seconds to ask if I had rung him yet. Now, however, I feel it is time to confide in her.

'Aww, I'm so pleased you called him, Amelia. This is exactly what you need to do. I think Patrick is the perfect distraction for you, well, and for me too. Ooh, I'm loving this. Now we just need to find him. Think back, did he say anything about a job?'

I delve into the deepest parts of my brain for help. We didn't really talk that much, but he did say something about his office being nearby. He may even have mentioned a company name, but it meant nothing so I would never be able to remember it. He had a fancy pen though. When he wrote the number down, I remember seeing this amazing fountain pen.

'I remember something!' I exclaim. 'He had this pen and I mentioned how amazing it was, and he said that he wrote a lot for his job. He could be a journalist.'

'Well, that's amazing. We can easily find a journalist; there must be articles online.'

'I don't know, because this was a long time ago and not everything was on the internet, like it is now. What if he changed professions?'

'Journalists don't change professions. He might even be super famous by now,' says Sian. 'Right. You head back to work and I'll do some googling for you.'

I rush back to World of Books, where I left Lisa on her own. She has a doctor's appointment, so doesn't look too pleased that I am five minutes late.

'Sorry, sorry!' I say as I rush in, looking slightly red in the face.

She huffs a bit and grabs her coat.

'See you tomorrow, nice and early, I hope. By the way, some new travel guides were delivered while you were gone. Can you sort them out for me?'

What I wish I could do is tell her that I'm leaving to follow my dreams. Since Mum has gone, I have been thinking about becoming a nurse more and more. I wish I could give something back to the community after seeing how those amazing nurses looked after Mum.

Of course, I don't say that though. My boss, Lisa, can be a bit prickly when she wants to be and I need to keep her happy if I wish to feed two hungry boys.

'Yes, most definitely. Anything else you need me to do?' I ask politely.

'That's all. See you tomorrow.'

The shop is quiet most of the afternoon, which is good as I can now unpack the delivery and will definitely manage to have all the books on the shop floor before tomorrow. Hopefully, this will make up for my earlier tardiness.

I can't help but notice one of the guide books is for New York. I am tempted to put it aside and use my staff discount. It would be lovely to read up about the places I visited so long ago. It has probably changed so much since I was there.

Finally, with the books in place, I check my phone in between customers, as Sian has been messaging back and forth. Her last message was to say that after an afternoon of googling there is no trace of Patrick being a journalist in New York. How odd. She has, however, come up with the idea of putting out a media appeal on Twitter for him to come forward, which is an absolutely ridiculous thought. Unfortunately, a customer had just walked into the shop and was looking for the latest Nigella cookbook when Sian messaged this, so I quickly agreed to a tweet. Which, yes, did make me a bit of a twit, and I know was a big mistake. If only that woman hadn't walked in right then, I would certainly have told Sian not to be so foolish.

I read her messages again now that the customer has left.

> I'll write something on Twitter appealing for Patrick. People love these stories. If we don't find Patrick, who knows who else might write to you?

My phone bleeps with another text from Sian.

> Hey, I'm a quick worker. It's on there. What do you think? 'Over 20 yrs ago, my friend met a man outside Tiffany's in NY. His name was Patrick and we want to find him. If U believe in #love, pls help us find him #Loveatfirstsiight #FindPerfectPatrick ♥

Oh no, this is dreadful. Some people have millions of followers. What if it was to go 'viral' as they say? Dick and Tanja may find out. They will laugh at me and think I am desperate.

I panic. I would never have agreed if I'd not been so rushed to reply. I should have left my phone in the stock room as I usually do. I'm not even allowed it on the shop floor. It's just that I'm worried school might call with an emergency. Oh, why did that customer have to come in then? I'm getting palpitations. Is this anxiety, or that extra coffee I had? Oh no. Sian needs to delete this immediately.

Okay, calm down, Amelia. Breathe. It takes two seconds to delete a tweet. I will tell her to remove it and all will be well. However, before I can message Sian, my phone bleeps yet again.

I'm a genius. Just put this on Facebook.

Do you believe in love at first sight?
What if you had met your soulmate but let
him get away? In 2000, a friend met a
gorgeous man outside Tiffany's in New
York on Fifth Avenue. Their eyes locked
and they knew they were destined for each
other. Unfortunately, my friend lost his
number and so they never met for the date
that he asked her for. I know these two are
destined to be together, even if it is a bit
late. Please share this post and let's
reunite them. Do you know a Patrick who
lived in New York in 2000? He is possibly a
journalist and carried a fancy pen. He wore
a suit and was tall, dark and apparently
very handsome.
Please contact me with any information.
Please share, share, share so we can find
Amelia's Perfect Patrick!

I ring Sian. She has to stop all of this immediately.

'Right. Delete it all now, Sian. Get it off Twitter and get it off Facebook. This could get too big. You have hundreds of friends on Facebook, Sian. And the story isn't exactly true, anyway,' I say.

'Yeah, I know, but we're not going to find him with a handful of followers, and this story sounds so much more romantic. Like you are totally destined to be together but you lost his number. Not that you kept his number for all these years and didn't even bother calling him,' she says.

'No, you have to stop it right this second. You can't do this without my permission,' I insist.

'You did give me your permission. I have it in writing. You said "okay".'

'Yes, well I had some woman in front of me wanting to make Nigella's cinnamon buns, didn't I? I didn't mean it,' I answer.

'Oh, come on. It'll be a laugh. Let me leave it on a bit longer. Just a teeny bit longer. You never know, Patrick might come forward right away and then I'll delete everything and nobody, except a few of us, will ever know. Deal?'

I hear the shop door chime go off.

'Shit, there's a customer,' I say.

'Okay, you go. Leave everything to me,' says Sian.

'Hello, do you have any books on Ikigai, please?' asks the customer.

'Iki… I, what?' I say.

'The Japanese art of Ikigai,' says the customer in a rather annoyed tone.

'I… Hmm, Yes. Okay,' I say, forgetting that my phone is still within earshot.

'Yes! Fabulous. You won't regret this,' says Sian to herself.

—

Perhaps it is all the stress pumping through me, but I decide to go for a walk in the park after work, as the boys have an after-school club. It is such a beautiful July day and it feels nice to get some air in my lungs. Forget-me-nots are springing up through the park, like a sign telling me not to forget my past.

I pass a couple of mothers pushing their prams. They look so proud with their newborns and are in their own maternal worlds as some runners juggle their way past. I remember pushing the boys like that. It is such a lovely feeling to be a new mum, even if you haven't slept since the moment your baby was born. I was so happy when the twins came along; it was one of the happiest moments of my life when the IVF finally worked.

In my late thirties, my body thought I'd left pregnancy a bit late. It did worry me that Dick wanted to travel and make use of my holiday concessions before starting a family, but I assumed I would be young enough to still get pregnant easily. After many disappointments, we were so fortunate that the second time we tried IVF it worked. Dick was ecstatic, and I thought he would spend more time at home and less time at work once we had the boys, which he did at the beginning. Once Jasper and Rupert were born, I stayed home in the day, weaning them and mushing up bananas and all things gooey. They were happy days, and I was so content. I had everything. Even Dick appeared satisfied for a while. Where did it all go so wrong? I hate to admit that there were good times. I daren't let them seep into my memory, or the sadness will flood back in. It's much easier to remember the bad times and convince myself it was always terrible.

I look at the runners; how I wish I could run like that. They obviously spot my desire to be like that, as one of them hands me a flyer. I read it with interest.

Wish you could run?
Join us every Wednesday for a beginners'
running club.

Could I run? I'm not sure I would ever be able to run. I can hardly breathe sitting down, let alone running. As

I look back at the woman who gave me the handout, she glances over at me and smiles encouragingly. I almost feel as if she is calling me to join. Can she see that running could possibly fill the empty void in my life?

We'll see. In the remote chance that Patrick and I were to be reunited, by some strange mystical power, then there is no doubt that I would need an emergency weight loss regime before he saw me after all this time. I will bear it in mind.

–

When I return home, I am feeling more upbeat than I have in a long time; that is until I see Dick's car parked outside. What does he want now? I will not let him affect me. I will not let him affect me, I repeat.

'Where have you been?' he asks.

'Out,' I answer curtly.

He opens the boot and hands me a big wooden box.

'Why are you giving me Tammy's box? What's happened?'

'Here, you can have Tammy back.'

'You've returned her already?' For once he is looking a little sheepish. Perhaps he feels bad about not letting me come to Disney and taking Tammy from us.

'Yeah, Tanja doesn't want her. You can keep her.'

'Tanja hasn't had Tammy twenty-four hours yet. What do you mean she doesn't want her?'

'She's in the hospital right now. Look, I have to go as she is having some tests.'

'Tanja is having tests?' I immediately wonder if one of her breast implants has exploded.

'Yeah, she thinks she has rabies. Look, I have to go.'

'How the hell could she have rabies?'

'Tammy bit her, okay. She was feeding her a strawberry. It must have been the nail polish that was the same colour, so Tammy bit her with those greedy little gums she has.'

I am laughing so much that I have to put the box down. Well done Tammy, extra tomato for you tomorrow. This has made my day.

'Dick... Shit. Richard! You do know that tortoises can't give you rabies, don't you?'

It's too late though; he doesn't hear me. He has already closed the car door to head to the hospital. I bet he wouldn't be in that much of a rush if it was me having tests.

I take Tammy back out to the back garden, where she belongs, and give her a little pat on the shell. However, I struggle to hold on to her, as my phone takes me by surprise as it vibrates in my pocket. It is Sian yet again.

Can you believe this? Up to 8,000 shares on Twitter already and 15,000 on Facebook.

Thank goodness I put Tammy down first. My hands are trembling. This is a nightmare of epic proportions.

Someone is bound to realise who I am now, and what if we find Patrick?

Chapter 8

Somewhere online — we will find Patrick

As soon as I wake up, I grasp about for my phone on the bedside table and feel my way around to switch it on. Then, with one eye open, I check for messages. Did anything exciting happen whilst I was asleep? Did Tanja Tart fall off the toilet and paramedics had to save her whilst her knickers were around her ankles? Are the photos all over the internet?

No, it seems everything is as it was when I hit the pillow. Except that between my WhatsApp and my emails there are twenty messages. The first email is from the valuers, about Aunt Emily. It seems that it isn't actually a painting but a photograph and is only worthy of a car boot sale. Apparently, it is of 'sentimental' rather than 'financial' value. My mood is dampened further by the fact that my next email is from Mrs Jones. Her news is even worse, as the dreaded class project has to be in by tomorrow. She has sent me a 'gentle' reminder as I forgot the last time. A 'gentle' reminder. I hate that line as much as I hate cycling shorts and Tanja Tart. There is nothing gentle about it at all. It is a statement that says, 'I know you always forget things so I am reminding you yet again'. Being gentle with me would involve not making the boys construct some super-duper creation out of home-made things that make *Blue Peter* projects look simple. Even the *Krypton Factor* wasn't that hard. This is definitely not good news at all.

The next few emails are spam. No, I don't want to help you find the lost bank account for the princess, or buy sex-enhancing medication, thank you. I don't even have sex and nobody would forget where they put $20 million dollars.

But then something makes me open my other eye. Both eyes stare wildly at the screen. With the time difference, and Sian being a renowned insomniac, she has been corresponding with men who all say they are Patrick. Being half asleep, I had almost forgotten what went on yesterday and am horrified as the reality takes hold. Sian has collated all the messages sent on social media, and emailed across an Excel spreadsheet of possible Patricks, and attached photos in another email.

There are fifteen men who have sent photos, saying they are Perfect Patrick. I glance at them quickly but I can tell immediately that none of them are my Patrick. One of them has bright ginger hair for a start. I don't know how he expects me to think that he is Patrick, unless you can go from tanned and dark-haired, to porcelain-skinned and gingery in the space of twenty years. One of the guys looks like he stepped out of Metallica; I do like his hair though. But no, Patrick would definitely not have long wavy hair. He was too immaculately dressed to be that relaxed looking now. One guy says he is twenty-five and remembers meeting me. I thought I was bad at maths, but even I can work that one out. Another man has no hair and is quite freckly – no, he definitely didn't have freckles. Why on earth would these guys pretend they are Patrick? Goodness, there are some bored people out there.

I check my nine WhatsApp messages.

One is from Jamie, asking if he can come around early evening to drop something off.

One from Dick, informing me he will pick the boys up later than usual this weekend, as he has a golf tournament.

And seven messages from Sian.

The first one sends shivers down my spine.

> Twitter, 256,198 retweets!!!!!! Facebook 412,000 shares!!!!!!! And now do you still think romance is dead? Look at all these people wanting you to find Patrick. Xxxx

Oh no. Is it too early for a glass of wine? This was my worst fear.

I am serving up Rupert's and Jasper's porridge when my phone pings again. I leave them to munch away as I check what the latest message is about.

I stare in disbelief as I see that Sian has sent me a screenshot of a message from a journalist who says she writes for a small newspaper in New York. She wants to interview me and help me find Patrick. She has asked for my email address so that she can send me a list of questions. I look at the response Sian has sent back and see that she has already given my contact details! I can't believe it. This is totally out of hand and bigger than anything I can control. I want to cry. I pick up the phone to tell Sian that she has gone totally overboard with it all.

'You must do it, Amelia. This is your big chance,' says Sian excitedly. 'If you don't answer the journalist, I will. I know the story anyhow. I'll answer the questions on your behalf,' she insists.

I hold the phone in my hand in despair. I know I need to put my foot down with her, but I don't seem to have the strength. I want to scream, 'Stop it this minute!' But the words don't come out. Also, this teeny part of me secretly wants to know whether this stranger can be found. You see stories like this in the news quite often. A lady who left her scarf on the bus, and the man who ran after her wants to find his dream woman, that type of thing. It's a bit different in a small town though; surely it's impossible to find someone in New York and from so long ago. This is a wild goose chase!

'Look, my lovely,' starts Sian. 'I know it's bigger than we thought it would be, but come on. Surely you can admit it is a bit of fun. I mean that bald guy I sent a picture of, he wasn't bad looking at all. He was quite hot, actually, in a Bruce Willis type of way.'

'Mum! Mum! Rupert's splat me in the face with porridge,' I hear Jasper scream.

'I didn't, it was an accident,' shouts Rupert.

'Oh, listen, I'm going to have to go. There's big drama here. Okay, okay. Just keep sending the photos then. I'll have a look at them when I sit down later after work,' I say.

'This is brilliant. I've got a feeling we're going to find him. I told Jamie all about it when I bumped into him in the Co-op last night. Even he said it sounds fun and you know how sensible he is. I'm thinking of getting some #FindPerfectPatrick T-shirts made, what do you think?'

'Mum, now. Rupert's smacked me with his spoon,' shouts Jasper.

'Look, I really have to go. Okay, okay. But absolutely NO T-shirts,' I say.

I must be mad, but my life has been so boring and miserable recently, this whole finding Patrick thing could give me and Sian something to focus on I suppose. Who knows, the newspaper might throw in a free trip to New York for us all.

With the boys successfully cleaned up and ready for school, I see that Sian has sent yet another message.

> Ooh, before you go to work, I'm thinking of getting some celebs behind us. What about Catherine Zeta-Jones? Or we could ask if we can post something on Humans of New York, they have millions of followers. If we get some big names behind us we're bound to find Patrick.

> Let's leave it as it is, okay?

I certainly don't want any celebrity in on the action.

—

With Sian and the boys all sorted, I head to work, which starts off uneventfully.

That is until Miserable Megan walks in for a famous Indian guru's latest book. Of course, I quickly spot her and rush to the stockroom on the pretext that I need to refill the historical romance section. This means Lisa has to take Miserable Megan's payment and I don't have to be fake.

Both of us know we don't like each other but pretend to smile when we see each other for Jamie's sake. I walked into a glass door, trying to avoid her, last week and I definitely heard her laughing from across the pavement.

By the time I leave the shop, there is a barrage of WhatsApp messages from Sian. It seems by 4pm we are now up to 650,356 shares on Facebook and 598,784 retweets. One of the retweets has come from a very famous comedian apparently, and so this has boosted the number of tweets. What did I say about not wanting celebs involved?

At 6pm we have 876,491 shares on Facebook and 764,983 retweets. When I finally get around to checking my emails, I see that Sian has forwarded me a new spreadsheet with eighty-five potential Patricks. I must ask her to wean them out a bit and no longer send me the obvious fakes. I now have people of all different ethnicities on there. If anything, Patrick could have had an Irish heritage, with a name like that. I know that he most definitely was not from China, the Middle East, or Somalia, like at least ten of the men who claim to be Patrick.

These are obviously very bored people, and there is no way I would romantically get involved with someone who would lie so easily. This is all futile. Patrick is a needle in a giant New York haystack. Even if the real Patrick did see any of this, he might not wish to respond, as he has since enjoyed a wonderful life without me.

Before I can think any further about Perfect Patrick there is one, much bigger, task I have to face. As much as I put it off, it is time to assist in the completion of the Man on the Moon project.

–

I find the boys sitting crossed-legged on the kitchen floor, which is littered with soggy papier mâché, UHU glue sticks and an assortment of paints.

'How you getting on there, boys?'

'Not good. We need a square shape and can't find anything to use.'

I look in the cupboards for a solution.

'Cornflakes box?' I say. They normally solve everything.

'No, we need it more square,' says Rupert.

Having exhausted all the kitchen cupboards, I look in the fridge. There is only one thing in there that is the shape of what they are looking for. I can't, can I?

I use the tap to squirt out the last remaining wine into a jug and remove the inside foil. The boys are mortified.

'We can't use a wine box, Mum!'

'What other solution is there? I can't find anything else. Look, paint it black or something and nobody will ever know.'

I pray to myself that yummy mummy Sophie Griffiths – whose little Isabel always has the best projects – doesn't realise what I have done. I know she used Möet boxes once for legs on a robot project they were making. However, Möet is a lot classier than boxed wine.

Jasper and Rupert carefully paint their project, making sure that they also splash half the kitchen floor while they are at it. Why do boys have to be so messy?

It is worth the mess, though, as for the first time ever our collaborated effort resembles what it is actually meant to be. It was definitely the wine box that we used for the main body which helped shape things up. We leave it on the floor to dry, and the boys finish off the rest of their homework whilst they wait.

I am getting tea ready when I hear my phone ring. Typical! My phone has been beside me all day and the minute I leave it in the other room it rings.

I run as fast as I can, tripping over the boys' creation as I do so. I watch in horror as I snap off the stand. We worked so hard on gluing that on, too.

I get to the phone and notice it is Jamie.

'Hi Jamie,' I say breathlessly.

'Hey, you sound like you've run a marathon. Don't tell me you've put on a gym kit and are running around the park?' he says sarcastically. 'I know how you always loved PE,' he chortles away.

'Of course I haven't, silly. I'm helping the boys with their school project, then I'm going to make a lovely apple pie and custard.'

'Sounds nice, can I join you? Although can I trust your cooking – you won't give me food poisoning will you?' he jokes.

'Don't be cheeky,' I say, teasing him back.

'In that case I take it all back. Please can I sample your delicious apple pie?'

'Okay then, if you must,' I answer.

'Well, open the door then,' Jamie says with a laugh.

'Oh my word, you were outside?' I say. It had slipped my mind that Jamie said he was popping around.

Jamie gives me one of his big smiles as he walks in.

'Did you not hear the doorbell? Are you going deaf in your old age?' He laughs.

'Oh, I'm so sorry. The boys and I were banging away in the kitchen… And I'm the same age as you, so I'd be quiet if I were you,' I say.

'Well, we're not getting any younger that's for sure,' he says, touching my arm. 'So, I haven't seen you since we went to your mum's. Are you okay? I noticed the new people have already made a few changes to the house. I wasn't sure if you knew.'

I try not to think of the new people who live in the house. To think that they have already ripped out my mother's beloved kitchen is utterly heartbreaking. I try to blank it out and not drive past any longer.

'Anyhow, the real reason I'm here is because of something else actually. As I said, I have a little something for you,' says Jamie.

'Oh, I like surprises. What do you have for me?' I say curiously.

'I'll go and get it from the car,' he says.

He walks in with a small branch in a pot.

'What's this supposed to be?' I ask.

'You remember your dad planted that tree in the front garden when you were born? You always talked about it… as well as the snowdrops he planted,' he says.

'Yes, I loved those plants. They all continued to grow after Dad died so many years ago. They were his legacy.' I smile.

I was the same age as the boys are now when my dad died. I think of Jamie and his dad. It is all so fresh for him, yet he seems so jolly and gets on with it all. I don't know how he can be so brave.

'Well, I drove past the house and noticed the new owners were cutting it down. I knew you'd be upset, so I asked if I could take a branch. I've put it in a pot and it says online that you should easily be able to grow the tree with a bit of TLC. Sorry, I couldn't get the snowdrops for you. Maybe one dark January night I will sneak in and dig them up for you.' Jamie laughs.

'Oh Jamie, I can't believe you would think of saving this for me. You are so sweet, thank you.' I give him the tightest, heartfelt hug.

'What are friends for?' he says, letting me go.

My mum and dad were so proud of that tree; it is devastating that after forty-eight years of being there the new owners would carelessly cut it down like that. To them it meant nothing.

'I thought you could plant it in your garden here and always have a piece of your mum and dad with you,' says Jamie.

'Yes, yes, that's exactly what I will do, wow. Thanks again. I am so touched. Are you okay? I mean after your dad and everything?'

'Yes, I'm fine. Don't worry about me. Megan's been teaching me meditation to deal with grief. Apparently, it helps,' says Jamie. 'There are some benefits dating such a spiritual person.' He smiles.

'Oh, right. Well, if that helps that's wonderful,' I say. 'But you know what else helps? Apple pie,' I add. 'I'd better pop it in the oven.'

As we move into the kitchen, Jamie spots the Man on the Moon project.

'It's broken. Mum broke it,' says Rupert.

'Well, she didn't mean to,' says Jasper.

'Yeah, but she did. She didn't look where she was going,' says Rupert.

'Let me look at it,' says Jamie.

The boys watch curiously.

He wiggles some things about, requests Sellotape and some string and within minutes the Man on the Moon is looking better than ever. We may even beat Isabel's creation at this rate.

'Well done, Jamie. That's amazing,' I say.

'Uncle Jamie saved the day. Yay,' says Jasper.

'Yeah, not a bad job at all, Uncle Jamie,' says Rupert.

Finally, we tuck into our apple pie, which turned out golden and perfect. Maybe I should publish a cookbook with Mum's lovely recipes. They don't make them like they used to. None of this sun-dried tomato and basil nonsense. It's all good old-fashioned dumplings, old school puddings and Bird's Custard.

'Well, I'd better be off,' says Jamie. 'Megan's insisted on taking me to Bath tomorrow for a few days. She's never been.'

'Oh, it's beautiful there. I went once with Dick,' I say, trying to sound positive.

'Yes, we're booked into a lovely hotel. Megan said it would do me good to have a break… You know, after Dad,' says Jamie.

That's nice of Megan. Maybe she isn't as bad as I thought. I feel as though I haven't done anywhere near enough to help Jamie, apart from attend his dad's funeral and assist with some of the floral arrangements. At least I knew who to recommend after Mum's service.

'You know I'm here for you, Jamie,' I say. 'Any time you want to chat, please pick up the phone, visit, whatever.'

'You have your own worries, Amelia. I wouldn't dream of being a burden,' says Jamie.

'Oh, my goodness, you'd never be a burden. Don't be silly. Don't say things like that,' I say. 'Shame you'll miss the divorce party though. Would have been great to have you there,' I add, trying to lighten the conversation.

'I know, but hey, you may have found your "Perfect Patrick" by the time I get back. And I know that Sian has a surprise in store for you at the party. I think it's more of a ladies' evening,' he says.

'What surprise? Oh no. What's she done now?'

73

'You'll have to wait. It's not scary, don't worry.'

'You have to tell me!'

'No, it's nothing to worry about. Forget I said anything.'

'How can I forget you said anything?'

Jamie taps his nose. 'You'll find out tomorrow.'

'Well, we'll miss you and thanks again. I'm sure Mrs Jones will be thrilled with these little munchkins tomorrow.'

The boys hold up the project, one each side.

'You'd better put it down safely, yeah, guys. We don't want it to have any further accidents.' Jamie laughs.

'Thanks. We'll look after it,' says Jasper.

'Yeah, thanks,' says Rupert.

With the Man on the Moon safely by the front door, all set for its imminent departure to school, I check the latest text message from Sian.

> Have 976,680 shares on Facebook;
> 899,078 retweets, but still haven't found
> Perfect Patrick.

Chapter 9

My house – divorce party

I have been reading up on divorce parties and there are some suggestions that they are good for closure. When your very recently divorced ex-husband is about to get married again, there is no doubt that you are in need of some form of closure.

I still consider it a little unconventional, but now that I am dressed up and Sian is here it feels a bit more exciting. Who cares what the party is for anyhow? It is a party thrown in my honour, I remind myself. It is a bit difficult to forget what the occasion is, though, since Sian has bought a divorce party pack. Scattered around the living room are signs saying things like, 'Just Divorced', 'She's No longer with Stupid' and 'We Always Hated Him'. Meanwhile, I am wearing a sash that says, 'Back on the Market'. In some ways it feels like a hen party, only for a single, middle-aged person, which is a sobering thought. And then there's the cake. Ah, the cake.

In fairness, Sian ordered one of my preferred flavours: chocolate ganache. It is the wording and decoration that are a little less tasteful. It is decorated with a bride and groom, like you would see on any normal wedding cake. However, the groom has been decapitated. I do hate Dick but that is a little harsh. His marzipan head is beside the bride's feet and what looks like a sparkly Jimmy Choo is kicking it. Scrawled in red-coloured icing is, 'Congratulations, No More Dick'. *Not that I ever had much of it in the first place*, I think, smiling to myself. The inscription doesn't read particularly well, and I am not sure if it is a double entendre or innocently meant that it is the end of Dick, as in the person. I think it is probably best that I start cutting up the cake as soon as possible.

I have been pleading with Sian to tell me what the surprise is since Jamie let it slip. However, she has flatly refused and says the surprise will be here at any moment. Imagine if it was that she'd found Perfect Patrick! I do hope not; I'm not ready to meet him yet.

There are ten of us waiting for the surprise to happen; Jane is one of them. She seems happy enough, although throwing back the drinks a little quicker than normal, but it is a party after all. It turns out that Markus had to cancel his fake date and so Jane is still none the wiser.

I pour her a big glass of vodka and diet Coke since she deserves it.

'How's Markus?' asks Sian. Personally, I can't bear to bring his name up.

'Oh yeah, he's good,' she says. 'Doing a lot of overtime at the moment. Sometimes he doesn't get home until midnight he's working so late. He wants Jade and Trent to go to private school, so he's working hard to pay for it.'

'So good of him,' Sian says with a hint of sarcasm.

'He's amazing, my Markus. I'm so lucky. I'd hate to be like this – having a "divorce" party,' says Jane, highlighting the word divorce. She looks at me pitifully as she says it.

'It's not that bad. At least I know Dick is a snake, unlike some people,' I snap. I immediately regret it and can't believe I said that in such a tone. It was the mix of alcohol and the way she said the D word that did it. Unsurprisingly, Jane gives me a bewildered look.

'Anyway, someone is here for you, Amelia,' says Sian, noticing the tension in the air. 'Are you ready for your surprise?'

'I'm ready,' I say.

'Now close your eyes.'

I do as I am told, and everyone in the room starts screaming and cheering. Is it Patrick?

'Keep your eyes closed,' repeats Sian.

What on earth can it be?

I am instructed to open my eyes, and there in front of me is certainly not Perfect Patrick, but three male strippers who all look quite slithery. Oh no. I don't mean to sound ungrateful, but a nice surprise would have been a voucher for a spa day, or a gift voucher to spend in M&S. I wasn't expecting this. Once again, I suspect this is more for Sian than for me.

Sian places one of my old records on the turntable as luckily we managed to fix the needle before the party. Man 2 Man Meets Man Parrish are now blasting out with 'Male Stripper'.

One of the strippers is sinuously gyrating his hips in front of me, while another two go around the room, dancing with each of the women in turn. Timed in perfect coordination, the three of them remove their tops to show their muscles, most of which are covered in what I'm sure are carefully considered tattoos.

I am beginning to feel uncomfortable with this man's groin in my face; I wish he would target Sian instead of me. I make an excuse that I need the bathroom and direct him towards Sian. She immediately seems pleased with the attention.

I don't want to be a spoilsport, but it has all been a little overwhelming. I think I need another glass of wine to get me in the mood and to escape for a minute.

I close the lid of the toilet and plonk myself down. However, it doesn't take long before I am interrupted.

'Amelia, Amelia. Are you in there?' shouts Sian with desperation in her voice.

'What is it?' I open the door to see a hyperactive Sian.

'You are not going to believe this, Amelia.' She looks in shock.

'Are you okay? You look like you've seen a ghost.'

'Well, I have. Kind of. One of the guys has the same tattoo that Jack had. You remember the cartoon on his right shoulder?'

'Oh, yeah, I remember.'

'This guy… well, his name is Rob… he has the same one on his left shoulder. How spooky is that?'

I give Sian a hug.

'Spoooooky,' I say reassuringly.

'Amelia, do you think it's fate? Do you think Jack sent me this guy from heaven?'

'I'm not sure, Sian. Maybe it's just a coincidence.'

I don't know what to say to her, but I am not entirely sure that any husband in heaven would send a male stripper to their grieving widow, but it is a coincidence for sure.

'Amelia, I've met the man I'm going to marry. I can feel it. You know how I always say I have psychic abilities,' insists Sian.

'You'd better get back to him then,' I say. I am genuinely pleased for her, but these guys are probably charging by the hour, so she had better get on with it if she wants his number.

I pour myself another Pinot Grigio and grab a willy shaped straw that is lying on the table. I was told that it was eco-friendly, so I don't feel too guilty.

The strippers are still dancing, but I notice that the good-looking, dark-haired one, with the cartoon on his shoulder, hasn't left Sian's side. Perhaps the feeling is mutual.

Looking around I can see everyone is having a good time, which is the whole purpose of any party, so that can only be a good thing. There is only one person who doesn't look so happy and that is Jane. I do hope it isn't because I was a little snappy.

'Are you okay?'

'I think it's the tequila. I feel sick. Can you get me a taxi?'

'Yeah, of course. Try and eat something and have some water. I'll get the taxi as soon as possible.'

I tell the taxi to rush. I don't fancy the idea of Jane vomiting all over my Laura Ashley sofa. I am such a terrible friend to her tonight.

'Sorry, I'm sooooo drunk, Amelia. I know I've drunk too much, but it's Markus. He makes me drink… He's not really working all those hours. He stinks of perfume when he comes home. I'm not stupid. Did you know that Dick was being unfaithful? I mean before you found out?'

Oh my, I don't know what to say to her.

'Well, there was his cycling. He did seem to go on long rides and never lose weight, or anything,' I manage.

I try to think how I can hint that her suspicions are correct, but now is perhaps not the right time with the state she is in. I am surprisingly relieved when she starts retching and is sick all over the sofa.

At 11pm the strippers' time is up, and Sian has Rob's telephone number written on her hand. The taxi for Jane arrives at the same time. What must the taxi driver be thinking of this mad house? He is greeted with a middle-aged woman staggering towards him and three scantily clad men walking out with a bag full of massage oil and squirty cream.

'Oh, that was brilliant,' says Sian. 'I'm missing him already.'

She blows kisses to Rob from the window as he leaves in a small van with 'The Banana Men' in yellow vinyl all over it. What a name.

'I haven't felt like this since Jack, Amelia. I'm in love.'

'Well, you'd better save his number on your phone then, before it rubs off your hand.' I laugh. She is like a teenager, so giggly and excited, although that might be the number of Bullfrogs she has managed to quaff too.

Sian pulls out her phone to put in the number. However, she starts screaming as she reads a notification.

'Oh my god, Oh my god.'

'Has he messaged already?'

'No, it's to do with Patrick. It's a Twitter notific… noticification…You know what I mean… I need to sit down. There's been over one million shares, Amelia. One million shares!'

'How on earth?'

'Facebook has 1.2 million shares, just over one million retweets.'

'And the story isn't even in the paper until tomorrow,' I say, remembering that I emailed the journalist her answers back.

'I know. But there's something else I need to tell you…
You'd better sit down. Get a glass of wine first though;
you're going to need it.'

I grab my wine and sit beside her.

'Are you ready for this?' she asks.

'I'm ready.'

'I think we've found Patrick.'

'You think you found Patrick?'

'I know we have found Patrick, Amelia. I can feel it
in my bones. I have officially found your Perfect Patrick!
Look, here he is…'

Chapter 10

Laugharne/New York – is this Patrick?

I wake up with a thumping headache and a house full of glasses, many still with remnants of wine floating about in them. It is going to take forever to clean this lot. I am beginning to wish we had held the party at Sian's house; after all, it was her idea. As usual, it's up to me to clean the mess she makes. I decide the cleaning will have to wait though; I can't face tackling it until I have had at least four cups of coffee and another sleep. Besides, this morning I have fifty messages waiting for me and even those seem easier to tackle right now.

One of the first emails I spot is from Roxanne, the journalist in New York. She has sent me a PDF of the newspaper article she wrote. I read over it.

Help Find Perfect Patrick

In August 2000, it wasn't only the sunshine that was sizzling hot that summer's day. British tourist, Amelia Simpson, was on vacation right here in New York, when she met a gorgeous stranger on the front step of Tiffany's on Fifth Avenue. A transatlantic love affair should have begun that day; however –

this is the sad part – Amelia lost the number of this tall, dark and exceedingly handsome man. We know that his name is Patrick and he worked near the Fifth Avenue district, but that's about all.

Have you ever passed someone and your eyes connected and you wondered if that was your soulmate? You glide up an escalator and see someone and your eyes meet? It's happened to us all, right? No? Well, this movie-worthy moment happened between Amelia and Patrick, so it is devastating that Amelia lost his number.

Come on, Manhattan, let's think. Are you Patrick? Were you waiting by the phone for Amelia to call you? Do you know Patrick? Maybe he told you about the time he met the woman of his dreams and she never called. He might be your colleague in work, your brother or uncle. Someone must know of a Patrick that worked around Fifth Avenue in 2000 and remembers this story. Patrick, we know you are out there somewhere.

Get in touch, please.

Okay, that's not too bad, although it is factually incorrect and besides, Sian thinks we have already found him. I don't have the heart to tell Roxanne that piece of information in my reply to her, as she is so excited in her email and seems to feel personally responsible for finding him. I build up an image of Roxanne in my throbbing head. Something tells me she is single and dreams of meeting her soulmate. She is young, I would imagine, and still enthusiastic about love.

She is definitely not divorced or she wouldn't be quite so ebullient about it all.

Sian forwarded me Patrick's message last night, but I wanted to read it through properly again with a clear head. She is absolutely convinced it is him because Sian has yet another of her 'feelings', and he fits my description of him precisely. Whilst very drunk after the party, she also consulted her spirit guide who confirmed this is the man we are looking for. I'm not sure that Sian in a drunken state talking to a spirit guide would give me any reason whatsoever to believe it is Patrick, but he most certainly has the exact same broody look that I remember. There is something about the way his eyes crinkle when he smiles that feels so familiar. Although I may not share Sian's spiritual beliefs, she could well be right for once. Even with a raging hangover I can see from Patrick's photo that he is as good-looking as ever. Forgive me for sounding so shallow. I secretly felt that he wouldn't have changed much, but I am surprised to see that his teeth aren't quite as perfect as I remembered. I assumed all Americans had perfect teeth. They are quite white, as you would expect; however, they are slightly crooked on top. They look cute though and quite suit him. His hair is exactly as I had imagined it would be now. Dark, with a slight wave, a hint of grey at the sides and thick on top. In his photo he is wearing his trademark well-cut suit, everything about him screams out that he is an older version of my Patrick. His message is short, but it certainly sounds like the man I met in 2000.

Good evening,
    I saw the media appeal for Patrick. Well, you found him!

I remember meeting a beautiful girl in 2000. She was so cute. I waited for her to call for so long, but she never did. I never forgot her. I didn't know her name, but I often thought of her. I would have tracked her down to the moon if I could have. My beautiful British girl. I am so happy to have finally found her. Please contact me as soon as you get this. I can't wait any longer. Drop me an email, call me, whatever, contact details below.

Yours always,

Patrick x

I need to message him back, find out a bit more information, but it all sounds quite credible. Sian was right: I think we have found Patrick. I ignore all the other messages waiting for me. I don't know why, but I have the feeling that this is the one. I don't need to look any further. He is my Patrick. I can't quite believe it. I look at his photo. It is as if we have met before. My tummy does somersaults as I study him. Why, oh why would I not ring him when we met? He's gorgeous! Looking at him I think of my previous life. The one before I met Dick, when everything was an adventure. What has happened to me? I seem to have lost myself. I lost myself being a mother, a wife and a part-time staff member at the bookshop. Seeing this message reminds me of who I was. The real Amelia with dreams. I was full of fun and laughter once long ago. Maybe I wasn't brimming with confidence, otherwise I would have met up with Patrick and followed my nursing dream, but I know that I was a different person to who I am now.

I feel the urgent need to write back immediately in case he disappears again. I don't want to lose him a second time. Maybe he will give me everything I have been missing – or he could be very married. If he is single, would he make my loneliness and heartbreak disappear? He suddenly feels like the escape I need and so I eagerly enter the email address he has given and start writing.

Dear Patrick,

Delete, too formal.

Hello Patrick,

Yes, that's better.

> Thanks so much for getting in touch. I can't believe it's you after all this time!
> Do you remember Tiffany's? It was such a beautiful day when we met. That taxi driver was so miserable. Are yellow cab drivers always like that?
> So, what's been happening? Are you a journalist I seem to remember? Are you married? Do you have children?

I don't know what else to write. Perhaps it is a little early to say I am divorced and talk about the boys, etc. I don't even know the guy that well. Yes, that's enough for now. He has my direct email, so the ball is in his court to contact me back.

> Anyway, lovely to hear from you.
> Love,
> Amelia x

I press send and await his response. I wonder what time it is in the States at the moment. Hopefully, he will reply with more information soon and then we can slowly get to know each other. I can't wait for him to respond. Sian was right: this is fun.

I feel a little guilty for being so happy, as one of my other messages has informed me that Jane arrived home early last night to find Markus with a woman on their sofa. I do consider myself slightly responsible, as I was the one who gave her all that vodka and tequila and the reason that she left earlier than planned. I didn't want her to find out like this, but Markus was being quite blatant about it all. Jane has now taken the children and is staying with her parents. I will give her a call later to see how she is. I am aware of how she will be feeling right now.

I hope Perfect Patrick doesn't have anyone in his life. I know he is only a pen pal at the moment, but I wouldn't want any partner of his getting the wrong idea. Even though I secretly hope he is single, I don't want to upset anyone. At least my message is written in a friendly manner. It is not like I have asked him to have WhatsApp sex or anything, unlike Dick and Tanja.

–

Ten hours later and there is still no reply from Perfect Patrick. Roxanne has messaged saying they already have some responses from the newspaper. I think I am going to have to tell her the news before too long.

By the time I go to bed there is still no response from Perfect Patrick. Strange, but I suppose I have gone over twenty years without being in touch, another day isn't going to make a difference.

I think about his smile, his eyes, and that beautiful hair of his. I do hope I hear from him soon. Perhaps my email wasn't direct enough. Does he realise that I am waiting for a response? Maybe I should have ended with an instruction, such as, I await your reply. Or, I eagerly await your reply – no, too keen. This is my first email to him and I am already useless at communication. But how are you supposed to write to someone gorgeous? I'm too embarrassed to ask Sian or anyone for advice. Sian would find it funny that I'm so out of the dating game that I can no longer communicate with a man. Are there any books you can buy that tell you how to communicate in a friendly and not overtly flirty way? The only letters I have received have been from lawyers over the past year or so. I am not used to communicating with a potential love interest. The only communicating Dick and I did more recently involved shouting. This is a whole new world to me.

Oh, come on Patrick, write back. I promise to be more forward if only you will reply.

Chapter 11

A mysterious location – WhatsApp

Monday

Remember me????

Sure.

I bet you're still hot. I'm sorry I didn't take you up on that date.

Lol, no issues.

So, is it too late to see you now?

Are you serious?

Well, if you don't ask, you don't get.

Okay, sure. Are you here at the moment?

No, but I can arrange to come and see you.

Oh, okay. Send me a photo. I don't even know what you look like anymore.

Tuesday

Beautiful pic, you have a lovely smile.

Aww, thank you. You're so sweet.

I'm a journo, I have a way with words ☺

Shame you're not a surgeon, you might have a way with your hands!

Ooh, naughty. I like it.

I'm always naughty.

Nice ☺

Wednesday

I like messaging you. I wish we'd met before.

Thanks, it's been fun hearing from you.

So, what you doing today?

Predicting a crash on Wall Street. Not very exciting stuff.

So cool. I looked for some of your articles online. Couldn't find them :(

Oh, honey, these damn paywalls. You have to subscribe and pay for the newspaper.

Ah, okay. Shame.

So, what's my honey doing today?

Messaging you, listening to the rain.

Sounds like typical British summer weather to me, I bet you're drinking tea – total cliche. ☺

No, a Pinot Grigio actually.

At this time in the day? I guess we do have a time difference between us. Listen, I have to run to a meeting now, honey. Speak soon!

Byeee, have a great day.

X

Thursday

So, did Wall Street crash yesterday?

Lol, no, not yet!

Hope your meeting went well.

It was only my boss, total slave driver.

92

Don't work too hard, you'll need some energy if I come over!

Lol. You really are a naughty one, aren't you! You're coming over?

Maybe we should get to know each other a little first, hey ☺

Maybe. But why take things slowly? Imagine what would happen in person!!!!!

Sounds tempting ☺

XXXX

Friday

Good morning, how was your evening?

Not as exciting as chatting to you, honey.

Nice. You know what to say.

Well, I have been published in all the best newspapers.

Woah, I'm super impressed. I don't know how you have time to message me.

I like to take a break every now and again from the stressful deadlines ☺

I'm glad to hear it.

Please send me some articles if I can't get them online.

Hey, I have to get back to work now, let's speak tomorrow.

Definitely. I'll miss you till then xxx

Message me when you wake up. Speak soon. XX

Chapter 12

Sian's house – the moment of truth

'You'd better explain everything right now, Sian,' I demand.

I keep staring at her phone in disbelief. I can't stop myself from shaking my head in disgust. Had I not seen the name Patrick pop up when I was looking at the selfie of her and Rob at dinner last night, I would have been none the wiser.

'Okay, okay. I just may have messaged Patrick.' Her normal confident persona has been replaced with someone I don't recognise. She is meeker and seems to have acquired a nervous laugh suddenly.

'Why would you message Patrick when you knew I was waiting for him to email me back?' I ask. I can't get my head around this at all.

'Look at his messages. He clearly likes you. Read again what he said about your photo. "Nice smile". Aww.'

'Sian, don't change the subject. Tell me why you would do such a stupid thing.'

'I knew if I left it to you then you'd be all polite and nice. I just wanted to get things moving along a bit, that's all. I'm sorry,' says Sian.

'But we know nothing about him. He might be married for all we know. What is wrong with you?'

I am so upset with her. I don't know when she was thinking of telling me. It is so fortunate for me that I saw Patrick pop up on her WhatsApp, or goodness knows how far it would have escalated. God forbid, she may have sent him nudes next and passed them off as me.

'Come on, I was only trying to help. I'd never hurt you. Surely you realise that,' says Sian.

'I know you wouldn't mean to hurt me, but can't you leave it to me? He's going to think I'm a right floozy now. What sort of start to any kind of relationship with him is this?'

Sian doesn't reply and looks away, her bottom lip jutting out. A habit she has when she doesn't get her way.

'I'm sorry, I just wanted to help. I want you to be happy. Look how miserable you've been lately. I thought we could have some fun and encourage him a bit.'

'Encourage him with me flying to New York for sex? Is that what you mean?' I ask incredulously.

How on earth could Sian be so naïve? We know nothing about the man. Sian might not always think of the consequences when she is up to something, but this is something else. What must he think of me? I don't even know that we can recover from this. How on earth can I contact him ever again after her flirty messages? She has given off the wrong impression of me entirely.

I don't normally storm out of Sian's house, but I need some breathing space from her. She might be my best friend, but sometimes she oversteps the mark and this is just too much. She has always been the same. This feels just like when we were sixteen. She told me that the school heartthrob, Kevin Williams, wanted to meet me outside the chippy for a date. She knew how much of a crush I had on him and I spent hours doing my hair. I turned up and he asked me what the 'F' I was doing there as he was there to meet Sian and proceeded to walk off. I cried all the way home. Sian insisted she meant well and was simply trying to fix us up. I didn't think I would ever forgive her then either. I slam her front door and walk out into the fresh air. I don't know what to think anymore. I can't even trust my best friend at times.

—

At home I get the biggest spoon I can find. I know I shouldn't.

Ah, Nutella. Why is it so easy to get through one of these massive jars in one go?

I feel truly lonely. The boys are at Dick's and I miss their company. When we were together as a family, we used to have a takeaway on a Saturday night, followed by watching some reality contest on TV. Now, every other weekend, they are over there, with Dick and Tanja Tart. The house is so empty without the boys. Maybe I should take up salsa dancing, or some kind of hobby to get me out when they are not here.

My phone keeps bleeping and I know it's Sian. I munch on some Pringles and sip some wine before reluctantly picking it up.

I see that she has forwarded me the WhatsApp chat, along with a huge apology. She states that she had no choice but to do this, as she knows that Patrick is what I need in my life. She says that sometimes a person is destined to come into your life at a certain point in time. Even if it doesn't work out, right then, at that point in your life, that person is meant for you. Like a guardian angel, only without wings and carrying a Creme Egg.

That does make me smile, but she is not off the hook entirely. Especially as I told her that I was disappointed Patrick hadn't replied. The number of times she sat there with a completely straight face, telling me she was sure that he would get in touch soon. Perhaps that is what hurts me the most: the lies.

As I read through the messages they have been sending each other, I die of embarrassment.

Shame you're not a surgeon, you might have a way with your hands, oh my, Sian. What an awful thing to say.

I take a sneaky look at Patrick's WhatsApp profile. I can't help but wish there was another photo of him. Instead, he has a poem, which I googled and discovered is Keats. It seems to be about dying, which is quite morbid.

When I have fears that I may cease to be,
Before my pen has glean'd my teeming brain,
Before high-piled books, in charactery,
Hold like rich garners the full ripen'd grain.

My WhatsApp profile has a picture of a cute fluffy dog, which I hope would portray that I like cute fluffy things. It is a little difficult to work out what Patrick's profile means. A poem doesn't give much away, except for the fact that he likes poetry. I suppose he is a writer and, as he said, he does have a way with words. But why this particular poem? 'When I Have Fears That I May Cease to Be?' Does it mean that he thinks he is dying? What if I have left it twenty-odd years to get in touch and now he is dying and he was, in fact, my soulmate all along?

That is probably not the case, but I should perhaps get things moving in the event that he does have some kind of terminal illness. I assume he can't be married after the messages he has been sending Sian, although I do need to be sure. How I can salvage things, though, I don't know. Looking at these messages, he must think I am some kind of sex maniac.

I need to find a way of messaging him while bringing it back down to my tone a little and definitely not Sian's. He also now has Sian's WhatsApp number and not mine. How on earth can I resolve this mess?

I want to find out more about Perfect Patrick first before I attempt to salvage anything, so I look him up on Facebook. It might even show that he has checked into a hospital and given them a review or is having treatment for something.

This is a bit of a task, though, as his surname still hasn't appeared anywhere. On his email it only said Patrick E. However, I enter 'Patrick E' into the Facebook search, as I am convinced that when people look you up, you only have to put in a name and they seem to appear. He knows my full name now, so he may have Facebook stalked me – you never know.

Sadly, 'Patrick E' doesn't bring up any positive results, which means that either I haven't been Facebook stalked, or I am wrong about Facebook stalkers. I google 'Patrick E' instead, but I don't think either of the results are him. One is a serial killer from somewhere in Texas and one was banned from an Irish pub for dancing naked with his Guinness. Fortunately, both photos look nothing like Patrick. No, there are absolutely no New York journalists fitting his description. I don't know much about the paywall that Patrick mentioned in his message to Sian, but it must be blocking us from finding his stories.

It is disappointing that I can't find anything, but I guess in the pre-Dick days nobody had the luxury of being able to find out more about a potential love interest with the click of a mouse. So, this is no different really. I shall simply have to find out more by asking him myself.

I go back onto WhatsApp and begin my dialogue with Patrick. I will somehow rectify Sian's forthrightness.

> Hi, it's Amelia. This is my new no. Just thinking of you. Hope you're having a fab day. X

The ticks go blue almost immediately; Patrick's read the message.

He's online right now!

Oh, bloody hell, he's typing.

Oh my god, Patrick is actually typing!

And then he stops.

Chapter 13

At home – cheap plonk with Jamie

'Hello, Sian says you're a bit upset with her,' says Jamie, who is standing on my doorstep holding out a bottle of Co-op Fairtrade wine. 'Thought you may need this,' he adds, pushing it towards me.

'Aww, come in, Jamie, that's so kind of you. Megan's not waiting for you, is she?' I say, looking around outside.

'No, no, she decided to stay on in Bath. There was some yogi guy she admires doing a special class. It involves being spiritually free and naked, so that was enough for me to know.' Jamie laughs.

'Oh, umm, right,' I stutter. 'Well, I hope you both had a good time away, anyway.'

'Yes, it was fine. But what about you? What the hell happened? It's not like you and Sian to fall out over something,' says Jamie, removing his battered old Barbour jacket and throwing it on the coat hook.

'We haven't fallen out,' I explain. 'She's just gone a bit overboard.'

'Sian said you were annoyed with her, but didn't elaborate,' says Jamie.

I explain what she has done and Jamie agrees that I should be annoyed with her but, as I would expect from him, he can see her point of view too. He is always so impartial and I do love that about him, but tonight it is annoying me. I want him to be solely on my side.

'I think she meant well. She does have your best interests at heart. She's really upset that she has done something to hurt you,' he explains calmly.

'I know, but she just took over. She has taken over from the beginning… I'll sort it out with her, don't worry. We've been friends for too long to let this come between us. It's just that… Perhaps it was all such a stupid idea after all. This whole finding Patrick thing.' I think about the fact that he still hasn't responded to my recent message. Why did he stop typing?

'Hey, come on, you. It wasn't that stupid. You had fun looking for him, didn't you? Don't tell me that a part of you wasn't curious about him. At least now you found him,' says Jamie.

'I suppose, but we both live on different sides of the Atlantic. We could never start a long-distance relationship, or anything.'

'Well, you only wanted a pen pal to start with, didn't you? Anyway, if you do ever decide to go to New York to meet him, I'd happily join you,' says Jamie.

'I won't be going to New York,' I promise.

'Well, just saying, if you do want to go, we could time it to go together. There's a conference coming up there with work and I have surplus air miles due to expire, so I can easily take a companion.' Jamie smiles.

'That's a lovely idea, Jamie. I would never leave the boys, but a nice idea. I would love to go back there one day,' I say.

'Well, just a thought if you fancied it. It would be good to have some company, to be honest. I don't know anyone in the office there, so it would be nice to have a friendly face with me.'

'Wouldn't you take Megan? She wouldn't like you going off to New York and not taking her, I'm pretty sure of that,' I say.

'She has some girls' trip to a health spa she can't get out of the week of the conference in October, so she can't make it,' he explains.

'Oh, I bet she's gutted. I can't imagine Megan being best pleased she might miss out on a trip to New York.'

'No, Megan is definitely a bit of a character,' he agrees.

Does he know how Sian and I feel about her? I laugh nervously.

Jamie laughs too, and it's as though we are both in on some private joke, but I'm not really sure what it is. He pours us both a glass of wine.

'Cheers. Here's to New York. Let's hope you can come with me.' Jamie grins.

'Yes, sure.' I smile. I would never agree to go anywhere without the boys, and so I only say that to please him more than anything.

'Hey, I rented a movie before I came over. I'd planned a night in and then Sian rang me all upset and I wanted to see if you were okay. You want to watch it with me? It's only on rent for 48 hours… It's *Sliding Doors*.'

'*Sliding Doors?*' I didn't even know you could still rent that.

'Wah! I love that movie; you knew that, didn't you?' I smile at him, despite Jamie looking away.

'Get the TV ready, Amelia. I'll run to the Spar and get some more Pringles. Looks like you've already gone through that lot.' Jamie points to the empty tube. 'Marshmallows too?'

'Sounds perfect!'

We have the most amazing evening, even if I do binge through the whole bag of marshmallows and only leave one pink one for Jamie. Why can't I binge on apples and lemon infused water, instead of everything that is bad for me? One small blip in my life and the emotional eater in me comes out like some type of cookie monster and there goes a whole family-size bag of Monster Munch.

'Do you still go running, Jamie? I'm thinking of joining that club down the park,' I say. I don't even know where the words come from, and they sound absurd out loud.

'I haven't had as much time as I'd have liked but, yeah, if you fancy starting at the club I can come with you for company.' He looks seriously at me as he takes his last sip of wine. 'Would you like to start running, Amelia?'

'I don't knowwww,' I find myself answering. Perhaps now is not the right time to think about starting a healthy new lifestyle. I quickly jam my mouth with Pringles, to stop myself from agreeing to any more idiotic ideas.

The evening goes so much faster with company. Being with Jamie is like throwing off your bra and putting on your favourite onesie. When you have known each other forever it is so easy to be around each other. I sink my feet into his lap, and he gently massages them. He doesn't even take any notice of the fact that my nail polish is starting to chip and my usual home pedicure is way overdue.

Chapter 14

Both sides of the Atlantic – hello Patrick

I wake up later than normal for a Sunday morning, as Jamie and I stayed up until the small hours putting the world to rights and chatting about my mum and his dad. Both were widowed young and both were in school together in the nearby village. Even though they had a lot in common, they never really talked to one another. They would just nod politely if they saw each other. It's wonderful to have this connection with Jamie, as it keeps the memories of our parents alive for both of us. I'm glad Miserable Megan stayed on in Bath, as it was exactly the type of evening to reminisce that we both needed, and it distracted me from the boys being at Dick's. You would think I would start getting used to it by now.

I can't wait for them to come home this afternoon. Until then, Patrick's messages are keeping me busy as he has finally messaged me back. One of my first assumptions about him is that he must be a bit of an insomniac, as he was up very late messaging me. Even with the time difference, he must have been up half the night. I read through the messages again, as though I need to memorise every single word. The first message he sent last night was quite touching. I had picked it up before bed, but decided it was best to respond in the sobriety that morning would bring.

> Hey, I've missed you. XX Hope you're ok.
> I'm getting worried about you XXX

It is so silly but my heart takes a leap as I read this line again and again, as I see that he was 'worried' about me. I know that I sound like a rather sad person here, but I don't think any grown male has been worried about me for a very long time. In fact, I am pretty sure that Dick never worried about me and wouldn't have cared if I had fallen off a cliff. Indeed, I remember when Dick read an article about women living longer than men and he uttered with complete disdain that I would probably live longer than him. So, no, I am pretty certain he never worried about my welfare, only the fact that I might outlive him.

I'm ashamed to admit that Patrick's comment makes me feel wanted and important for once in an extremely long time. I am an independent woman who doesn't need the validation of any man, but as a grown-up orphan, it's the thought of having someone who cares enough to say they were worried about me that hits an emotional nerve.

I read the response that I have just sent back.

> Great to hear from you, Patrick. You know
> you can contact me on this no anytime.
> Didn't mean to worry you. X

I had edited my message so many times that Patrick had gone offline by the time I had sent this. I immediately regret including the word 'anytime'. Reading it again I feel as though this may come across a bit needy. Fortunately, his response an hour later is very pleasant.

> Gee, thank God for that. I was beginning to think you were ignoring me. I missed you. ☺

He missed me! But then again, strictly speaking, he missed Sian and not me, since it wasn't actually me that he was messaging previously.

I read my response to him over and over, to ensure I come across as a confident divorcee and not the emotional overeating wreck that I am.

> Awww, no, I'm here, just some technical difficulties with my internet connection

Phew. I wonder if I should have put a smiley face at the end there? Although, would that be a sad face if I was having difficulties? Oh God, I am useless at this sexting stuff, although smiley faces aren't officially sexting, surely.

He doesn't seem to have been too concerned that there was no smiley face, or kiss, as his next message is quite sweet.

> I'm glad to hear you're okay. So, you're coming to see me, are you? Maybe that's not such a bad idea. I'd love to see you, sorry if I sounded a bit off before. I had some work stuff on my mind. Xxx

Perhaps it is all the flirty messages that Sian sent that has given him the wrong idea and now he wants me to fly over so he can get his wicked way with me. Well, I won't be having a wicked way with any man, so he is in for a surprise there.

I try to learn more about him. He says that he has Irish roots and his ancestors are from Waterford. I tell him how it is such a small world as my crystal wine glasses are from there too. I talk to him about family stuff and listen to what he says about his life. I tell him about my boys and prevent myself from bringing any bitter stories about Dick into the conversation. In return, Patrick admits how he never had children, or a wife, as he was afraid to commit to anyone, following a childhood trauma that he doesn't elaborate on. Now, at fifty, he has a boss he hates and no family to carry on his legacy. However, he does enjoy polo and has won many cups for best polo player and the like. As if he wasn't already perfect enough!

After seeing a photo that he has sent of himself at a polo match, I imagine him galloping around the field in his white jodhpurs like some hero in a Jilly Cooper novel. In the photo he looks like the type of man who would hold you tight and make everything feel okay again. I can't stop myself comparing him to Dick. He didn't dream of kissing me passionately in the past few years. In fact, if I had tried to hug Dick, he would often push me away. This is why I am so flattered and captivated by the slightest hint of Patrick's attention.

I am still staring at the phone, dissecting every comment and its meaning, when a new message flashes up from Patrick.

> Hey, honey. Sorry, I had to go offline for a bit. So, is it morning or afternoon for you now? This time difference is driving me crazy. XX

> It's afternoon, Patrick. So, what you been up to? XX

> I had a polo match.

> Fantastic, did you win?

> No, I was so pissed. We lost at the last minute.

> Oh, okay!

I'm quite surprised. I never imagined him swearing over WhatsApp somehow. It just doesn't fit with the Jilly Cooper hero bit really.

> Anyway, enough about my day, how's yours?

It's so nice that he asks me so many questions. He seems so interested in what I have to say. Again, I compare this to Dick, who couldn't care less how my day was going. Though I suppose as a journalist, he is used to asking people questions.

> Not much, there's never anything exciting happening. Although I have a Medieval Festival to attend in a nearby castle next weekend x.

> Do you live in a castle? That's what I love about you British people, you have fun accents and live in castles. xx.

Before I can answer his ridiculous assumption, his next message takes me by surprise.

> Hey, I realized that I only ever heard your accent the one time you called me. We should Skype one day so we can see each other, wouldn't that be fun?

The one time I called him? So, Sian has spoken to him and pretended to be me as well? What the hell did she say to him? I must speak to her about this.

> I'd love to!

I find myself answering, despite the thought of Skyping him making me especially nervous. It is one thing sending a photo of myself that has been carefully selected and possibly airbrushed a little, but another seeing me on Skype. What about those times when the camera gets stuck and your mouth is half open? Skype Face, I call it. You can get stuck like that for ages when the signal gets a bit weak. I really don't want Skype Face with Patrick.

> Great, then let's set up a time now.

I don't reply as I think of ways to avoid Skyping.

> Ah, checked my diary and I can do 9am
> NY time tomorrow. Does that work for you?

I want to say no, but instead find myself forced into typing a total lie and besides, I am off tomorrow.

> Yes, definitely. Looking forward to it
> already! ☺

I find myself saying.

By tomorrow, I need to lose five kilos, have a few subtle highlights done, find something to wear and get a full facelift.

Or I could Skype him in a very dark room and tell him that the light bulb has blown.

Chapter 15

A very dark room – time to Skype

My first problem is my outfit. I need something that says, 'it's my day off work, I'm in the house, chilling, and this really is no big deal'.

Unfortunately, I also need something that will appear elegant whilst making me look fantastic. It doesn't take two minutes of searching in my wardrobe to discover that I won't be finding anything that fits either of these requirements. All that is in there are jeans that are way too small, maternity dresses that I still can't bear to part with and a few jumpers that have seen better days. I pluck a few bobbles off my favourite jumper as I consider what I can do.

Rummaging about again, I finally find a white shirt tucked at the back of the wardrobe. I bought it for an interview for a job in Morrisons a long time ago. I didn't get the job, so not sure it is particularly lucky, but it will look a bit smarter than the rest of my clothes. I remove it from the hanger and try it on. It is very tight and the bottom buttons are bursting at the seams when I do them up. It might still work though.

Placing myself strategically in front of the computer, I try and work out how much of me he will be able to see. If I get it at the right angle, I can get only my top half in and he won't see the buttons that are threatening to erupt at any second. I can't find anything else that looks classy, and a white shirt works for every occasion. For all he knows, I could have teamed it up with the perfect pair of size 10 jeans and a classy belt. I have no choice but to opt for the shirt.

As for the venue for my Skype session, I choose the back bedroom, as with the weather being a little dull this week, the room is permanently pitched in darkness. I chuckle to myself as I realise the lighting is perfect.

I am still not leaving things to chance, though, and have put on at least four lashings of concealer, some Flash Balm to brighten up my skin and have given my hair a fresh blow-dry, which has made my hair look a little lighter.

I am carefully applying my pale pink lipstick when the familiar tone of the Skype ring begins, precisely at 9am EDT. I like the fact that he is punctual, at least.

'Hi!' I answer casually.

'Hi, trying to get the picture working – one minute,' says Patrick.

My heart is leaping about now. I wonder if he can see me yet. I certainly can't see him.

'Is that better?'

'Oh yes, that's better,' I say.

There he is, looking at me from across the Atlantic. My heart wants to melt. He has a black jumper on which, even over Skype, you can see the definition of his chest through. Wow! He is certainly in shape; it must be all the polo.

'Can you see me?' I ask. In fact, I'm hoping there's something wrong with the camera and he can't see me at all.

'Um, yes, but it's very dark. I can see more of an outline of you really. Can you maybe improve the lighting, so I can see you a little better?' he asks.

'Sorry, there's a problem with the light in here. Some sort of electrical problem, and this is the only room I can pick Skype up properly,' I lie.

'Oh, okay… Weird. Anyway, nice to hear that beautiful British accent.'

'Nice to hear your lovely American accent too,' I say, hoping he doesn't pick up on the fact that Sian and I sound slightly different. Fortunately, he is still blissfully oblivious to Sian's stupid stunt. I don't even know how I could ever explain that, so I brush the thought to one side and hopefully he will be none the wiser.

'So, what shall we talk about?' I add.

'You…'

'Haha, well, my life isn't so exciting.'

'Oh, Britain is such an awesome place. I went the year before I started my PhD. I inter-railed around Europe. You're lucky to have so many amazing places in your fabulous country.'

'Wow, what did you study?'

'It was a journalism thing – all research stuff. I enjoyed my year off more.' Patrick laughs. 'In fact, you know, I must have met you not long after I'd got back,' he adds.

I feel myself blush slightly.

'Yup, I still can't believe you came up to a stranger like that,' I say.

'I always go for what I want. I don't waste time,' he says. 'Life is so short. You know how I mentioned a trauma in my past? You see my parents were killed in a car accident when I was five years old. I grab life with both hands; you don't know what can happen. I don't know how long I have left.'

'Oh no, I'm sorry, that's awful. I lost my dad when I was young and so I can only imagine how it must have been.' I want to ask him what he means about not having long left but can't bring myself to say it out loud.

'It's okay. I was just a kid; I don't remember much. I only know that you have to live your life. Don't waste time, that's my life motto. Although I should probably find a new job since I am wasting my life with my mean boss.'

'You seem well qualified; I'm sure you could get anything. How come your boss is so bad? What did he do?'

'It's a she, not a he.' He laughs.

'Aww, she's mean to you.'

'Harriet, yup... I'm not able to leave my job right now. I wouldn't find anything else that pays so well. There aren't that many jobs around in the current market. You said you work in a bookshop. Do you like your boss?'

'No, not really. I mean, she's okay, but my dream is to do something different,' I say.

'Yes, what would you like to do?' he asks. 'Set up a charitable foundation, or something?'

A charitable foundation? Don't you need to be one of those rich classy American women to do that?

'Umm, no.' I laugh. Perhaps my outfit has given him the wrong opinion of me. 'My dream is to become a dementia nurse and help others the way they helped my mum.'

This is the first time I have ever told anyone of my secret dream. Not even Sian knows; somehow it feels easier to confide in someone so far away.

'Can't imagine that being a dream, but... Anyway, when you coming to New York?' Patrick asks.

'I'd love to, but I've some other things going on right now,' I say, disappointed that Patrick didn't say anything positive about my dream job.

'You live in a castle; you can do anything you like. You're not "skint" as they say over there, are you? You don't have one of those castles with a leaky roof, do you? Do you have a butler?'

'I don't live in a castle, Patrick. I live in a cottage.'

'Castle, cute cottage, those roofs made of straw, all the same. I love British houses. I should have been an architect. Anyway... When are you coming over?'

'I don't know that I can. I can't really leave the boys and...' I want to say that I don't know him that well, but he interrupts.

'Can't their dad take them? Surely mothers get time off too. All mothers deserve some free time. I'd love to show you the sights, wine, dine and... you know the rest.'

I hope he doesn't mean what I think he does. Surely not.

'Please come and stay in our wonderful city,' says Patrick.

'I hardly know you, Patrick. And I could never stay at your place, even if I didn't have the boys,' I say.

'Oh, honey, I would never dream of you staying at mine.'

Why on earth did I say that? Perfect Patrick is bound to be a gentleman, apart from when he is being led astray by Sian, of course.

'It never entered my mind that you'd want to stay with me,' he adds. 'I know of lots of hotels in Manhattan; many won't break the bank, though that won't matter for you I'm sure. Hey, I think a colleague of mine may have written a piece on getting a good hotel deal downtown. I can send you the feature if you're interested?'

'Okay, well, that would be nice. I'd love to read about the hotels in Manhattan anyhow.'

'Don't read about them, come over and check them out. We waited over twenty years for this date, let's finally have it!' Patrick says excitedly.

Oh, why can't Patrick live in Tenby, or somewhere closer? I can't go to New York. I haven't got the money and, much more importantly, I have got the boys. They come before absolutely anything in the world. There is no way I would ever jaunt off to New York in a million years.

'Okay, well, send me that article and I'll have a look into it,' I manage.

'That would be awesome. Please say you'll come; we'll have the best time, I promise. Can I ask you one more thing? You seemed quite up for some fun when we first talked. Now you seem so much more, um... what shall we say... reserved,' says Patrick.

Oh no, I don't know how to explain this.

'Hellllooooooo!' Without warning, and before I can answer, a lady's voice sounds in the background.

'Shit. Heinous boss on the loose. Can we chat again tomorrow? Gottago.' And the line goes dead.

Chapter 16

Aldi – an unexpected phone call

Over the next few weeks Patrick doesn't stop messaging. When I wake up, instead of opening my eyes to spam, or rants about homework from Mrs Jones, I receive heart-warming messages.

This morning I am greeted with:

> Hello beautiful Amelia, wishing you the
> most wonderful day. Xxx

So many positive adjectives to wake up to! I have even started humming along to the radio as I take the boys to school, and I practically skip into work. Patrick has remained a secret from Lisa, though, as she can be a bit of a gossip-monger. Last week she asked me if I was taking something!

I'm heading to Aldi after work, to try and find something edible for tea that the boys won't waste, when I notice a WhatsApp call trying to come through. Of course, my first panicked reaction is that the boys have been smacked over the head by the school bully and are now in hospital. Thankfully, it is nothing like that. It is Patrick and he is calling me on a video call. A video call in the middle of Aldi! Oh my, I can't think of anything worse. My hair is scraped back into a greasy ponytail as I didn't get time to wash it this morning, as previously planned. This was all thanks to Rupert spilling his corn-flakes over him and me having to quickly iron yet another school shirt.

A lady in front of me is fighting to get to the poppy-seeded bread rolls whilst I juggle my basket and a French stick. The French stick is threatening to topple over my basket at any moment. How on earth does he expect me to pick up a video call in this situation? I stare in horror at the screen as the ringtone blares out. Hopefully, he will have left a message by the time I get out of here.

However, by the time I return to the car there is still no message from him explaining what his call was about. I wonder if the phone had gone off in his pocket and he didn't mean to call. Curiosity gets the better of me and I decide to ring back on my terms. That means definitely no video call. He picks up right away.

'Amelia, how are you?'

'All good, thanks. I'm not sure if you tried to call me?'

'Hey, I did indeed. I was calling to say hi, see how your day's going. What you're up to, that kind of thing. I've missed you.' My heart immediately skips a beat. I am reminded once again that someone missed me who was over the age of ten.

'That's nice.' I don't say that I missed him too. It's nice to hear from him, but I am not sure I am at the missing stage quite yet.

We exchange a few pleasantries, what the weather is like with both of us, how work is going at the moment, when his tone changes. He clears his throat and something instinctively makes me feel nervous.

'I have to tell you something, Amelia. I don't know if it will affect your feelings for me but...' I knew something was coming.

'Go on...' I say.

'Amelia, I just want to tell you that...Well, I get a bit depressed at times, to be truthful. My therapist says it's because of my parents, all the trauma I've been through. I also have an illness to deal with... But, for once in a very long time, I feel as though I have some hope in my life. You give me a reason to want to get up in the morning.'

The poor man, no wonder he suffers from depression having lost all his family and suffering with an illness. I hope he doesn't ever feel suicidal and that is what his poem means. Or is it the illness that is the reason for the poem on his phone? Perhaps it isn't surprising that he struggles to get up in the morning with everything he has to deal with. How terrible.

'Oh, Patrick. Why would this change my feelings towards you? I'm so sorry to hear this. Are you okay? I mean does your therapist help? If you ever need someone to talk to please know that you can tell me anything.'

'Yeah, she's a great help. You and her... Well, I guess you both saved me.'

Goodness, it just proves that you never know what goes on in someone's life.

I saved him! Well, along with his therapist, of course. But the most handsome, polo-playing journalist that I have ever met has been partly saved by Me: Amelia. His candid confession floors me.

'I'm sorry you're going through this. I just want to give you a big *cwch* and...'

'A couch?' says Patrick. 'Like my psychiatrist's one?'

'Umm, no. Never mind. Look, I totally understand what you've been through and how difficult it must be for you. I know when Sian's husband died, she was depressed. I think she still struggles; you just wouldn't realise. I'm sure it's more common than you think.'

'Yup, grieving is so hard, no matter how long ago it happened,' says Patrick.

'Absolutely,' I agree.

An awkward silence develops and I try to think of ways I can change the subject, but I'm not sure if he wants to talk further about his grief, or perhaps disclose his illness. I don't want to misjudge the situation and seem brusque. Fortunately, Patrick changes the subject first.

'So, umm, yeah, anyway. Now I got that out of the way... I just wanted to say hello, I guess. It's a shame I couldn't see more of you every time we Skype, but that's why I thought of calling you on a video chat. To have a frank discussion with you. And I wanted to see you, Amelia. I know this might sound odd but I feel so drawn to you. Like we did when we first met all those years ago, I guess. It's like time stood still when we talk. I could very easily fall in love with someone like you.'

Has Perfect Patrick tried to say he could fall in love with me, whilst I am in the middle of the Aldi car park? I would pinch myself and check that I wasn't dreaming, except two cars in front of me have just collided and so I am definitely not in a dream.

'Well, I'm glad we get on so well,' I say, trying to drown out the noise of the angry exchange going on outside.

I am confused about my feelings. I am not in any real rush to fall head over heels in love with anyone after what I have been through.

It is as though Patrick reads my mind though.

'I don't mean to come on strong, Amelia. I hope you don't think that. It's just that life is short, as I always tell you. It's not often you find someone so compatible and I don't know what tomorrow has in store for me, I take medication that prolongs my life but...'

'What? Medication that prolongs your life? Oh, my goodness, what's wrong?'

'Oh, I shouldn't have said that. I'm so sorry, forget I said that. I've said enough for one day.'

I sit staring out the windscreen. What on earth is Patrick not telling me?

'We need to make every single day count, Amelia. That's why I decided not to waste my time. I'm not going to play games with you. This is why I wanted to be honest,' he says.

Maybe this is why he works so hard. The poor beautiful man needs money for his medication. They do say it is very expensive in the States. We are so lucky to have our NHS.

'I've had such bad times, Amelia. Now I want the remainder of my days filled with love and happiness. I want to meet up with my beautiful British lady again.'

'Oh, Patrick. That's so lovely. I hope I can make you happy. I truly do.'

'Then say you'll fly to New York, Amelia. Fly to New York and meet me, then my dream to see you again will come true.'

Chapter 17

A Welsh castle – The Annual Medieval Day

'Are you wearing tights, Jamie?' I can't stop staring at his skinny little legs in a pair of white tights.

'I'll have you as one of my wives if you're not careful, Amelia,' laughs Jamie.

Bless him, I should probably stop laughing now, but he really doesn't suit Henry VIII. He would have been much better dressing up as a court jester or something. He is far too slim and his white tights just emphasise his comical matchstick legs.

Sian is dressed as some kind of warrior queen and is squeezed into a very tight basque. Part of me is relieved that Rob has to attend a hen party in Bristol later so couldn't make it. He would be fawning all over her in this. She looks as though she might burst out any second, so as her friend, I may have to keep an eye on her modesty as the day progresses. Especially as she is already guzzling mead and it is only 11am. My peasant girl costume, however, is loose enough that I have none of those worries. In fact, walking around in these loose rags is quite comfortable and airy. There is even plenty of room to enjoy the medieval feast laid out in front of us. I grab a chicken drumstick and bite on it as I walk around.

The sun shines down on us, and I feel so grateful that I am finally emerging from all the misery of the past year or so. I am with my amazing best friends and, for the first time, am beginning to see a whole new future in front of me. I don't know how long Patrick and I will have together, but perhaps I should make the best of any time we have left. I feel immensely positive as I send Patrick a selfie of the three of us at the castle. He answers immediately.

Hey, I knew you lived in a castle! Ha! I laugh at Patrick's response.

I return to sipping on my mead and consider what Patrick's friends are like. I hope he has close friends who support him with his medical condition, whatever that might be. He hasn't talked about any friends really; he seems a bit of a workaholic. Perhaps he throws himself into work to take his mind off things.

'Ooh, isn't that the boys over there, with Dick?' says Jamie.

'Oh yes, it is, and Tanja Tart too. Look, she's dressed as a wench, how appropriate,' says Sian.

Fortunately, Dick and I are not often in the same circles. He had his golfing friends, who only ever discussed their golfing prowess, and I had Sian who baulked at them all. Therefore, we don't often bump into each other. However, he has the boys for the weekend and had warned me that he would be here with them today. Thus, it comes as no surprise to bump into them. Before I approach, I take a glug of mead to drown the hurt of this being the first time that we are not here as a family unit. I want to shield my boys' innocent little eyes as Tanja picks up a leaflet she has dropped. Perhaps she genuinely forgot to put a skirt on with the belt she is wearing. She certainly doesn't look very medieval with her silicone breast implants bobbing about. I think she should be flogged personally.

'Hi boys, don't you look cute. Your hats look lovely. Lucky we had all that felt left over from World Book Day, hey? You having a nice time?'

'Yes, Mummy. Dad took us to do some archery,' says Jasper.

'Yeah, and he missed and nearly killed someone. Didn't you?' says Rupert cheekily.

'No, I did not,' says Jasper.

'Yes, you did,' says Rupert.

'Don't lie,' responds Jasper.

'You're the liar. Liar, liar, pants on fire,' shouts Rupert.

'Oi! Stop it, you two,' I demand.

They finally quieten down, and I notice how Dick and Tanja have no control over them. I can't imagine what will happen when they take them on holiday.

We all stare at each other awkwardly until Dick finally breaks the silence.

'So, we need to discuss the dates for Disney. I was thinking next month? I need to use up the holiday time,' he says.

'Yeahhhhhh!' shouts Jasper.

'When's that conference in New York again, Jamie?' asks Sian.

'October.'

'Isn't there a half-term in October?' says Sian incredulously. 'You can time it perfectly, Amelia. Didn't I tell you you're destined to meet Patrick? It's all lining up for you. The Disney trip, Jamie being there. You must do it,' she whispers.

'Message Patrick and tell him you're coming. Go on,' she says a little louder.

'I don't have the money, Sian.' I laugh. She does get carried away.

'Who's Patrick and tell him you're coming where?' says Dick.

'None of your bloody business,' says Sian, before I can answer. 'Come on. I can't bear to be around this wench any longer,' she adds, pointing a long finger at Tanja. 'I'm off to check out the jousting.'

'Sorry, she's had a bit too much mead,' I explain. I don't need any animosity lingering in the air. It's not nice for the children to witness and so I change the subject quickly.

'Do you want to talk about Disney then? Half-term would probably be best,' I say.

'Yay,' says Rupert.

'Pleeeeeese,' says Jasper, making a cute face and jumping about as if he needs a wee.

'Sure, let's go half-term week. I'll have a look when I get home,' says Dick.

'Daddy, that's brilliant,' shouts Jasper excitedly. 'And now your shares have gone up, we can bring back a present for Mum.'

'Your shares have gone up?' I repeat. 'The same shares that plummeted so badly they left you penniless when we signed the final settlement and you had no money because of them?'

Dick and Tanja turn to each other nervously.

'Dad said he knew he'd invested wisely. Didn't you, Dad? He told me I need to invest my pocket money wisely too,' says Jasper innocently.

'Did you intentionally buy shares you knew were going to go down and then rise back up, so it looked like you had no money?' I ask Dick. Why did I not realise this before? It is just the type of thing he would do.

'Umm, no. Right, we have to go. Rupert said he wanted to watch the horse thing… Umm, I think there are horses somewhere. Come on,' says Dick, pulling the boys in his direction.

'Yayyyyyyyyyyy, let's see the horses,' says Rupert.

'Horses, horses,' chants Jasper. The boys shake each other in excitement. At least I think it is excitement and not another squabble.

'See you tomorrow then, boys,' I say, giving them a big hug. I shoot Dick a filthy look.

'Oh my god, Jamie. Did you hear that about the shares? He did it on purpose, I swear. He knew those shares were going to do that and then he'd get his money back,' I say.

Jamie puts his arm around me. 'Come on, you know what he's like. You can't let him affect you. Dick is, well, you know, a dick.' He laughs.

–

Jamie and I walk away and attempt to locate the part of the castle where the jousting is taking place to find Sian.

'Now the boys are sorted, say you'll come to New York with me and meet your famous Patrick. Sian and I have talked about it loads and both agree you desperately need this break. I think it will help you put everything into perspective and realise there is a big world out there. A world away from Dick and his dodgy dealings,' says Jamie.

'I really don't have any spare money right now. I don't think so. Perhaps I should start buying lottery tickets again,' I joke.

'It won't cost you much because of the air miles, Amelia. Please come with me. To be honest, I'm being entirely selfish. I don't want to have to walk around such a wonderful city alone; I really want your company.' Jamie smiles.

He makes me giggle as he dances around in his tights, shouting, 'Come to New York, come to New Yorrrrrk!' Until we spot Miserable Megan coming towards us. Her face looks like thunder.

'There you are,' she says to Jamie. 'I've been looking every-bloody-where for you.'

'I'm so sorry, Megan. We bumped into someone and were chatting over the other side. You made it a bit earlier than you thought, that's wonderful,' says Jamie.

Her face softens at this.

'Yeah, class finished early, luckily. Goodness, look at the state of her,' says Miserable Megan, looking towards someone.

Jamie and I look in the same direction and see Sian leaning against the castle wall on the east wing. We have only been here a few hours. I knew the combination of a warm autumn day and half a gallon of mead would be disastrous for Sian.

'What you think?' says Jamie. 'Time to get her home?'

'Yup, I think so,' I agree.

I don't mind that our day has been cut short, as the appearance of Miserable Megan is as though a dark cloud has appeared.

Once I get Sian home safe and sound, I start in the direction of my house. It's not a long walk from Sian's, so I choose to take a detour. I don't feel quite ready to sit in an empty home yet. I spot the park straight ahead; it is abandoned as everyone is at the castle. I plonk myself down on one of the swings; the gentle breeze whooshes against my peasant dress. It is nice to have the park to myself; I relish in the peace and quiet. I swing gently and think about the day and how emotional it was. Life is beginning to improve, but seeing Dick and Tanja with the boys, as if they are one big happy family, is something I still find difficult. However, I am pleased I got through it so well. I may have wanted to flog Tanja Tart, but at least there were no tears. I consider what Jasper said about the shares. Poor Jasper, saying that so innocently. I become more enraged with Dick and what he has put me through. So, his shares have gone up. Sky-rocketed probably. Dick and Tanja must have planned this all along. I wouldn't be surprised if he had siphoned money into an account with her whilst I was busy helping mum. Now they have the money to take our beautiful boys on the holiday-of-a-lifetime. I, meanwhile, can't afford a trip to a caravan in Porthcawl.

It feels so unfair that I had to lose Mum's house because of his choices, but I believe in karma. I hope that one day he will realise that he lost a beautiful family who loved him. He had everything he ever needed but was greedy. Nothing is ever enough for him. He may eventually realise that Tanja isn't enough for him and, by that time, I will have happily moved on with my handsome New Yorker. This thought certainly cheers me up.

Chapter 18

A furniture store two months later – Fundraising

'It's been months that Patrick has been harassing me to visit,' I say as my phone bleeps with yet another message from him. I must put my phone away, as Sian and I are trying to study the kitchen bins in Tremendous Value Furnishings.

I am not quite certain why we are in the bin section, as we are here to look for a new bed for Sian as Rob wants to move in with her. What is everyone's rush at the moment? Although Sian has always rushed into things headfirst. She is so ecstatic that she is considering purchasing a remote-controlled massaging bed in preparation for her new housemate. I had never heard of such a thing before and it's almost £3,000!

At the moment, though, I feel like pushing her onto the bed and putting the massage on high-speed until she tells me exactly what happened with Patrick on the phone. For months now I have tried to get it from her. I did try and squeeze it out of her at the castle, when she had drunk far too much mead, but to no avail. I am also tempted to stick her in one of the super-speedy rocking chairs and not stop rocking her until she tells me. Both thoughts have crossed my mind. Sian absolutely refuses to divulge what she said when she spoke to Patrick all that time ago and insists that she has done me a favour and that's all I need to know. I will never get it out of her.

'You have to visit Patrick. It's in your destiny,' Sian keeps repeating. 'I know he's gorgeous, but he's obviously lonely and has something missing in his life. That thing missing is you. This is so romantic, Amelia. You're made for each other. Imagine Dick's face when he finds out that someone so gorgeous has fallen in love with you. Just maybe make sure Tanja never meets him though, hey,' she adds.

I know Sian wants me to go to New York and it's all super exciting for her, but it isn't quite as easy as she feels it is. She isn't a parent and doesn't understand that the boys are my number one priority.

'It's impossible for me to visit him and not on the cards,' I say.

'Come on, you can easily go when the boys are in Disneyland, but you'd better hurry and organise something quickly,' says Sian.

'I don't know. I want to be home in case the boys need anything. What if they forget something?'

'But they'll be away, Amelia. If they forget their favourite sweater, or teddy, you won't be able to get it to them anyhow. Do you want to sit at home pining for the boys the whole week they're away? I think not.'

'No, I agree it would help having something to take my mind off an empty home, but I don't have spare cash lying around for a holiday either. I have other priorities. Jamie said he might have some air miles for the flights, but I'd still need a hotel, spending money – it all adds up.'

'Money is the easy bit. You sell the picture. It's going to be worth millions.'

'No, I meant to tell you that I got the estimate back ages ago. It's bad news.'

'They said it's worth two million pounds and not three,' laughs Sian.

'No, it's not worth anything.'

'Are you serious?' she asks.

'Yes, that's why I'll definitely not be going to New York in the near future,' I say.

'Oh sweets, there must be something you can do. You can't let this opportunity pass you by. You deserve a little holiday. What about the other things you found in the attic? Obviously, the ankle warmers aren't worth anything, but there has to be something of value… I have an idea, your record collection? Are there any collectables?'

'Apart from a Haysi Fantayzee picture disc, I very much doubt it.' I smile.

'Come on, you have a good selection there. I saw hundreds of records in that box. Even if you sold all of them to a second-hand record shop, they must be worth something. Look, let's forget the bed,' says Sian. 'Let's go back to yours and go through that box. I won't give up until I get you the money, and then perhaps you'll agree to splurging on a well-deserved break.'

–

Opening the box at home, Sian is frantic to find something of value. She puts the records in heaps. Novelty songs in one pile and anything she thinks could be of any importance in another.

'Nik Kershaw, everyone loved him,' she says. 'Let's see how much it's worth on eBay.'

Flicking through her phone, Sian looks disappointed. 'What? How can Nik Kershaw start at 79p? He's a bloody legend. Wham! Fantastic. Let's try that,' she says hopefully. 'Oh, well, that's £10. Look, one seller's asking £65 for it!'

'Sian, even if I put them together, I'm never going to make enough and there are bigger priorities right now,' I say.

I admire Sian's tenacity, but I have to be realistic.

'This is about you for once; not electric or gas bills, but YOU.'

Sian pulls out a few more records as my WhatsApp bleeps with another message from Patrick.

> Did you get the article I messaged you on the NY hotels? XXX

> No, I didn't get anything XX

> Oh, technology, hey. Always lets you down. Never mind, Well, anyhow, why don't you look at flights and keep me updated? XX

> Ok. Will let you know. Xx

I return to Sian and the records, putting some of my favourites in a pile to keep. It will be nice to have some spare cash, and I don't have the space to keep all the records. Regardless of any New York trip, selling the records is a useful thing to do.

'There must be over a hundred records, so even if we sell each one for an average of a pound, it's more than a hundred pounds – it's better than nothing, Amelia,' says Sian excitedly.

Finally, with the records all bagged up in bin liners, we pick the boys up from school and head straight into town.

–

'Can't we go straight home?' complains Rupert.

'No, we won't be long. We need to get rid of the records and then we can go home,' I reply.

We head to Zebedee's Vinyls together, struggling to carry the massive number of albums and singles. The four of us have a couple of bags each, each one extremely heavy.

A feeling of relief hits me as I put them down onto the counter. The grungy-looking guy, wearing a Led Zeppelin T-shirt, gives us an amused look.

'Where the hell did you find this lot?' he says, peering into one of the bags. 'In an attic somewhere?' He looks at us half jokingly, half suspiciously.

'Yes, we did, actually, they're my old records,' I explain.

He looks through the records with disgust on his face.

'Bloody hell, you liked some crap music. No Ozzy? No AC/DC? Alice Cooper?' He's smirking to himself now.

I wish he would say how much they are worth, instead of criticising my choice of music.

'Yeah, okay. So we have different tastes. How much can you give me?' I say, getting impatient.

He picks up a Nana Mouskouri record, 'Only Love'.

The man laughs and slams it down on the counter.

'Hey, careful. I used to love that record,' I say.

'I'm not sure I'll give you anything much for this lot,' he continues.

He starts putting some of the records in piles and suddenly stops at one of the singles that I don't particularly recognise.

'Sex Pistols. Now that's more like it,' he says, pausing to look at the cover. 'This is a classic all right,' he mutters to himself.

'Okay, whatever. I only bought it second-hand to impress an ex-boyfriend. I don't even like them. I prefer a-ha. Now how much will you give me?' I ask, getting more annoyed with him by the second.

'Tell you what. I'm feeling generous today. Give you five hundred quid for the lot,' he says, finally smiling.

Sian looks at me excitedly. 'Five hundred pounds! That's more than we thought, take it.'

'Okay, we'll take it,' I agree.

'Wait, one second,' says Rupert. 'I think we should have more money. There are lots of records there. Did you check the prices?'

'Yes, shhh, it's okay. They're old records anyway; five hundred pounds is better than nothing.'

He is so like his dad. Always determined to get every last penny.

'Let me check the price on eBay,' says Rupert. 'You know, just to be sure.'

'Sian and I already checked the prices on eBay, sweetie. The average price is about ninety-nine pence, so we are getting a good deal. Shh, let's just take the money while he's in a good mood,' I say.

'Give me your phone, Mum. I don't trust this man,' says Rupert.

I am so embarrassed.

'Sorry about that. Kids, eh,' I say to the guy, who is now giving Rupert evil stares.

'Let's look at this record…' He picks up the Sex Pistols record. Oh no, of all the records to pick up. Why couldn't it be Keith Harris, or the Roland Rat record underneath?

The man pushes the Nana Mouskouri single in front of Rupert.

'Oi, kid, try this one.'

'No, it's okay. I have this one now,' says Rupert. 'Mummy, why would a record have the S word on it and why would you buy such a thing?' he asks.

'Long story, my darling boy, I have no idea. I agree that it is a funny name. Maybe you should try the other single instead and we will leave this at the bottom of the pile.'

I try to take it from him but he is determined, and when Rupert is determined nothing gets in his way.

I am cringing when my innocent eight-year-old types in the words 'Sex' followed by 'Pistols' and waits for the page to load.

We all stand around awkwardly for a while. The man is drumming his fingers along the till impatiently when Rupert starts making a scene.

'This man is trying to rob us,' he shouts. 'It's selling on eBay for eight thousand pounds.'

The man turns his head away. I'm sure I hear him mutter the words, 'Little shit.'

'Show me the page, Rupert,' I say.

Rupert shows me the listing, and I see what he means. There is the exact same record on there, selling for £8,000.

We show it to the guy, and he looks at us horrified.

'Smart kid you've got there,' he says, making a face at Rupert. 'Look, I'll have to speak to my boss. Give me a minute.'

Rupert high-fives the three of us.

'Told you, didn't I?'

'Yes, you little clever clogs. I'm very proud of you. I'll give you extra spending money for Disneyland for that,' I promise.

Five minutes later, the man opens his office door and pops back out.

'Look, boss says we'll need to check over everything, but he thinks we can give you £7,850 for the lot. That's fair enough. Some of your other records aren't worth wasting the vinyl for. We can transfer the money to your bank account later.'

Rupert goes to open his mouth, but I tell him to be quiet. I know what he's thinking. If we try and sell it directly on eBay, we could make more. I am completely satisfied with the £7,850 though, and there are no fees.

'I really didn't like that guy,' says Sian on the way out.

'Me neither,' says Jasper.

'He was a horrible man,' says Rupert. 'You're lucky I was there.'

'We were indeed, my little munchkin.' I give him a hug.

'I think you two boys deserve a big ice cream before going home.'

'With sprinkles?' Rupert asks.

'Definitely with sprinkles.' I grin.

'Yayyy!' They both shout.

'And, after that, you, Amelia Simpson, need to think about planning a holiday. Time is running out,' says Sian.

'I don't know about a holiday, but I'm glad you made us go through the records,' I say. 'I only wish we'd have done it sooner. Then it could have been me taking the boys to Disney.'

'No way. It's meant to be,' says Sian. 'Dick is supposed to take the boys because you need some fun of your own. You need to chill a bit. Go to New York and live a little.'

'Oh, I don't know. I still don't think I'll book anything. Imagine what this could pay for around the house? The boys need new school shoes and...' I say.

'Stop making excuses,' says Sian.

I choose to ignore her and grab the boys' hands.

'Come on. Let's hurry for that ice cream,' I say quickly changing subject.

Chapter 19

Laugharne – all going wrong

'Amelia, I'm so happy today that I bought you flowers.'

'Flowers! Wow, that's so kind of you, Patrick,' I respond.

I don't know when I was last given flowers. Probably on the day of Mum's funeral, but they were obviously more for her than for me. It is a shame that Patrick hasn't actually handed them to me, as I have a lovely vase for them. However, there he is on the other side of the Atlantic, holding out the most stunning bouquet of pink and white lilies. How beautiful. I wish I could lean over and smell them. Though maybe it is for the best. I would hate to get a pollen stain.

'I chose them carefully, especially for you, Amelia,' says Patrick via Zoom in my dark back bedroom.

'Well, I love them.' I giggle.

'I will buy you so many flowers when you come over. I just want to hold you in my arms and never let you go,' he says.

Looking at Patrick on the screen in front of me, this thought sounds very inviting. A lovely *cwtch* with this handsome New Yorker sounds just what this Welsh woman needs. However, there are so many things I could get the boys with my windfall. I'd feel guilty spending some of it on myself.

'If you come to New York, I promise I'll arrange the hotel for you, so you don't have to worry. I may need your credit card details, but I'll do all of that. If I book it for you, I'll get you a cheaper rate. Hope that sounds good for you,' says Patrick. 'Umm, just so you know, though, I wouldn't be able to pick you up at the airport if you do come – those transatlantic flights sure do arrive at difficult times – but the hotel, I'd arrange that for sure,' he continues.

Of course, I don't tell him, but if I did make it to New York I wouldn't dream of letting him pick me up. I want to make a good impression on him when he first sees me. I don't think coming off a transatlantic flight stinking of spicy airplane food, too many vodkas and general travel-induced stinkiness will somehow create the first impression that I want on him.

'Yes, I really wouldn't need you to come to the airport if I fly out. You're busy; I understand,' I say.

'I'm so glad you understand, baby. You're my number one, but you know what my job is like and then there's my polo… I have to stay fit. I worry about my health, you know…'

'I understand. Tell me more, Patrick… About your health, what is it? I don't really know what's wrong.'

'I feel like we don't need to talk about it, you know,' he says. 'It is like we know everything about each other. We have this undeniable connection. Like a rope that binds us together.'

'Well, no, I still want to know more, Patrick. We have so much to talk about. Perhaps you know more about me than I do about you. You're so good at listening,' I say.

I'm not sure I like the mention of a rope tying us together, to be frank. I hope he doesn't want to tie me up. I haven't had sex for years, let alone anything remotely kinky. I don't want to flare up my sciatica or anything.

'You don't know me as much as you'd like to because you talk too much.' Patrick laughs.

'Well, yes, I do talk a lot. It might be a Welsh thing. We love chatting to people. If I come over I promise to give you a chance to speak,' I tease.

'Great, but do you think we would do much talking? I mean…'

He stares into the camera with his beautiful hazel eyes that are not the colour of the Med, as I envisage when I think of him, but more like a Brazil nut you'd find in a bag of Co-op mixed nuts. His long eyelashes blink flirtily. I feel my cheeks redden. I am so not used to flirty moments in my life.

'Ahem. Well, um, I don't know, Patrick. As you know, I like talking. I enjoy learning about people. It is very interesting and…' I realise I sound utterly boring and out of my depth. My sexiness level is an absolute zero.

'Okay, we could talk.' Patrick smiles. 'I love talking to you. But you know what I would love even more?'

I hold my breath, dreading the next words. What if he says he wants to make love to me? I don't know how I will respond. I would never be brave enough. No, that is definitely not happening.

'What would you love, Patrick?' I ask, dreading the answer.

'To love you until my dying breath.'

I let out a relieved sigh. Well, not because of the dying part, but that he doesn't want sex. What a relief.

'Oh, phew. Haha. Yes, that would be nice,' I answer clumsily.

'Could you love me, Amelia? I have told you that I can see myself falling in love with you.'

'Well, I, umm… I suppose I could. But it takes me time to fall in love, especially as I've been so badly hurt.'

'We're not all the same, Amelia. You have to learn to trust again one day,' says Patrick.

'I know; I am getting there,' I say.

'I'm glad, because I would never want to hurt you. I hope you believe this. Let's just see how things go and take it one step at a time, hey,' he says.

'That's great, I would like to take things slowly. A bit like my tortoise.' I laugh nervously. Why do I say stupid things when I get nervous?

'But you don't always have time in life, Amelia. Remember that. So try not to put off what you can do today, hey?'

I think that saying normally means for chores and things, not rushing to fall head over heels in love with a stranger across the Atlantic. His mention of timing yet again makes me probe further with my earlier question.

'How much time do you have, Patrick? What are you trying to say here?'

'My darling, Amelia. Nobody has much time left. It's like one of those egg timers. You reach fifty and the egg timer starts going faster and faster,' says Patrick.

'What on earth does that mean?' I ask. He does say some strange things sometimes. Perhaps it's the cultural differences. 'Patrick, are you holding something back from me about your illness?'

'Yes, I am. But I don't wish to talk about it when I'm so happy. Please come and see me and we can talk,' he says.

'It's just not possible at the moment, Patrick. You are lovely and perfect, but… The circumstances are too difficult to come over,' I say.

'Why do you make things so hard for yourself? You said your sons are going away with their dad tomorrow. Your friend will be in New York. Why can't you come? This is crazy.' He is starting to sound annoyed.

'It's not as easy as you think. I'd need to ask my boss for time off. I have so many responsibilities. I can't jump on a flight the way other people might be able to with no commitments,' I explain.

'Well, I don't see where any of this is going. If you don't come to New York, there is not much of a future. It's your choice,' says Patrick abruptly.

I look in horror at his perfect features on the other side of the Atlantic. I don't want to stop communicating with him, but I can't possibly arrange anything now.

The boys leave in less than twenty-four hours and I've faffed about so much that I have left it far too late to go to New York, even if that means I will lose Patrick.

Chapter 20

At home – saying goodbye to the boys

Dick arrives early morning to pick the boys up on the way to the airport. Tanja looks at me disgustedly from the passenger seat of the car that is waiting outside. I can't help it if I am still in my towelling dressing gown. It was more important to have the boys all packed up and organized. Self-conscious, I wipe at the butter stain from yesterday's toast that covers my left boob.

'Oh, Jasper, Rupert, let me give you a double hug,' I say as we bid goodbye.

This is horrible. It was bad enough when they went on the school trip to a Welsh language camp in Pendine for a few days, but this is Florida I am sending them to – and with Tanja Tart. I want to cry my eyes out and have a little tantrum. Of course, I don't. I put on a brave face and wish them all a wonderful holiday with a smile on my face.

'Mum, I'll miss you, but I promise to bring you something nice back,' says Jasper.

'Yes, Mum, we'll find something for you. Would you like a big Mickey Mouse?' asks Rupert.

'Ooh, anything you choose would be lovely, Rupert,' I say. 'That's so thoughtful of you.'

'Right, boys, time to get in the car. Don't want to miss the flight,' says Dick from the doorstep, refusing to come any closer.

I hand over the luggage to Jasper and Rupert, and they carry it towards the boot of the car.

'No room in the boot. Tanja's suitcase filled it up. You'll have to squeeze in the back with the bags,' I hear Dick saying to the boys.

Of course, her suitcase has filled the boot, I mutter to myself.

I maintain the smile until the car is a dot at the end of the road, and then my chin starts to quiver and I burst into tears behind the closed door.

Calm down and think of the positives, I tell myself.

I can have a long, hot soak in the bath without the boys needing to urgently search for something that they haven't used for the past five years.

I can eat all the Maltesers in the bag without having to offer them any.

I can join the runners at the park, as I don't have to rush home from work. Is that actually a positive? I'm not sure.

I can…

Before I finish the mental list of things I can do, I see that Lisa is calling me from her mobile. I hope she doesn't want me to do extra shifts. There go my plans for running in the park.

'Amelia, are you already on your way in?' she asks.

'No, I was going to have a quick cuppa and then start getting ready. I'm a bit later than normal because the boys have just gone off,' I explain.

'Right, well, for once I'm glad you're running late. I'm ringing to say, don't bother coming in. There's been a leak from the flat above; the ceiling's collapsed in the shop. We're going to have to close for at least a week, by the looks of it. I've spoken to the insurance company, and they said I have to get two quotes from builders before they even look at the claim. I can't get a builder till Friday. It's going to take ages to sort. They'd better give compensation for loss of earnings.'

'Oh no, well, shall I come in and try and help move the books, or anything?' I ask.

'No, luckily the books are fine, but the seating area and the lovely pink sofas are ruined. Absolutely bleeding ruined,' says Lisa.

'Oh dear, what a nightmare. Well, if I can do anything at all,' I say.

'No, until the insurance sorts everything out there isn't a lot we can do. I'll ring you next Monday when I know more,' she says.

I put the kettle back on and make a fresh cuppa. What am I supposed to do with no work and no boys? The house is small, yet I suddenly feel as though I am rattling around in it.

By 10am I'm incredibly bored. I call Sian to explain that I have an unexpected week off and see if she fancies lunch.

'Oh, I'm sorry, I've got to visit Rob's mum this afternoon. Ivy had a fall and is a bit down in the dumps,' she explains. 'We're thinking we might stay over with her for a few days. Are you okay?'

'Yes, fine. No problem. Of course, that's much more important. You go and help out. I'll see you when you get back,' I say.

'Why don't you see if Jamie can still get you those air miles, Amelia? Go on. What else are you going to do this week? There must be a flight available somewhere. It's now or never,' says Sian.

'I don't know. We'll see,' I say.

I put the phone down and make yet another cuppa and sit down to watch daytime TV. This is nice, I tell myself, it's not often I get any time for myself.

Ten minutes later, I can't bear to hear the woman on telly explain about the bunions she had removed. I walk around the house aimlessly. I enter the boys' bedroom and feel sad as I look at their empty beds.

I wish I was in work; it would be much better than this quiet home.

At 1pm I message Patrick. I apologise for being so undecided and explain that I have a week off from work unexpectedly.

'Well, honey, what are you waiting for? Get on the flight,' he says. This idea is getting more attractive by the second.

By 2:01, I am even more bored and by 2:29 I can take no more. I can't bear to be home alone like this. I pick up the phone to Jamie.

'Hey, if I was to come to New York with you, do you know if those flights on air miles are still available?' I ask.

'Well, I can certainly check. It would be amazing if you could come with me. Give me two minutes. What about a hotel though?' says Jamie.

'If you can check availability on the flight, I'll ask Patrick about the hotel he mentioned before,' I say.

'It's a deal,' he says.

I message Patrick and ask if he can find out if the hotel has any rooms for this week.

I have never been so spontaneous in my life and it feels exhilarating.

Patrick answers five minutes later.

> Honey, yes, it's available. If you give me your card details, I'll book it for you now because I get a discount, remember? Xxx

> Okay, let me double check the flights and I'll get back to you xxx

Jamie finally rings back to say that he can't get me on the outward flight he is on, but there is a last-minute seat available on tomorrow's flight to JFK.

'It's a bit soon for you, but you might be able to make it. We'll be on the same flights back, if that helps,' he says.

'Book it,' I blurt out. 'As Patrick says, life is short. Let's do it.'

'This is going to be fantastic, Amelia. This makes my business trip so much better having you there. You know, having company,' says Jamie.

I ring Patrick to tell him the good news.

'Oh baby, I get to hold you and spoil you and do all the things I've wanted to do for so long. Maybe you can meet my friends, we can go for dinner… I'm so happy. Is my beautiful Amelia happy too?' he asks.

'Yes, I am,' I say. 'I truly am. I can't wait to see you and see New York again.'

With everything in place, I realise that I need to do some urgent shopping, as I am not in the slightest bit prepared for a trip to New York, so head to the shops quickly.

I am at least two stone heavier than I have made myself out to be, and so my first stop is the ladies' lingerie department to invest in my first ever pair of Spanx-type things; at least that way I will look good with clothes on. It is not like he is going to get to see what is underneath my fat-busting protective layer.

I pass all the racy red, glamourous black and pastel shades of underwear and head to the big pants section. I look for underwear that will immediately shrink me from a size 14 to an 8. I am not going to be greedy and want to become a size zero or anything, a size 8 will suffice.

I eventually find a massive pair of black knickers that promise to give you a flat tummy and drop a dress size; how very different to the red thong that Patrick may think I still wear. I choose a size larger than normal, as they look so tight and I would like to have the option of breathing while being sucked in. I'm also worried about getting deep-vein thrombosis in an artery in my pelvis somewhere, especially after the long flight, so I want to keep as much of my circulation going as possible.

Near the knickers stand, I notice a padded bra that makes you look two sizes bigger. Ironic that I need my pants to make me look three sizes smaller. Why does it have to be that my bottom is ample but not my chest? I sometimes wonder if my body got things the wrong way around. Not to worry, though, as thanks to this miraculous underwear, at the age of forty-eight, I am finally going to have the body I have always wanted. Patrick would probably be a little disappointed if he discovered my pendulous breasts under the superfluously padded bra, but never mind as he may never find out.

Since we will not be having sex at any point, I do wonder what sort of places Patrick will take me. He did say we would go for dinner. I hope dinner isn't our first date, though, as it would be so embarrassing if I started to choke on a shiitake mushroom as we exchange pleasantries. I do hope he is not one of those people who eats noisily and makes some kind of chomping noise.

As I consider Patrick's eating habits, something catches my eye in the clothing section. It is the most beautiful black floaty dress. Not only is it utterly fantastic, it also has a tag saying that there is 50 per cent off; there is even a size 14 left.

As I am looking at it, a woman beside me goes through the rail, stopping at my dress. She touches the fabric, gently stroking the silky material. I watch in horror as her hand starts heading for the hanger. I have this strange primal urge and grab the hanger before she can, almost pushing her out of the way. I'm sure there is something wrong with my hormones at the moment.

She gives me a startled look, and I run to the changing room with my dress. I need to lock the fitting room door in case she comes after me. I hear her ask the assistant if she has any other size 14s, to which the answer is a resolute no.

Unfortunately for the lady, the dress fits me like a glove and goes in at all the right places: it is perfect for a first date. Perhaps I should go for something a little less glamourous and sexy, but I'm going to be in New York, after all, where everyone oozes sophistication, and I desperately need something new. I certainly don't want to dress in my normal fashion that says I am a mum of twins who has gone through a bereavement and a divorce in the past year, and who hasn't had sex in a very long time.

This is my 'dress of hope', a dress that makes me feel empowered, sexy, glamorous and is a dress of a divorcee who is about to embark on a whole new life.

It might only be a dress in the sale for some, but to me this is the beginning of something wonderful. It's the start of a bright new future with love, happiness and an intelligent, handsome polo player sweeping me off my feet.

'I'll take it,' I say to my reflection in the mirror.

Chapter 21

Somewhere over the Atlantic – the future is bright

The distinctive musty aircraft smell hits my nostrils as I approach the crew member who is reaching out to check my boarding card. I hand it over and notice I am shaking. I haven't admitted it to anyone, but I am so nervous about everything right now: flying alone, being without the boys, and, of course, meeting Patrick. I may as well be an unaccompanied minor on a flight for the way I feel.

The male flight attendant smiles at me as he hands back the boarding pass, which is tucked away in the passport. I was lucky to find it behind the microwave last night. I'd almost forgotten I had left it there after needing it as proof of identity for the lawyer all that time ago.

'We've upgraded you to upper class, Mrs Simpson.'

Oh my, the words I have always wanted to hear.

Except, I didn't actually hear them. Instead, I am now sitting in an economy seat – the seat I rightly deserve thanks to Jamie's free air miles. I am at the back near the toilets. I do seem to go to the toilet a lot more nowadays. I think it is the endometriosis, so I suppose it will be handy to be so near the lavatories. I mustn't complain. It turns out that I am also the first to get served, as the drinks trolley starts at the back of the cabin. So, it is a bit of a win–win situation really.

'What would you like to drink?' says a tall, blonde cabin crew member shortly after take-off. She reminds me of Jamie's ex-wife. I am now glad he isn't on the flight out with me. I know he has Miserable Megan in his life, but I wouldn't want him to get upset by being reminded of Melinda. Emotions are so much stronger at 39,000 feet I find. I'm forever crying when watching an in-flight movie, even if it is a comedy.

'White wine, please,' I say politely. I try to divert my eyes and not keep staring at her. I can't help myself, but I am curious as to how she got her hair into such a neat bun. My hair would probably look like a bird's nest if I tried that. How come some people can do these wonderful things with their hair? I do envy them.

The lady smiles, dazzling me with her dental-advert-worthy white teeth, and hands me the wine, showing off her equally perfect manicured red nails as she does so.

'Here, have three. It's a long flight,' she says kindly.

'Oh, wow, thank you!' Perhaps it is as well that I am not in charge of Jasper and Rupert right now.

'Cheers,' says the lady next to me as she lifts up the glass of gin and tonic that she ordered. Until now she hasn't said anything, which I really didn't mind.

'You on holiday?' she asks with what I assume is a New York accent. I notice that it sounds a bit similar to Patrick's.

'Yes, kind of,' I respond. 'I have a friend there... I'm going to meet up with him.'

'Hmm. A male friend, huh?'

'Um, yeah.' I blush. 'Well, he's... Ah, long story... I... You? Are you going home, or...?'

'Give me your hand,' she demands, not answering my question.

'What?' I ask. What on earth does she want my hand for?

'Give me your hand. I read palms. Let me see how your visit will go,' she insists.

She is starting to make me feel uncomfortable now. I don't want my palm read.

She grabs my hand and pulls it over to her. Does it say in my palm that fortune telling freaks me out? If I did believe in fortune tellers, I really wouldn't want to know if something horrible is going to happen.

'You've had a tough time,' she says, looking at a crease in my palm.

How can she possibly tell that from looking at my hand? Is it because I haven't used the pomegranate and aloe vera hand cream that Sian bought me last Christmas? Perhaps my skin feels a bit rough but…

She draws her finger along another crease in my palm. I notice her enormously long nails as she does so. They are painted a bright shade of purple and scratch me slightly as she runs her finger along.

'You've waited a long time to get with the right man. But he's here now. You've found him,' she adds suddenly.

I almost spit out the wine that I am slurping at nervously.

'I've found the right man?' I ask. I suddenly feel like a Jane Austen character who has been waiting for the perfect suitor. Does he have a big stately home in the country too?

'Yup, your man is in New York.' She laughs. 'You'll marry him. Bitter sweet though, as someone important will be missing from the wedding.'

Did she say I was going to marry Patrick? And that's Mum. If I was to remarry, unlike my wedding to Dick, Mum would be missing.

'This man in New York, he is definitely the one for you. No question about it. He's tall… handsome. Yup, you two are the perfect match,' she says. 'I dun know why, but you should have realised this sooner. Both of ya took your time.'

'Oh, well, yeah, I took twenty years to call him. How do you know all of this?' I ask. She knows so much that I wonder whether I should begin to believe what she is telling me.

'I'm a natural… I have waiting lists in New Jersey,' she says with a laugh. She then takes her drinks napkin and writes down what she has told me.

'Will he die early?' I ask as she starts writing.

'You'll both have a good life… now, there, that's all I can see. Remember what I said,' she says, handing me the napkin. 'When it happens, I want you to look at this again and see I was right. Don't forget me.' She gestures to the screen in front of her. 'I'm going to watch…'

She puts her headphones on and tells me nothing further. She can't stop now. I want to know if the boys will get good careers; will Jasper improve his science skills? I need to know more, but that is it. That is all she will tell me. I wonder if she is right? I am not ready to marry again after Dick. I would certainly never want to go through that again. The boys don't even know about Patrick; this is all a bit sudden. They'd have to get to know him and absolutely adore him for me to marry him. How can it possibly be true? But how did she know as much as she did? I have too many questions for her to just start watching telly like that.

The more wine I drink, the less absurd this all seems. I suppose if he was so perfect, we would have to have some kind of commitment eventually, especially with such a long-distance relationship. If he hasn't got many years left, we would have to get a move on. I guess I could marry again one day. I never planned it, but, well, Dick is getting remarried. I don't know. I never would have expected it, I have to say… Oh my goodness. 'I'm going to marry Patrick.'

Surely not.

Chapter 22

New York — good to be back

Four messages bleep on my phone the minute I switch it on in the airport terminal. The most important one is from Dick. I feel so relieved to see that the boys are enjoying themselves, although I miss them so much that I feel like getting an internal flight to Florida. I think I would swim there if there weren't so many alligators down that way.

> Boys are having a wonderful time.

> Watched you land safely on a flight tracking app, so off to bed. Miss you lots, Sian xxx

> Let me know when you land, honey. Not long till I see the gal of my dreams, can't wait! Xx

I see the boys must have been using the debit card again. I bet it was on the flight to play some sort of game. I should never have entered the number onto their iPad. As for Patrick, aka 'the man I'm going to marry', I will message when I get to the hotel. I don't want to appear too eager.

The gal of my dreams, bless him, he hasn't even seen me properly yet. He might be in for a shock. I still can't believe the palm reader said that I would marry him though. I never would have thought that would happen.

As I wait at the luggage carousel, I see the palm reader once again. She picks up a leopard print suitcase – an item I didn't know existed. She waves over at me and shouts something. I just about manage to hear her in between the chattering and squeaking of luggage wheels.

'Remember my words… Have a good life with the man of your dreams…'

I smile over and am about to respond when I notice my suitcase appear. The relief is immense as I desperately want to escape the airport. Even though I managed to get some sleep on the flight, I am still exhausted from all the travelling.

On the drive towards Manhattan, the city lights wake me up a little. A surge of adrenalin hits me as the Manhattan skyline peeps out at me in the distance. What a skyline. It doesn't matter how many times you see it in real life, or in the movies, it never fails to take your breath away.

It certainly feels like it was over twenty years ago when I was last here. I don't think I would know my way around at all; it almost feels as though this is my first time here. Nothing seems familiar.

We weave around different blocks, which I personally would call streets. They all look so similar that it is hard to get my bearings. Although it is almost midnight, people are rushing about the blocks like an army of little ants.

The cab pulls over at the hotel, and I wish we were in the wrong part of town. I can immediately see from the grubby, air-polluted, stained look that a five star this is most certainly not. However, if I try to put a positive slant on it, then it has to be said that it does have that New York buzz to it, even if that involves listening to police sirens all night. It is basic, but it was reasonably priced, so I shouldn't have expected much more. Crammed into a back street of Manhattan, I discover that the street it is located in, and the room itself, are equally as compact.

I still haven't messaged Patrick back, so I am not surprised when my phone starts to ring. I have barely put my bags down when I see his name flashing up on the phone.

'Hi, where are you? Your flight landed hours ago,' he says the minute I pick up the call.

'Sorry, busy getting a cab and then looking at all the sights… I should have messaged…'

'No harm done, baby. How do you like your room?'

I look around and see the longest ever dark hair on the migraine-inducing blue and yellow carpet. Yuck. Has this place even been cleaned?

'Oh, it's perfect,' I say sarcastically.

'Great. I knew you'd love it,' says Patrick, totally missing the point. He must think I don't have very high standards.

'Did you check out your bathroom yet?'

I haven't dared go in, but I can see the shower curtain is pulled across. It looks like the type of bathroom where there would be a murderer waiting behind the curtain. I can't help wonder if this is the sister accommodation of Bates Motel.

'No, I haven't. I'm not sure I fancy it,' I say. Even though I would love to freshen up I am too scared to go in.

'The bathrooms are fantastic there, Amelia. Surely you have a big bath, which I hope to share with you soon, incidentally.' Patrick laughs.

A big bath? From where I am standing, I am not even sure one of my thighs is going to fit in the bath, let alone me and Patrick. Also, that is a bit forward of him. Then again, maybe I should be a bit more open to the fact that he might get to see me naked, now that we are supposed to marry and all. The thought makes me panic again. Marriage and sex with someone else, is such a terrifying thought.

'Ha, I don't think we will fit in the bath together, somehow,' I manage.

'You have the suite though; right?'

'I don't know. It's a regular room, I think.'

I look around, wondering if this is actually a suite and see a mouldy looking banana.

'There might be a fruit bowl,' I add.

'Oh, cool. I'm sure you're in the suite then. I did ask them to upgrade your room.'

'You asked them to upgrade me?' I ask. That's so sweet of him.

'Yeah, I pulled a few strings, you know.'

'Oh, thank goodness, because if this is the suite, I cannot even imagine the regular rooms,' I say.

'You don't sound too pleased with your room, Amelia. Is something wrong?'

'No, nothing wrong. I'm tired. I'm sure the room will look amazing in the morning,' I say, doing my best to sound a little more grateful for the upgrade. 'Yes, I am just tired. I'm sure everything will look so much better after a sleep,' I reiterate, but when I look at the crumpled old bed linen, I know this is a lie. Do they even change the sheets between guests?

'Okay. Listen. You have a sleep, okay. I'll see my beautiful princess tomorrow. I'm sure you're just jet-lagged. Night night, darling. Love you.'

'Love you.' I don't know why, but the words escape from my lips. Maybe a part of me is falling in love with him even though he has put me in the worst dump I could have imagined.

Just as I resign myself to sitting on the bed, my phone rings again. Maybe it is Patrick calling back. I am pretty sure there has been a mix up and I am in the wrong hotel.

'Hello,' says Jamie's chirpy voice. 'You landed okay? Did you get to your hotel yet?'

'Oh Jamie. I did, but it's horrible. Hang on a minute.'

I listen carefully as I hear someone knock and then attempt to move the door handle.

'Oh my god, Jamie. Someone's trying to get through my door. It sounds like they're trying to get a key in the lock. They're rustling something.'

'Right. Put your safety locks on quickly. What's the name of your hotel again? Give me two minutes and I'll call you back.'

There's some commotion outside and then I hear a security guard. I press my ear against the door.

'Sir, is this your room?'

'I'm looking for someone,' I hear a man's voice say.

There is more knocking on the door.

'Ma'am, are you okay in there?'

I don't respond. I'm too scared to speak. I notice my phone ringing on the bed. I am terrified that if I answer the men outside will hear me, but I can see that it is Jamie calling back.

'Hello,' I whisper down the phone.

'Right, there's an Uber on its way for you. I've booked a room where the company have put us up, okay. The taxi will be downstairs waiting for you in two minutes. Start grabbing your bags and head out. I want you to stay on the phone with me the whole time, until you get into the cab.'

'I'm too scared to open the door,' I say.

'I'm with you. Do it. Get out of there now. The taxi is waiting, just run if you have to.'

I unlock the bolt and peek outside. The men have gone.

'Oh phew, Jamie. The men have gone.'

'Great, now keep walking.'

'Excuse me, miss. Missy, excuse me.' I hear a voice behind me.

Oh no, it's the man who was outside my room. I recognise the voice. He's shouting for me. He's running up to me.

'Miss, please. Stop.'

'Do murderers say please?' I ask Jamie.

'Missy, you left your sweater downstairs,' the man says, catching up with me.

'Oh my gosh. I am so sorry. I thought you were a... Never mind. Thank you,' I say.

Although the man was not a murderer, I still feel immensely relieved to leave the hotel as I sit in the cab.

–

Walking in to where Jamie has booked me, I feel so much more comfortable.

It is a typical business hotel. All functional and quite minimal. I'm so busy looking up at the bright, spotlighted ceiling that I bump into someone carrying a briefcase.

'Sorry!' I say. The man looks at me with disgust.

'Tourists,' I hear him mutter. I obviously don't look like I'm on a business trip then. What is he doing with a briefcase at this time of the night? Shouldn't he have finished work by now? Is everyone in New York a work-aholic?

I am soon checked in by an attentive receptionist and given the key for my standard room. I open the door with my key card and am pleased to see that there are no vagrant hairs in the room. Not even a hideous carpet.

I throw myself on the comfortable bed. I want to snuggle under the sheets, but they are tucked in so tightly I don't quite have the strength to loosen them. Instead, I get up and search for my nightshirt and hang up my 'dress of hope'.

I am still searching for my nightshirt when Patrick replies to an earlier message. I had sent photos of my new hotel, after explaining to him that I had to leave the hotel he had arranged. I thanked him for his trouble though.

> Glad you're happy, honey. Sorry that didn't work out. The location was amazing; I guess it would be better in the day. Off to bed now but look forward to seeing you tomorrow. Tiffany's, Fifth Avenue, 1pm. Just like old times XX

> Great. See you then. Look forward to it XX

I do consider putting a few more kisses, seeing as he has tried his best with the hotel arrangements and I feel rather ungrateful. However, he has only put two so I think better of it. Treat them mean, keep them keen and all that. What is much more important, is the fact that it is now officially less than twelve hours until my date.

I am about to be reunited with Perfect Patrick after all this time.

Chapter 23

A dodgy deli – not the perfect start

I wake up with a pounding headache, probably due to the combination of wine and dehydration from the flight. On top of it all, as I slept in I have now missed my hotel breakfast. Today has not started out as perfectly as I had hoped, seeing as it is THE BIG DAY. Ideally, I would have woken up dozens of pounds lighter, refreshed and glowing, and not with what feels like a woodpecker gnawing at my temples.

I decide to search for a deli and get a bite to eat even though I am so nervous that food is the last thing I feel like right now. However, I certainly don't want my stomach to give out a big growl if Patrick and I were to have some kind of embrace upon meeting.

I find an average-looking deli and greet the server.

'A plain ham sandwich, please,' I say.

The server looks at me completely vacuously, and I have to repeat myself five times.

'Ham, please. Ham, ham, ham, ham?'

He can't understand my Welsh accent, or the fact that I don't want a ham on rye, like the New Yorkers seem to eat. I try to think how they speak in New York.

'Haaaam?' I plead desperately. It is no good, though, he just isn't getting me.

I try to think what people eat in the movies. What would he understand? The queue behind me is getting longer and I hear someone shout for me to hurry up. In my panic, I point to a wilted sandwich in the display fridge.

'You want this? Jeez, woman, why didn't you just say pastrami on rye?'

Sheepishly, I pay for it and take my wrapped sandwich from the counter top. I keep my eyes to the floor as I walk past the waiting customers.

I find a metal chair outside the deli and attempt to eat my sandwich. I take one bite of it and know that it's inedible. I didn't want rye in the first place. I open the sandwich up to inspect its insides. Is that mustard? I hate mustard. I take some of the pastrami out and wipe the generous serving of condiment off.

As I finally nibble on the pastrami, I can't help but people watch. It is such a busy street. A smart young couple holding hands are first. They look so in love that you can't help but feel happy for them. Next is a powerful-looking woman in a suit, quickly followed by a punky-looking guy with ubiquitous piercings. He glares at me and obviously doesn't appreciate me people watching, so I look at my phone and begin to text.

It is high time I texted Dick to check on the boys anyhow. They should be up and about by now and hope-fully settling into the different time zone. Fortunately, Dick comes back immediately and says they are all fine, that the boys had pancakes for breakfast and love the food in the hotel. I am relieved to hear that. I know Dick is a good father really; it is that Tanja Tart that I am more worried about. I will speak to them later. They won't be able to keep it to themselves if there are any issues with her.

Satisfied that the boys are fine, I message Sian and tell her about my escapade last night. She finds it hilarious that I thought a man returning my sweater was a murderer. It is okay for her; she wasn't in a dodgy hotel in a big city all alone. I will be grateful when Jamie arrives. Hopefully, if his flight is on time, we may even catch up this evening.

I put my phone and my sandwich down. I can't manage much more of it, my nerves are starting to get the better of me, plus it's awful. I throw bits of rye to a grateful passing pigeon. Unfortunately, he quickly lets his fellow bird people know and a flock swarm the table next to me.

'Oi, lady, no feeding the pigeons. Did you not see the sign?' shouts one of the staff.

The man who served me earlier comes out to see what is going on. He gives me an evil glare.

'What is wrong with you, woman?' he says.

I apologise and get up quickly to leave. It is time I head back to the hotel to start my transformation anyway. It is going to take me forever to get ready for the most important date of my life.

It was difficult enough trying to find a shirt for Skype the first time we met; preparing for today was a whole different situation. Ultimately, I had to invest in an outfit that portrayed a sophisticated, confident divorcee, even if the reality is that I am an anxious, nervous wreck meeting the possible love of my life for a casual walk along Central Park. It was me who decided on the Central Park bit. Patrick said he'd meet me at Tiffany's and then I said we could walk over to Central Park, even though it is a bit of a hike. I wanted to stay public in case anything went horribly wrong and he is a murderer and not the man of my dreams after all. Although I could get dragged into a bush by him, I suppose. Hopefully, there would be some bright spark walking his dog who could save me though. I hope dogs are allowed into Central Park. Surely, they must be.

Anyway, I have invested in a pair of the best-fitting jeans I have ever found for this special occasion. My thighs don't even look their true width in them. As for the top, that was a little more difficult.

Although the jeans were flattering, every top I tried on revealed the most hideous muffin top. Not even a muffin top, more of a complete-chocolate-gateau top really. Eventually, I discovered the most beautiful chiffon blouse. It is cream, embroidered with gold, has floaty chiffon sleeves and is so dreamy. As it has a camisole top underneath you can't see my muffin top, nor any stretch marks courtesy of the twins. It is definitely one of those pieces that you want to keep in your wardrobe forever. The only downside is that it is a bit cold for autumn in New York – but looking good is the objective here. This is far more important than keeping my chest warm today. Luckily Mum can't see me.

As for my shoes, I have decided on some pumps that I bought on the high street, and I think I have managed to coordinate the perfect look. For once, I feel like I have stepped off the pages of *Grazia*, thanks to this beautiful top and a couple of Advil. I used my curling irons to give my hair a bit of oomph and I am quite pleased with how that looks. Even my skin doesn't look too tired with the luminous foundation I have on, thanks to my spending spree in Duty Free.

It's soon 12:15. I have no idea how far away I am from Fifth Avenue, so I decide to give it a good forty-five minutes to walk it. I do hope that is enough time.

Whilst walking past Bergdorf Goodman, admiring the imaginative window displays, my phone bleeps. I panic that it could be Patrick cancelling. I am in such a hurry to check my WhatsApp that I drop my phone. Reading it upside down on the pavement I see that it is from Jamie. Thank goodness.

> Managed to get Wi-Fi on the flight. Text me as soon as you're finished. Good luck! Landing in about two hours. Was thinking of an Italian someone told me about for dinner. That's if you're not too busy with Patrick. ☺

I manage to write,

> Sounds good, safe landing

before I spot Tiffany's, right in front of me.

Oh my, oh my, oh my. He is there. Patrick is standing outside Tiffany's, and he is beyond drop-dead gorgeous. He really is Perfect. Maybe I should cancel the walk, as I think I may have to sleep with him immediately.

Chapter 24

Tiffany's – meeting Perfect Patrick

Stay calm, Amelia. Stay calm. My head is spinning; I am going to collapse. Is this a panic attack? Am I going to collapse? Has anyone got any Valium?

Oh shit. He has seen me. Wave Amelia, wave. My arm won't move. Okay, it is moving slightly. I manage to lift my arm. I thank my lovely chiffon sleeves for hiding the bingo wings that are now flapping about like one of those Canadian geese.

He waves back. Oh my god. Those big muscular arms are waving back at me.

I don't think I can breathe. Can I breathe? Help, is there a paramedic around? I'm going to faint. I think I need some kind of inhaler.

My legs are like jelly, more jelly-ish than normal. I feel like they are going to go from under me. He's coming up to me. What on earth do I say?

'Hey, Amelia. Wowee. Finally, we meet!'

Wowee? That sounds like something the boys would say. Just please don't let him say amazeballs.

Patrick hugs me and kisses me on the cheek. The most loving and gentle kiss I have ever experienced. I am never going to wash my face again.

'Hi!' I manage to squeak. 'So good to see you.'

'So, umm, Central Park?' he confirms.

'Yeah, sure.'

Amid all the excitement, I realise that I haven't even noticed what was in the window at Tiffany's. I am so busy sneaking glances at Patrick that I could be anywhere in the world right now; even if I was in a flagship Christian Louboutin store I wouldn't realise.

'So, how's the new hotel?' Patrick asks politely.

'Oh, nice, thanks, Patrick.'

'I'm so sorry the hotel I booked didn't work out. One of the guys at work said it was a cool place. I feel terrible you didn't like it. I promise to make it up to you. I said I'd spoil you. That's all I have ever wanted since we met back in 2001, umm-ish,' he says with a big smile. 'To spoil you forever.'

'Close, 2000.' I laugh.

He may not remember the exact year, but once again I am flattered. Someone wants to spoil me, he is beautiful, lives in glamorous New York and... doesn't have long left, my anxiety quickly reminds me.

The leaves are turning the autumnal shades of purple, orange and magenta in Central Park, so it looks absolutely magnificent. I want to pinch myself. I am here with leaves scrunching beneath my feet, with the most charming man I have ever met. He is so different to Dick – a man who didn't want to be with me – who never wanted to do anything. I am with someone who plays polo and lives what life he has left to the full and, as an added bonus, is ten times better looking than boring old Dick.

I never thought I would say it: but thank you, Tanja Tart. Thank you so much.

I stop myself. Why am I thinking of Tanja Tart when I am here with my beautiful future husband?

'You're quiet,' Patrick says as he takes a long look at me. Oh no, I do hope the sunlight hasn't accentuated that stray hair on my chin that I forgot to pluck. I feel around my chin nervously. Shit, yes, it's still there.

'Oh, sorry, I was thinking of something,' I say, smiling at him.

He takes my hand and holds it tight. It is the most wonderful feeling I have had in many years. My heart is bursting with happiness.

We are walking along, hand in hand, taking in the giant skyscrapers that shadow Central Park when we come to a bridge. Patrick seems to know his way around the park extremely well.

He stops and pulls me to one side.

'This is called Gapstow Bridge. I often come here to chill when I am stressed at work. I love looking into the pond. I could stay here for hours,' he says, while pulling me closer.

He looks into my eyes and, before I can say anything, he kisses me.

I don't ever remember being kissed like this. Did Dick kiss me like this when we met? I know it has been a long time, but I don't remember him ever kissing me like this. He seemed clumsier and his lips were hard somehow. Patrick's lips are soft, his kiss is so delicate, so passionate, so, well, yummy. I want this feeling to last forever.

'Oh, Patrick.' I draw away and catch my breath. 'You certainly know how to kiss.' I actually feel like giggling like some kind of school girl right now.

'I've wanted to do that for a very long time,' he says with a big grin.

'Well, that was worth waiting for, that's for sure.' I laugh.

172

He draws me close again and kisses me for round two. I could definitely get used to this. He is the best kisser I have ever known. This time he slowly moves his arm down my back. Oh God, I hope he doesn't feel all the lumps and bumps.

We pull away from each other once again and look into each other's eyes. There is no denying the chemistry is electric. Why on earth did I not take him up on that date? Why would I not call him? I suppose it was all about fear and lack of confidence when I was younger. He asked me out; I should have gone. I resolve to never doubt myself again.

My wonderful Perfect Patrick is holding me so tight that I can feel something in his pocket. Oh no, it is a bit embarrassing, but at least he seems to feel the same as I do. Oh, now it seems to be pulsating.

'Fuck, what now?' says Patrick abruptly. He digs into his pocket and fishes his phone out. Oh! It was on vibrate. I thought it was a bit of a weird sensation.

'I'm on my way, I'm on my way. Okay, don't worry. Calm the fuck down. I'll be there,' he barks down the line.

I am surprised by his tone on the phone. It is as though someone suddenly flicked a switch. It makes me intrigued as to who is on the other end.

'Listen, I have to go,' he says as he ends the call. 'I've been called away. I may have to travel tonight.'

'Oh no. We are just getting to know each other. Do you have to leave?' I say disappointedly.

'It's that boss of mine. I'm going to have to run. I'll message you later.'

He gives me one of his amazing kisses and runs. He physically runs down Central Park, leaving me standing there all alone.

I feel as though I have been handed the most amazing Christmas present and someone has taken it away from me.

Chapter 25

Manhattan – I've lost Patrick

Jamie is already waiting for me inside the trendy little Italian restaurant he has chosen for us. Even though the restaurant is bustling, I quickly spot his familiar blond head and rush over to the table.

'This looks fabulous,' I say, looking around at the unusual décor. It has metal pipes on the ceiling and a Vespa tucked away in the corner. My mum would probably have said it needed someone to plaster the ceilings, as those pipes shouldn't be exposed, but it all adds to the charm of the place.

'I've taken the liberty of ordering you a Manhattan. Hope that's okay? I thought you needed more than a boring old spritzer when you're here in New York,' says Jamie.

'Perfect.' I grin. 'So, flight all okay?'

'Not too bad,' says Jamie. 'Got a bit of news to tell you though. Should we order first?'

'Hope it's nothing bad,' I say curiously.

'No, not really. Probably for the best. Let's order the food first, then chat. We only have the table for an hour or so.'

We pick up the menus as we wait for our drinks. There is so much choice I don't know where to start. Everything sounds delicious.

'Ooh, grilled sardines,' I say.

'Ooh, bruschetta,' says Jamie.

'Ooh, pasta with lobster,' I say.

'Ooooh, ravioli stuffed with meatballs.' Jamie laughs. 'Think it's going to have to be three courses for me.'

'Absolutely. Have you seen the tiramisu they have over there?' I say, looking at the fridge full of cakes.

The server comes with the Manhattans, which are presented in Martini glasses with a juicy-looking cherry on the side of the glass.

'Cheers,' I say. 'I've never tried one before.'

'I haven't either,' confesses Jamie.

'Ooh, it's a bit strong, but… Yes, nice,' I say as I take a sip.

'Hmm, lovely,' says Jamie, taking a huge slurp.

'So, what's the news?' I ask.

'Ladies first. How did your date with Patrick go?' asks Jamie.

I start telling him about the date. The amazing date that was far too short.

It's typical, but the server comes up and interrupts me as I am in full conversational flow.

Jamie orders the grilled octopus to start, and I order the sardines.

'For main course, it has to be the lobster pasta,' I say, my mouth watering. 'Do you have any garlic bread?' I ask.

It doesn't look as though I am going to be kissing Patrick again tonight, so I think I will be safe with the garlic. I still haven't heard anything from him, which I am a little concerned about. I am beginning to wonder whether he had some kind of code with someone: if I wasn't how he remembered me, then they should call him and he would pretend to be called away. Then again,

I think back to the palm reader: she seemed to know her stuff. Then there was that kiss, surely that gave away his feelings for me. There must be some kind of simple explanation. I guess it is because he has to work hard to earn the money and, if that means an urgent business trip, that is what he must do.

'So, you were saying…' Jamie says, turning back to me.

'Well, this may sound really weird, but a fortune teller told me I was going to get married to Patrick.'

'What?' Jamie screams, making half the restaurant turn around. 'You're not going to marry a guy you don't even know. Has he asked you to marry him?'

'Well, no. A fortune teller I met on the flight told me. So, if that was to be true, I suppose it doesn't really matter that our date was cut short. We would have the rest of our lives together,' I explain. Although it is anyone's guess how long that will be.

'What about the boys? You don't know this guy properly, Amelia. You're normally the sensible one. Sian I would expect this from, but not you. How can you be sure he's "The One"?'

'I'm not sure he's the one, but the fortune teller told me he was. That's all,' I explain again. 'It's all a bit strange, I agree. I suppose you can't rule anything out though. Life does have a habit of surprising me,' I say.

The grilled sardines arrive, and I order another Manhattan. I notice Jamie looking uncomfortable.

'Is your octopus a bit chewy?' I ask.

'No, why?'

'You don't seem very happy, that's all,' I say.

'I'm fine. Let's just eat,' he says.

'Oh, look, text from Sian,' I say, looking down at my phone. I know it is rude to be on your phone when you are at the dinner table, but I was checking in case Patrick had messaged.

> How's Perfect Patrick? Jamie said he was meeting U later. Have fun, I'm off to bed now. Tell me all tomoz. Love U xxxxxx

'Oh, so you've been in touch with Sian today?' I say.

'Yeah, I told her I was looking forward to catching up with you tonight. I promised her I'd keep an eye on you. That's why I'm so disappointed in you rushing into things, Amelia,' says Jamie.

'I'm only saying what the fortune teller told me. Of course, I'm not going to rush into getting married. Do you really think I'd do that to the boys? They come first, for goodness sakes,' I say.

'That's such a relief, Amelia. Great news. I just want you to be happy but take your time.'

Our main courses arrive and we gobble them up as we chat about Jamie's dad. I didn't realise it was his birthday today until Jamie told me.

'To your dad,' I say, clinking glasses. 'The first anniversary of everything is the hardest. Remember when your dad went out and bought that XR3i convertible?'

'Yes, Mum went nuts with him. Bless, she died not long after and Dad thought the car was cursed. I'll never forget, she accused him of having a midlife crisis and said he would run off with a dolly bird next. Oops, sorry,' Jamie adds, remembering my circumstances.

'It's fine, Tanja isn't really a dolly bird,' I say.

'Oh, and do you remember when your mum went ballistic and said you'd been drinking cider with Sian?'

'Yes, all Sian's fault once again,' I agree. 'My mother stopped me from going to the rugby club disco for months.'

'Yes, it wasn't quite the same without you and your crazy dancing,' says Jamie. 'Remember, you loved that "Time Warp" song? You thought you knew every step for the dance.'

'Oh, don't. Nooo.' I laugh.

Our desserts interrupt our memories and I stop talking immediately when I see the huge slice of tiramisu on the table in front of me.

Like the rest of the meal, it is absolutely superb.

'I'm so stuffed,' I say to Jamie. 'I really shouldn't have eaten all that.'

The server comes along and clears our plates the minute we put the spoons down.

'I think they want the table back,' says Jamie.

'Yes, we'd better think about heading off,' I agree.

'Are you ready for a surprise I've arranged for you?' asks Jamie. 'Thought we could make a night of it; hope you don't mind.'

'No, of course. What's the surprise?' I ask.

'Ah, you'll have to wait and see,' he says.

As we wait for the bill to arrive, Jamie opens up about his conference that starts tomorrow and tells me what it is all about. It sounds pretty awful and is for some IT thing about fraud, or something. I want to know what the surprise is, but it is only fair I pretend to listen to his IT talk.

Finally, the server returns with our change, and I put my jacket on.

'I hope that was enough of a tip,' says Jamie. 'I'm always scared I'll get it wrong.'

'I know, me too,' I agree as we head out the door.

We flag down a yellow cab as it drives past. I wonder where Jamie's taking us next.

'To 219 West 49th Street, please,' directs Jamie.

'Where on earth are we going?' I ask.

'You'll see.'

—

I love being in the yellow cabs, looking at all the sights. It is so beguiling and magical and I look forward to bringing the boys here one day. We could even end up living here if I were to marry Patrick. I wonder if they would like it here; it is so different to the countryside that they have been brought up in.

'We're here,' says Jamie.

I look out the window to see crowds of people queuing. I eagerly jump out of the cab.

'This is your surprise,' he says, putting a protective arm around me as I get pushed by some Italian tourists.

We are standing outside the Ambassador Theatre, and there is a huge billboard advertising *Chicago*.

'Wow, we are going to see a musical!' I say, thrilled.

What a fantastic opportunity. I haven't had time to think about sightseeing and enjoying New York. This is about as awesome as it gets, a show on Broadway!

'Is Catherine Zeta-Jones in it?' I ask Jamie.

'No, she was in the film.'

'I know someone who went to school with her,' I say, proud of my claim to fame.

'Amelia, everyone in Wales claims to know someone who went to school with her,' Jamie says, laughing.

'Fair enough. Oh, I did speak to Keith Chegwin on the radio once,' I quickly add.

'Okay, you win. You know more celebs than me.' Jamie laughs.

We happily sit down in the mezzanine row of the theatre. Jamie has chosen our seats carefully and we have a clear view of the stage.

The curtains part and the stage comes alive. This is so exciting!

I never really knew the story of *Chicago* but it is set in the twenties. There is a lot of dancing about and some fabulous jazz music, which makes it invigorating to watch. The only thing is that it is actually about a chorus girl called Roxie, who kills her husband's mistress. I have to wonder why Jamie would bring me to see something involving an extramarital affair like this. Does he think I should have done that to Tanja Tart? No, surely not.

In the interlude, Jamie tells me that the show has been on for twenty years, so it was probably on when I came to New York the last time. That is a coincidence; maybe that is why he thought of this show for me.

'Why did you choose *Chicago*?' I finally ask him.

'I don't know, because I thought you'd enjoy it,' he mutters.

Oh, so there was no ulterior motive. I really must stop analysing everything and instead enjoy the moment. I have had the most amazing day ever. A walk in Central Park with my possible future husband and now a Broadway show with one of my best friends.

We leave the theatre, amid the masses of crowds, and look for a cab once again.

It is easier that we are now staying in the same hotel, as we can take the cab together.

'I've had so much fun, Jamie,' I say as we practically stumble into the lift. 'Those Manhattans are a bit strong though, don't you think?' I add.

Jamie is busy agreeing with me when the doors open for his floor.

'Right, this is me. Take care, Amelia. I'll see you when I have some free time, okay. Don't forget, please don't do anything silly with Patrick,' he says.

He reaches out and gives me a hug.

'Okay, I'll try to be sensible,' I say.

I hold the lift doors open as Jamie gets out on his floor.

'Hey, what was it you wanted to tell me earlier, by the way? You said you had some news and then we started talking about everything else.' I remember.

'It was nothing important,' he says.

'Come on, tell me. Or I won't sleep wondering what it was,' I say.

'It was only about Megan… She dumped me right before the flight, that's all.'

'What?' I say in disbelief.

The lift doors close with Jamie on the other side. I desperately try to press the button to open them, but it's no use as I am on my way up to the fifteenth floor.

Poor Jamie. Why didn't he say something earlier? That is so typical of him, he probably didn't want to spoil our lovely evening. Surely, I should have realised that something was wrong though. Did I miss a sign? I suppose I never even asked how Miserable Megan was. Had I asked, he may have told me and I would have been able to talk about it with him. I should have asked about Megan; it's just that I didn't really want to know how she was.

Oh, Jamie. As always, he has tried to make me happy with a lovely evening and hidden any pain he is in. He really is too good for this world.

Chapter 26

Sacramento — where is that?

By the time I reach the room and pull my phone out of my handbag, I have nine missed calls from Patrick. I read over the text he sent me half an hour ago. He must have sent it when we were in the cab on the way home.

> Sorry I had to leave. Tried calling so many times, I hope you're not mad at me. Flying to Sacramento on an urgent assignment. Message you in the morning. xx

I am at least grateful that his disappearance wasn't a ploy to escape from me.

I tap 'Sacramento' into my phone: where on earth is that? Perhaps I could have gone with him. It would have been fun to have gone on an assignment with a journalist.

Lying in bed, the feelings of happiness and joy I had all day have washed away. I suddenly feel a bit sad. Miserable Megan has dumped poor Jamie and I feel a bit dumped too. Plus, I wish I was reading bedtime stories to the boys. It doesn't feel the same going to bed without kissing them goodnight. I message Dick to tell them I'm saying night night. Tears start to prickle my cheeks.

Everything feels pointless. I flew out to see Patrick and now he has been called away and I don't even know how long for. I only have three days left here; what if he doesn't come back by then? And Jamie… Why on earth would anyone dump him? That's Megan for you, I suppose. Sian and I said it would end in disaster. I will put money on it she is running off with the yogi she met in Bath.

Jamie doesn't respond to my message checking to see if he's okay; he must have fallen straight to sleep. For me, on the other hand, it is a different story. It seems to take forever to get to sleep even though I am sprawled out on a lovely queen-size bed. I must eventually fall asleep, though, as I wake up dribbling all over my synthetic pillow.

-

I get ready for breakfast, popping on my favourite comfortable jumpsuit, so that I have plenty of room to scoff bagels. Unfortunately, Jamie had to leave early to register for the conference and is having breakfast at the convention centre. I hope his head wasn't too bad after all the drinks last night.

Although the hotel is targeted at business travellers, a man and a woman who are definitely together sit on the table beside me. I wonder if she is the CEO of a multimillion-dollar corporation and he is her limo driver, either that or the man is having an affair with his PA.

The man leans over the table to feed the woman – how romantic. Nobody has ever fed me toast; I wonder if Patrick would feed me toast.

The red-haired woman with the toast-feeding man takes a big bite of it, crunching at it seductively, and they both share a private joke. I feel an enormous pang of jealousy. Why can't that be me? I wonder if they ever argue. Maybe the reason they get on so well is because they don't have to live with each other every day.

I take comfort in the enormous buffet. I have already had eggs benedict, which would normally fill me for at least an hour, but I can't help going for seconds, thirds and fourths. At this rate even my one-size-bigger Spanx aren't going to fit. That is if Patrick ever returns and I get the opportunity to wear them.

I am biting into the most delicious pain au raisin when I see my phone light up.

It is Patrick on WhatsApp with his morning greeting. Today, it is a little different though.

> Hey, blueberry muffin XX

Blueberry muffin? Is that because he thinks I am fat and spotty?

> Blueberry muffin???? xx

I type back, noting he is still online.

> Lol. I want to eat you for breakfast, of course. Xx

I burst out laughing in the middle of the dining room. That is the cutest thing I have heard, unless he is genuinely a cannibal, of course.

> Haha, very funny. I love it XXXXXX

Okay, I got a bit carried away with the kisses there, but I really miss him and want to see him.

> Good news – I leave Sacramento tonight. Be back in NY by tomorrow morning Xx

> Soooo happy to hear that. It's weird coming all the way to see you and you're not even here! Xxxxxx What assignment are you doing in Sacramento anyway? XXXXX

> Office stuff, to do with the company I work for. They have offices in Sacramento. Long story, quite complex xx

Two kisses. Hmm, I even gave him capital kisses.

> You'll have to tell me when you're back then. I'd love to hear more about your work xx

I'd better calm down on the kisses.

Listen, gotta go, boss is here. I have to be in the Manhattan office for 10am for a breakfast meeting, but I'm free tomorrow evening. Can we meet then? XX

That would be wonderful Xx

I'm thinking Japanese. Is that good for you? XX

Oh, yes, Japanese is perfect. Xxxxx

I am well aware that I have added too many kisses there, but who cares if I seem overly keen? I *am* overly keen.

Patrick will be back soon, and we are having dinner in a Japanese restaurant. I am in heaven once again. I feel like I am floating on a cloud – a big, fluffy, wonderful cloud.

Chapter 27

Streets of Manhattan – time to shop

Whilst I examine some Lego in an enormous toy shop on one of the main streets, my phone rings for what seems like the billionth time. I am trying to decide between some Star Wars Lego or this Mindstorm Lego robot stuff. I know the boys would love the Mindstorm thing, but it is super expensive. Will the boys even keep it safe, or will they lose half the pieces as usual? I ignore the phone until I decide to take two smaller boxes of Lego instead.

With my decision finally made I can check my phone. I see that it is Dick. My stomach lurches immediately. I wasn't expecting him to ring. He wasn't due to call me. Why is he calling? I spoke to the boys when they woke up. They were all excited about their day ahead at some amusement park.

The minute he speaks I drop the two boxes of Lego. My hands are shaking as I press 'Jamie' on the phone.

'I need you urgently. Can you meet me at the hotel?' I ask between sobs.

'Okay, but can it wait a while? I'm just at the conference,' he says.

'No, it can't wait. Please, can you meet me at the hotel now?' I ask urgently.

'Okay, I guess I can be there in about ten minutes. What's this all about? Are you okay?'

My walk back to the hotel is one big daze. I bump into so many people.

'Watch it, lady!' shouts some rude man. If only he knew what was wrong, then perhaps he would have some sympathy for me.

My eyes are blurry with tears, and I wipe my white sleeve against my smudged black mascara. I don't care that the waterproof mascara could stain this top forever. It will be a reminder of the worst day of my life.

Once I reach the lobby, Jamie comes running in.

'What on earth is so urgent? What the hell?' he asks as he notices my blotchy, tear-stained face.

A smart young woman in a suit stares at me as I sob all the way through the lobby, but I really don't care who is looking at me.

'I'll tell you in the room. Let's go up,' I say.

'Okay. I've managed to get out for the rest of the afternoon, so no rush back,' he says. 'It's just some teamwork exercise later, nothing important.' He mutters on, but I am not listening to any of it.

I open the door and my knees go from under me. I collapse in a heap on the floor. I have been brave for so long that the moment I enter the room I can't take it any longer. The whole hotel must have heard my desperate screams.

'You have to calm down and tell me what's going on,' says Jamie, lifting me on to a nearby chair.

'It's that Tanja Tart. She's... she's... lost them,' I say. The reality hits me once again. Saying the words out loud makes it all real and the pain strikes me again.

'What do you mean, Tanja Tart has lost them?' Jamie asks, bewildered.

I sit down, then stand up again. I can't sit down in this state of panic. My chest is so tight. I try to focus on my breathing. I need to calm down and think rationally.

'We don't know the full details yet. The police are there with them and taking statements. Dick said he would ring me as soon as there are any further updates,' I say.

Jamie places his hand on top of mine, but I pull it off, unable to remain still. I am going to wear the carpet out in a minute; I have walked up and down this room so many times.

Despite being told that Dick will contact me with more information, I try to call him. However, his line is constantly busy. I couldn't focus in the shop and don't even remember what he said properly. I heard the words 'Jasper and Rupert are missing', and then my head went all blurry and I thought I might faint.

The boys have been missing for two whole hours. They could be anywhere by now. Someone may have sold them to human traffickers; they could have dyed their hair green and they are now completely unrecognisable. The nasty folk who kidnapped them could have removed their kidneys to sell, or anything. Oh, my gorgeous boys, please don't remove their kidneys. Their beautiful, beautiful kidneys. How on earth am I supposed to cope? I need to speak to Dick immediately. Why can't I get through? Why is he not calling me? He is the only one who knows what is going on.

'Amelia, please sit down. It's not going to help anyone running around the room like this,' says Jamie. 'Can I make you some tea?'

'No, I don't want anything. Why would I want anything? I only want my beautiful baby boys!' I shout. 'My babies. I should never ever have let them go away with Dick and Tanja. You could see they couldn't manage the boys at the castle. Why did Dick leave them with Tanja Tart?' I sob.

Jamie puts his arm tightly around me.

'I don't know that he really left them with Tanja Tart. You said that the boys ran off when Dick went to pick up her caramel latte,' he says.

Is that what I recalled to him? I don't even know what Dick said. I am in a state of confusion; thankfully Jamie remembers what I have told him.

'That woman. First my husband, now my boys. I hate her. Hate her, hate her, hate her,' I scream.

'Try to calm down a bit. Focusing your hate on that woman is not going to get the boys back. We need to focus on finding them now and keeping in touch with Dick,' says Jamie.

I know this makes sense, but right now I need to pour out my pain and hatred on that horrible woman. If it wasn't for her, so many things in my life wouldn't have happened and now to lose the boys. This is the final straw.

'Dick is their dad and I'm sure he is terrified. I don't think Tanja Tart will be his favourite person right now, either,' says Jamie.

'I should think so too. And where are the police? Why aren't they ringing me? I'm their mum,' I say.

I'm their mum and I wasn't even with them. What sort of mum am I?

'They need to be out there looking for the boys at the moment. They'll be busy,' says Jamie. 'I'm sure they'll find them; the park they were in is massive. I've had a look online. They could be anywhere there,' he adds.

'That really isn't helping, Jamie. They could be half way around the world by now. Put the news on,' I demand. 'Maybe there's something on the news.'

There are so many channels it is difficult to find any news. It is mostly repeats of *The Bold and the Beautiful* and *Judge Judy*.

We finally find an American news channel who are talking about some shark that has been spotted on a beach. What if they have been eaten by a shark? Were they near the sea?

I start to imagine the next set of headlines. You know how the media twist these things.

MUM LEAVES KIDS IN THE COM-
PANY OF TANJA TART FOR NEW
YORK ROMP AND KIDS GET EATEN
BY SHARKS.

News reporters will be interviewing Mrs Hopkins in number 9, and she will be saying, '*She was a terrible mother. She was always late for school with the kids and she once made a school project out of a wine box*'.

She will definitely make me sound like an alcoholic.

She has never liked me since Jasper's ball smashed through her prize petunias. I so hope the news reporters don't knock on number 9. Please knock on sweet old Mrs Charles in number 12 instead.

I try Dick's number once again. It finally rings out.

'Hi,' he answers. I feel as though I will explode with anger at him.

'How could you have lost them?' I scream.

'It wasn't my fault, okay. They ran off. They were there one minute and gone the next.'

'Well, you shouldn't have taken your eyes off them, you idiot. Why would you not watch them? How could you trust that horrible woman to look after them? She couldn't look after the flaming tortoise,' I scream.

'Because I thought they were old enough to behave for one minute. I didn't know they'd run off,' Dick says. 'I'm so sorry. I'm really sorry.'

For a moment my anger starts to subside. I can hear he is very upset and it must be difficult for him too, but I still can't help but be furious with him for leaving them under her watch for a second. Those parks are so busy, anyone could have come along and grabbed them while that floozie wasn't looking.

'Where are you now?' I ask.

'In the security office. The staff brought me in here while the police and security check everywhere. They're not letting anyone in or out of the park now,' he explains. 'Oh, hang on, the policeman's coming,' he adds.

I hear voices mumbling in the background, and then Dick says, 'I'll call you back in a minute. There's been some kind of development.'

Chapter 28

Two sides of the States – seeing is believing

Jamie and I stare in disbelief at the photo that has been sent to my phone. There in front of me is Jasper, looking through a glass window, with Rupert helplessly watching on the other side – their hands touching through the pane.

The good news is that they have both been found. The bad news is that Jasper was discovered inside a claw machine in an arcade and the staff can't find the keys to open it.

'What on earth is he doing?' I ask Jamie.

I honestly don't know whether to laugh or cry. I am so relieved they are safe that my emotions are everywhere and I am a little hysterical. I think once he gets out of the machine then I might be able to laugh about it, but for now, I am immensely concerned that the staff can't find the keys.

'They'll have to get the fire brigade out; can't someone call them?' I say anxiously.

'I'm sure they'll find the keys in a minute. You don't want them to smash the glass. It might injure Jasper,' says Jamie rationally.

I try to figure from the picture if Jasper is in any discomfort. I mean, is there enough oxygen in a claw machine for a nine-year-old? It is not like this is a subject taught at school, 'how to survive being trapped inside a claw machine'. Perhaps I will petition for this to become part of the curriculum when I return.

I simply have to pray that they find those keys. Isn't there a master key somewhere? My phone is practically glued to my hand now as I wait for the next bit of news.

'Come on, why don't we go to the bar and get a drink while we wait?' says Jamie. 'I'm pretty sure it's time for a drink after the day you've had.'

'I don't think I should be heading to the hotel bar when my child could be suffocating in a grabber machine, Jamie. My god, you can tell that you're not a parent.' I regret the words immediately even though Jamie doesn't show any hint of emotion.

'Sorry, I shouldn't have said that. I don't know what I'd have done without you today. I owe you, really. But, look, I should get on the next flight and get home. I'm not even in the mood for a holiday now. My poor boys have been through so much trauma. I wasn't even there for them in their hour of need.'

'Your flight is in 48 hours; I don't think it's going to make much difference now. Plus, I'm on your flight back – you never know, I might be able to upgrade you.' Jamie winks at me, but I am in no mood for his flippancy. My child is stuck in a claw machine, possibly struggling for oxygen and about to get hypoxic. I really couldn't care less about business class.

'I should never have left them. Everything is all my fault. They'd be safe at home if I hadn't come to New York. Perhaps they wouldn't be in Florida right now. Maybe they'd have gone at a different time and this wouldn't have happened,' I say. The guilt hits me again.

'They wanted to go on holiday, Amelia. Come on, they were allowed to go on holiday with their dad. You did nothing wrong. Dick probably didn't really either; it's that silly woman. Look, stop with all the guilt, will you? We all know what you've been through with Dick and how unhappy you've been. Come on, stop all of this, you deserve a break and you're a great mum,' says Jamie.

'Really?' I ask. I don't feel like it right now.

'You are such an amazing mum. You live for those boys and do everything you can for them. Don't be so hard on yourself,' he says.

The phone rings and I see it is Dick. Please let him be calling to say that Jasper is finally out.

'He's out. They got him out!' he says with relief in his voice.

'Oh, thank God. Don't ever let that woman be on her own with them again, do you hear me?' I say. I signal to Jamie that Jasper has been released from his temporary prison.

'Are you away? Your phone ring's funny,' says Dick, taking me by surprise.

'Yes, I decided to take a break in New York,' I say.

'Was that what Sian was whispering about like some school kid at the castle? Oh my god, you planned this, didn't you? No wonder you wanted me to take the kids to Disney. Have you got a new man?' says Dick.

'First of all, I asked if I could take them to Disney, so no, it was not planned. And would you really care if I did have a new man?' I say. 'You can't have it both ways, Dick. Remember you're getting married.'

'Oh,' I hear down the line.

'Is that a hint of jealousy?' I ask. Dick doesn't answer.

'Can I speak to Jasper now, please?' I am beyond desperate to hear my baby boy's voice. I hear Dick grunt something, and then Jasper comes on the phone.

'Mum, that was seriously cool,' he says excitedly.

'What on earth were you trying to do?' I ask.

'I bet Rupert the candyfloss money that I could climb in and get the big SpongeBob SquarePants out. I was trying to be fugal, like Daddy recommends,' answers Jasper.

'It's frugal,' I say. 'And technically that's actually stealing, Jasper. I can't believe you would do such a thing.'

'Sorry, Mum. I thought Dad would be happy that I saved a few dollars and got a free SpongeBob. Rupert said it was a good idea.'

'No, I don't think even Daddy would be happy with that money-saving idea,' I scold him. 'I will speak to you when you're back and Rupert too. Neither of you are out of trouble yet, young man.'

'Ohhhh,' he groans. 'By the way, can I put the video on YouTube? A nice lady videoed it.'

'No, you cannot put it on YouTube,' I say sternly. 'Now give the phone back to Dad.'

'Sorry we gave you such a shock, but I had to let you know they were missing. Anyway, no harm done. All okay now,' says Dick.

'I'm glad you told me. You can't keep something like that from me,' I say. 'I suppose you must be pretty shaken up too,' I add.

'I'm all right. Had a bit of a scare. Remember when you thought Rupert wasn't breathing in his cot that time? We sat in the nursery watching his chest, waiting for it to rise. Then it finally did and the relief was immense. Well, that's how I'm feeling right now,' says Dick.

'I'll never forget it,' I say. 'Now try and relax. Just don't take your eyes off them again.'

In that moment, all the hatred I have ever had for Dick subsides. We are both the parents of these wonderful boys and have that common bond. Neither Tanja nor anyone else will ever take that away from us. I finally feel at peace with him, even if I am slightly smug that he could be a teeny bit jealous at the thought of me meeting someone else.

'Everything okay?' asks Jamie once I put the phone down.

'You know, I am actually,' I say. 'I never thought I'd say this, but everything's going to be okay.'

No sooner have I put the phone down than there is another bleep. I have the shock of my life as I see a photo of a huge diamond ring on the incoming message.

'Jamie! Oh my god! As if there haven't been enough surprises for one day. He's just proposed,' I scream in excitement.

'He's proposed,' says Jamie shocked. 'Patrick has proposed?'

'Oh, sorry, no, no. Not Patrick. Rob. It's a message from Sian. Rob's just proposed,' I say. 'I'm so happy for her. I know it's a bit sudden, but they're so well suited. She says they're going to get married in Gretna Green, and she wants me to be her chief bridesmaid,' I add. 'He's only just given her the ring. She doesn't waste time that one,' I say, laughing.

'That's so awesome,' says Jamie.

'I know, isn't it?' I agree.

'I tell you what, why don't we upgrade that drink I suggested? I know it's only 4pm, but let's go for a drink somewhere special to toast them,' says Jamie. 'There's a champagne bar not too far away some of the guys on the conference were talking about. Fancy a glass? My treat.'

'After the day we've had, why not?' I answer with huge relief.

–

The Champagne Bar at The Plaza is absolutely stunning. This is the most beautiful hotel I have ever seen. I feel as though I am on a movie set. Wherever I look is perfect.

I order a Kir Royale while taking in the splendour of it all.

I send Sian a photo of our drinks.

To you and Rob

My tongue tingles with the beautiful bubbles of the Kir Royale as we sit by a window overlooking Fifth Avenue. I can just imagine coming here with Patrick; in fact, he is probably a regular. Maybe the barman even knows him. I wonder if I should ask him. I would definitely imagine this to be his type of place.

'Same again?' Jamie asks.

'Oh, go on then,' I find myself saying automatically.

Dick has messaged to let me know that the boys are back in the hotel safe and sound and it is as though nothing has happened. Having this information means that I can now unwind a little, plus my bubbles are so delicious that I can't resist another.

Jamie comes back with the drinks and our conversation turns to his ex-wife, Melinda. I suppose she was in my head because of the doppelganger flight attendant.

'Do you ever see her?' I ask curiously.

'No, the last I heard she had three children. She moved to Spain after the divorce and that was the end of it,' Jamie responds.

'Do you ever feel sad about not being a dad yourself?' I ask. I still feel awkward about my earlier remark and try to judge whether I hit a nerve.

'Honestly, for a few years after the divorce… Ah… Well, that's why I took myself off to London at the time and threw myself into my career. Now I've climbed the IT ladder as it were, I won't deny there's an empty gap in my life, especially now I've lost dad, but who knows what's in store…'

'I always wondered why you never married again.'

'Well, between work and my dad it didn't occur to me… and I don't want to get hurt ever again.'

'Hah, I know that feeling.' I smile. It seems Patrick, Jamie and I are all deterred by the same thing, unlike carefree Sian.

'I hope you're not too sad about Megan,' I say.

'No, we both knew that wasn't going anywhere. We had completely different interests. It's a complete put-off when you go for dinner with someone and they just pick at a salad. I'd much prefer to go out with someone like you, who loves her food. I don't mean go out with… I mean… You know, dine with and I don't mean who loves her food… I mean.' Jamie sits there awkwardly. 'What am I on about? Must be the champagne. I'm making no sense. I'd better be going before I say something I shouldn't,' he says, standing up.

'What do you mean, "say something you shouldn't"?' I ask.

'It's absolutely nothing,' he says.

'What? Are you okay? You're not sick too, are you?'

First Perfect Patrick, now Jamie. I'm starting to worry about everyone.

'No, I'm not sick,' he says reassuringly.

'Well, what are you talking about then?' I ask.

'Absolutely nothing. Look, we really should be going,' he says, getting up to leave.

'But we haven't finished our drinks. I'm sorry, I shouldn't have asked those questions… It was rude of me.'

'No, it's fine. Honestly. You need an early night anyway. Go and chill in your room maybe. Aren't you planning some beauty appointments early tomorrow? You have to get ready for that big date in that fancy Japanese restaurant, after all,' says Jamie.

'I do indeed,' I say.

I quickly swig the last drop of champagne, there was no way I was going to waste that. I look at Jamie's glass and am very tempted to lean over and finish that one too, but think better of it. We are in a swanky place, after all.

I am so happy when I get back to my room that I sing the Alicia Keys 'New York' song to myself. How amazing life is suddenly. My best friend and I have drunk champagne in the swankiest bar I've ever been to and, more importantly, my boys are safe and well. Tomorrow, I have a date with a very handsome man and I have some pampering to look forward to before that. Life suddenly feels very perfect indeed, I think to myself.

Chapter 29

A back street salon – a little pampering

Following a very early night, I find myself lying on a white, paper-towelled couch the next morning. I close my eyes and relax. I haven't been pampered for ages. In fact, I think the last facial I had was in the lead up to my wedding.

A tall Eastern European therapist, with heavily pencilled eyebrows, scans my pores and prods my skin around in the quest to discover quite how dehydrated my epidermis is. Naturally, it turns out that it is very dehydrated, and she has already recommended that I buy all the moisturising serums and creams that she suggests. After a lot of tutting, she mixes lotions and potions together and meticulously prepares my facial scrub. My skin is going to look as good as new after this.

'Okaaay, I see vat I can do, but I not magic person,' she says as she begins slathering my skin with some kind of tingling concoction.

'You're not a magic person?' I repeat.

'Don't think you look after skin?'

'Well, um, yes, I do but…'

'You need more than vacial – you need cosmetic surgeon. Botox for shuuur. I making peel now. Better for you, before you leave maybe you have some Botox shot. Ve have special deal and you need this very bad.'

I thought I was going to come out of here pampered and polished; I feel like I am being scrutinised and tortured. I do try my best to look after my skin. Though, of course, there was the one night I had too much to drink and slept in my make-up. This must be the reason for the open pores she is complaining about.

'Also, too much hair on lip,' the direct lady suddenly says. 'Better ve do vaxing after. I can do upper lip and Brazilian, two for price of one. For special offer today only,' she adds.

'I don't want a Brazilian. I only came in for a revitalising facial. No, no, please,' I insist.

'Okay, ve do another special offer of leg and lip vax. Ve do that, yes?'

'Okay, well, I guess my legs are in need of waxing.'

I had planned on shaving them before dinner, so I find myself agreeing to the waxing. I must be crazy, but she is very persuasive.

After my facial, she places the hot wax on my upper lip. It feels as though it is searing through my skin, similar to a steak on a hot griddle. I am sure after a peel, or any kind of facial, you shouldn't wax, but she has assured me that I will be okay as they have some kind of special wax that can be used.

'Ouch!' I scream as she violently tears the waxing strip off my delicate skin.

'Quiet, you vant to go about with micetache? We have to do zis,' she says, pulling my face towards her harder.

I feel myself dig deeper into the couch, trying to squirm my way further down to escape the clutches of this mad woman. It reminds me of when I go for a smear and shimmy up the bed as the clamp thing appears in front of me. Unfortunately, as with my gynaecologist, this squirming about only makes her grip tighter.

Eventually she shows me a mirror and I can see that my lip is definitely hair free. A little red, but definitely hair free. Maybe it was worth the pain after all.

'Now legs,' she says. I swear she is laughing to herself. I am left in no doubt that she is definitely enjoying herself a lot more than I am.

I get up feeling light-headed after all the anguish, but I am immensely proud of the fact that I have managed to have my upper lip and legs waxed without passing out. I also succumbed to the Botox but, as she used numbing cream beforehand, this wasn't anywhere near as bad as the waxing.

'I have a manicure and pedicure booked next,' I say. At least that has to be enjoyable, surely.

I soon realise that I will never come back to this salon, as although my toes are now a beautiful shade called 'romantic rose', my toenails have been filed and cut into a round shape and I do fear that this will cause ingrown toenails when they start to grow. My cuticles have also been cut down to the max and are bleeding in places. So, I certainly will not be giving this place a five-star review. I only came in for some pampering but am leaving in pain and bleeding. No wonder they have so many special offers on.

The girl on reception looks at me in shock when I pay my bill. I think perhaps they were expecting a massive tip, but there was no way after that experience that I would give them anything extra. I am relieved to open the door to the outside world, after breathing in the pungent aroma of acetone and nail polish for too long. I decide to take a short stroll and get some fresh air to clear my lungs, although I don't know that the pollution of the city is much better for you. I am going to have a little sleep before meeting Patrick tonight, so I don't want to be too long meandering about the city. I still get moments of jet lag, as my sleep pattern is all over the place and then when I finally get to sleep, I have to get up to catch the hotel breakfast.

As I walk along, I see a nice-looking man, who must be in his thirties. He stares at me and kind of smiles. I must be oozing some kind of positive vibe here because everyone is looking at me. It is so good for my confidence after years of Dick not even glancing my way.

They say that confidence shows and since being in New York I really think that I am finding myself once again. I am no longer someone's wife; I am my own person and I can't wait for my date tonight. Freedom really isn't so scary.

With my head held high I walk in what I think must be the direction of the hotel. Although I actually have no idea whether I can walk there or not really, since I came for my appointment directly from some Banana Republic store. However, after what feels like I have walked to the moon and back, I finally reach the hotel, where I catch sight of myself in the mirror.

OH. MY. GOD. What on earth has that evil woman done to me?

Chapter 30

Turning Japanese – pass me the saké

Globules of blood are dripping down my face where I was injected with Botox, and a red rash covers my upper lip in the perfect shape of a moustache. It is not even a small, discreet moustache shape, but more in the formation of one of those handlebar moustaches. No wonder everyone was staring at me. That young bloke was not admiring me in the slightest. I should never have got so carried away in the salon. I just got talked into it all as the lady was so pushy. I have only five hours to make myself presentable before tonight. How on earth am I going to manage it? I consider telling Patrick that I have food poisoning and can't make the date. That would be devastating though. I have waited so long for this. I finally get to see him again and now look like Frankenstein. I am so mad with myself and, of course, that wicked woman.

I search for solutions on the internet and type in 'rash after waxing'; there must be something that can be done. As for the bloodstains, I will have to gently mop those up.

Most of the help online advises to apply a cold compress, along with medicating creams. I can't really look for a pharmacy in this state, though, so a cold compress will have to do. From the safety of my room I call room service for an ice bucket.

When it arrives twenty minutes later, I hide behind the door and reach out my freshly manicured hand to grasp the bucket. Grabbing one of the hotel hand towels, I place lots of ice inside. Ah, that feels nice and cooling. I make one for my forehead too, seeing as that seems to look a little bit swollen.

Relaxed on the bed, with the ice bucket beside me, I can't help but feel sleepy. I close my eyes and hope that by the time I wake up, the rash and any swelling have calmed down.

--

Four hours later I am woken up to a message from Sian.

> Hello, lovely, how's it going? Just wanted to wish you luck with Patrick. Think it must be almost your dinner time?? Message me as soon as you can. Obvs if you're busy don't worry… If you know what I mean. Hehe. Xxx

> OMG, Sian, nothing like that will happen. Don't be so naughty. That's def more you than me!!!!

We message back and forth for a while about her fabulous engagement and then the Jamie and Megan situation, which we are both secretly relieved about.

Then I realise Sian is right. It is almost dinner time.

I had planned on spending hours getting ready, and I am shocked to see that I now only have forty-five minutes before I have to grab a cab and head to the restaurant. How am I supposed to get ready in forty-five minutes?

I run to the bathroom and see in the mirror reflection that my lip and surrounding area are still red. It is going to take me longer than ever to get ready for the date of my life if I am to disguise this rash.

I am in a panic as I swap my handbag over, look for my lip gloss, try to fling on my sandals and search for my key card to get back in. What did I do with it?

Finally, I find the key under the hotel notepad. As I open the door, something makes me turn back and make the bed. You never know, Patrick may want to come back for a coffee, or something. I quickly pull the sheet over and realise that ice has melted all over the bed, leaving it soaked through. I consider calling housekeeping to change the sheets, but if I am going ahead with this date, I really don't have time for that right now. It will have to do. Anyway, he won't come back, I'm sure of it.

–

I find a cab easily and flag it down. I am definitely not walking anywhere tonight in the sandals that perfectly coordinate with my 'dress of hope'. I only wish that Patrick notices the shoes and not the facial eruptions. It still hasn't subsided that much, although the copious foundation and concealer have helped a little, and my long fringe hides my swollen forehead. I can kind of get away with it, but if he kisses me and the make-up comes off, or my hair moves, then he will definitely notice something is very wrong.

Patrick is as punctual as ever. As soon as the cab pulls up, I see him waiting there. I like that he is so punctual. Another perfect quality of his.

'Wow, you look ravishing,' he says, giving me a kiss on the cheek.

Ravishing, ooh, I've never been called that before.

I laugh nervously.

'So do you,' I manage, even though I am not sure you should ever call a man ravishing. Ruggedly handsome, or something, but not so sure about ravishing.

I have to say that I am not used to compliments and so don't really know how to handle them, or equally, how to give them. Gosh, what do I say next?

I am so incredibly nervous tonight. I could, in fact, be even more nervous than on our first date. What happens if he asks to sleep with me tonight? Do I do it? I mean it is very early days, but if he was to be my future husband and he is dying, then it is not like it is a one-night stand, or anything. Does dating etiquette even apply if someone doesn't have long left? I push these questions out of my mind. I am sure the Spanx things I am squeezed into will decide for me anyhow. I don't think they can be removed, even if I wanted to remove them.

'Shall we get a drink in the lounge first?' asks Patrick politely.

I could certainly do with a drink to calm my nerves, so I quickly agree.

I also have to confess that I am not looking forward to eating in front of him due to my choking phobia. Plus, I am a bit of a nightmare when I see nice food as I have no self-control. I gulp it down as fast as I can and make a complete pig out of myself, which may explain my phobia. What if I can't control myself with the restaurant's legendary black cod? Perhaps I should order the sushi and then I won't touch anything and can tell Patrick that I am watching my figure.

The waiter comes along and asks if we need a menu; however, Patrick says we don't need one as he knows the menu off by heart. I am fine with that and am happy for him to order, as I would take almost everything on the menu, apart from the sushi, if I had my way.

'Shall we order the black cod?' Patrick asks.

'Oh, yes, sounds delicious,' I say. Now he's going to see me for the glutton that I truly am.

'Rock shrimp tempura?' he asks. Oh no, all my favourite dishes. I love shrimps.

'So, tell me about your day,' says Patrick, sipping at his expensive glass of Sauvignon Blanc.

'Sorry, can I get some lemonade for this?' I ask the waiter as he darts past. I am mortified, but I can't drink the expensive wine straight. It is a bit strong for me. I can see by Patrick's face that he is a bit shocked by my uncouthness.

'Oh, um, sorry. Where were we? Oh, my day. Umm…Yeah, it was okay. I found a salon, got some waxing done…' As the stinging has subsided, I realise that I had forgotten about the redness for a while. I pull my hand to cover my mouth self-consciously. I do hope he hasn't noticed any remaining telltale signs.

Patrick grins. 'Woah, nice. Did you get a Brazilian?'

I am horrified. I didn't even know guys knew about these things. Though, fortunately, he didn't say anything about getting an upper lip waxed, so can't have noticed that. I suppose Brazilians are more socially acceptable than lip waxes nowadays.

'Oh, um, no, um, not at all!' I say flustered.

'Well, I coulda waited until later to find out, but a guy's gotta ask,' he says, laughing.

The tone has suddenly changed. All the pleasantries have gone out the restaurant window and it quickly becomes apparent where he thinks tonight will lead to.

'More wine, please,' I shout to the nearest waiter.

I need more wine than ever before. I cannot do this sober. The thought of having sex with someone who isn't Dick is so frightening. I know I must do this if I am to move on. I really do need to have sex with someone new, as scary as that sounds, but...

I practically grab the wine from the waiter, pour some lemonade in and glug it down in one.

'Are you nervous?' Patrick asks.

'Is it that obvious, Patrick?' I smile.

'I want you more than anything right now, Amelia. There's nothing to be afraid of.'

He looks straight into my eyes, and I melt yet again. Yes, I have to do this. I am ready. My heart is on fire. He wants me more than anything? Does that include winning the lottery, or a multimillion-dollar polo match? Does he want me even more than that scrumptious black cod or the saké that is in front of us?

'Wow, I'm flattered. You really do say the nicest things, Patrick,' I say.

Patrick picks up a tempura shrimp and leans across the table.

'Here,' he says seductively.

I open my mouth and bite into the shrimp.

He fed me a tempura shrimp! I am definitely ready to sleep with him.

Chapter 31

The hotel – the time has come

I did quite fancy the blueberry cheesecake, but Patrick said there was only one dessert we would be having tonight and it was not on any menu. I see what he means as we can hardly get into the hotel lift before his hands are everywhere.

He suggested my room, since his apartment is a mess and he hasn't had time to organise his cleaner due to his recent trip. I suppose that is fair enough and we should make the most of the hotel room.

We are hardly through the door before he pulls me passionately on the bed and I land on top of him.

'What the hell?' screams Patrick, feeling around him.

'Oh, yeah, an ice bucket tipped and oh, um...'

'Jeez... Let me take my pants off, they're soaked,' he says.

Gosh, he is so direct.

Oh, he meant trousers. I keep forgetting they call trousers pants in the US. What do they call pants then? So many cultural differences, goodness.

As he removes his trousers, I decide that now might be a good time to rush for a quick pee and get the Spanx off before he discovers them. This gives me the ideal opportunity to sort myself out whilst he deals with the wet patch.

'Just need the bathroom, sorry.' I excuse myself and lock the door as quickly as I can in case he starts rummaging for towels, or anything, to help him clear up.

I breathe in as I struggle with my underwear, hoping that this technique may assist in their removal. Why, oh why, do these have to be so hard to get on and off? I am desperate for the toilet, as I haven't been able to go all night and, with my bladder, it has been extremely uncomfortable. I don't know if it is the Japanese saké but lifting one leg up is proving to be very difficult. I smash straight into the toilet seat as I roll down the tiniest bit of underwear and I think I am going to wee myself.

'Are you okay in there? What you doing?' comes Patrick's American drawl from the bedroom.

'Yes, yes, I'm fine. Thank you,' I shout.

Stuff it, I will have to cut them off. Discovering some nail scissors in my toilet bag, I cut down one side even though the material is superstrong. There! I did it. I cut through my pants and pee at the same time. Oh my, the relief is indescribable.

'Come on, I'm waiting,' shouts Patrick.

Finally opening the door, I see him lying on the bed. Completely naked. Oh gosh, I don't know what to do. I haven't seen a naked man for… oh, I don't know how long. Yikes.

Still in my dress, I attempt to hold in my wobbly bits and try to push my boobs out at the same time as I walk towards him. He gets up and starts kissing my neck. He puts his hands through my hair. I pull my fringe from him and tidy it up a bit.

He is completely in charge as he takes control and hoists up my dress. Thank goodness I managed to take the underwear off in time.

'Ooh, I like it,' he says as he moves his hand further up my thigh. I hope he doesn't think I have been like that all night.

'Oh, I was wearing underwear earlier... I just...'

'Shh, stop talking, my baby...'

He strokes me in a way that I can't even move. I want to kiss his neck and work towards his chest, but I am too transfixed by his touch. All I can do is relax my body and ensure that I remember this feeling forever. He is certainly nothing like Dick, who only cared for his own pleasure. The kisses are getting harder and more passionate. He tastes of the earlier Sauvignon mixed with saké. I finally manage to use the energy I can muster to return the kisses. I kiss along his beautiful chest; it has just the right amount of hair. He really is quite amazing, even his body hair is perfect! Every inch of him is perfection. His abs, his thighs, his arms. I guess it is from all the polo he does. I want to keep on kissing his body and never stop. I put my hands through his thick dark hair. It is so silky and smooth and smells so fresh, like he has stepped out of the shower, even though he has been out all evening. Finally, he puts those big strong arms around me and lifts me onto him.

–

Twenty minutes later we are snuggling in bed. I am curled up into his arms with my head on his chest. I don't ever want to let go. Maybe he is my perfect future husband.

'I think I was in love with you the first time we met,' Patrick says.

'Wow, really?' I had never believed in love at first sight before.

'Yup, seeing you for those five minutes I knew you were different to any of the American girls I hung out with. You were special,' he says, stroking my hair.

'Oh, Patrick. I wish I'd called you when we met. I made such a big mistake. We missed out on all those years together,' I say.

'We're together now, that's what matters,' he replies.

He kisses me on the lips, and I start to melt once again. He is so good.

'I was surprised you remembered me when Sian and I searched for you,' I say eventually. Maybe one day I could tell him the truth about it being Sian who was the person he spoke to on that initial phone call, but now doesn't feel the right time.

'I knew it was me you were looking for right away. Then, when you explained about the red thong in the taxi, yeah... Well, I was so pleased to hear that story of how we met. I was surprised it took you so long to call though. But, hey, the red thong. There aren't many girls with that story.' He laughs and starts nuzzling my neck. 'Hmm, that thong. Are you ready for round two?' he asks.

'Oh, yes, I am so ready,' I whisper back into his ear.

Chapter 32

The hotel room – waking up with a sex god

Patrick is so perfect that he doesn't dribble in his sleep. His mouth isn't even open. He just lies there like some kind of angel with his lips gently pressed together.

I have been watching him now for at least ten minutes, desperately trying not to wake him up. While he sleeps, naked beside me, I study his body. I search for signs of his illness, but on the outside there are no indications that educate me further. Who am I to know what is going on inside his lovely body though? Life can be so cruel. How can an illness ravage such a perfect man?

I could watch him sleep all day. However, I have to drag myself away from him, as I must ensure that I have natural-looking make-up on before he wakes up. I cannot have him see me first thing without make-up. It will be different once we are married, as then it will be too late for him to change his mind. For now, I must always be as perfect to him as he is to me.

Peering in the mirror I see my upper lip is still red, but half of my face is too, so I can blame it on the stubble rash which is good news.

I put on the make-up as quickly as possible in case he wakes up. However, twenty minutes later and he is still sleeping like a baby, albeit a very beautiful one. I know that I said I could watch him sleep all day, but I didn't literally mean it. I start to get a little impatient as I want to talk to him and have another of his fantastic *cwtches*.

I clang a coffee cup against another on purpose – that should do the trick.

He starts to stir as I bang about the coffee maker.

I have no idea how he drinks his coffee, so I try and make a guess.

'Hey, sleepyhead, time to wake up,' I say, handing him the coffee cup.

He groans a little and I realise that he is not a morning person. No wonder he is always up so late.

I pass him the cup, careful not to spill any. He takes a sip of coffee and spits it out all over the bed.

'What the fuck! Did you put milk in this?' he asks, opening his eyes dramatically.

Oh no, so he obviously doesn't take milk. This is awful; I have slept with him and I don't even know how he takes his coffee. It serves as a reminder that I still don't know everything about him.

'I'm so sorry, Patrick. I had no idea how you liked your coffee. I tried to guess. I take milk so… I just assumed…'

'This is serious, Amelia. I'm lactose fucking intolerant. You could have killed me.'

'Um, no, I wouldn't have killed you. I'd have given you a bit of an upset stomach, perhaps.' But then I remember his mystery illness. What if I had killed him? I feel horrendous.

'Do you need an EpiPen, or anything?' I ask helpfully. 'Is there something I can get you?'

He looks at me with horror, startled by my ignorance. I realise that the lactose intolerance could be related to the illness. What if I could be the reason he dies sooner? What a silly thing of me to do to him.

'I'm so sorry, Patrick. If you told me more things about your health and your problem, then maybe I'd have known you were lactose intolerant. Is it to do with your illness?' I ask.

Patrick doesn't respond.

'You just won't talk to me about it. I don't know anything. You promised you'd tell me when I came over. Let me make you another coffee and we can chat,' I say.

'I'm going to be really sick now because of you. I've got a lot on at work today too,' he says.

'Well, you spat most of it out so hopefully you didn't ingest that much, Patrick.'

He ignores me as I try to placate him and instead picks up his fancy watch, which is on the bedside table.

'Shiiiit. I slept in. I need to shower.'

He jumps into the shower while I make another coffee, which I have now found out should be black with two sugars. As I pop the coffee on his bedside table, I hear him talking in the shower. It is only then that I notice he took his phone to the bathroom with him. Why would he take his phone to the bathroom? Unless, of course, he has tummy problems because of his milky coffee and plans on being in there a while.

I hear the words 'landed thirty minutes ago, see you later'. Why is he pretending he has been on a plane somewhere?

He eventually walks out of the bathroom like some divine being. A white towel is wrapped around his waist and his cute dark hair is still wet.

'Sorry, boss was asking why I wasn't in the office yet. I had to make an excuse,' he says, waving his phone around.

I find myself forgiving him for his outburst, even if he was being a total diva. He is possibly dying, though, so perhaps outbursts can be excused. Fortunately, his mood has mellowed following the shower.

'Sorry I overreacted a little.' He smiles at me. 'I'm a bit of a health freak nowadays. I didn't mean to get mad at you.'

Surely, if he cared that much about his health he wouldn't take two sugars. He was also knocking back quite a few glasses of Sauvignon last night, but maybe he is just living out his last days.

'That's okay,' I say. I pull at his towel and hint at round three. He suddenly forgets that he is late for work.

Round three wasn't quite as amazing as rounds one and two, partly because the bed was now covered in coffee and it was quite difficult to position myself in the right place. In addition, it's nice to snuggle for a while afterwards and not have what could be your future husband rush into the office.

I have to say goodbye to him, which is a horrendous thought. I leave tomorrow morning and he has already told me that he has something on at his polo club tonight. It would have been nice to have been invited, but apparently it is strictly members only and not even partners are allowed. It is disappointing that he has to go, but he is giving some trophy out so he absolutely can't miss it.

'So, my gorgeous, Amelia. It's au revoir, we will meet again soon. I will come to Wales as soon as I can, okay. I can't wait to meet the boys and, of course, meet with you again,' he says as he stands by the hotel room door.

'Okay, but I hate it that you have to leave. I wish I could stay with you all day today. It's my last day here. I wanted to spend it with you.' I think I may start to cry now.

'Me too, my sweet Amelia, but I have a deadline by five, and I've been with you instead of working on the interviews. You know what my boss is like. She is already looking for me,' he says.

'I know, but there's more to life than work.'

'My darling, I'll see you in a few weeks. I promise. We'll be together very soon. We have the rest of our lives together.' He smiles and leans down onto my neck and gives me one of his spine-tingling kisses.

Was that a proposal? Did he just say we have the rest of our lives together? Was this what the fortune teller meant, perhaps? I am obviously not going to say yes; he hasn't even met the boys, but I do wonder if that is what she saw.

Now the tears really start to fall. How can I carry on my day without those amazing kisses? Can I take his lips back home with me?

Patrick wipes away a tear from my cheek.

'I love you, Amelia. You are truly special. Now I must go.'

I watch him walk to the elevator. My potential future husband is walking away and I don't know when I will see him again.

I shout after him, 'See you soon, Patrick.'

He blows me a kiss, and the lift doors close. I am tempted to chase him down the corridor and follow him to work. I don't want to say goodbye just yet.

Chapter 33

An alleyway – following Patrick

I feel like Cagney and Lacey, only it is just me, Cagney, as I try my hardest to keep up with Patrick. He has been on the phone the whole time since I ran out and followed him. I can't believe I caught up with him after he left me; it is amazing how quickly you can get ready when you really have to. I can't get close enough to hear his conversation, or he might spot me. I am not spying, or anything, I am merely curious. I want to see what his office looks like, so the next time he chats about work and all his deadlines I can lovingly picture him at his desk.

He walks for ages until I think that I may have to give up. I fear that I can't keep up with his pace much longer. For a dying man he certainly walks fast. Fortunately, he stops by a fire hydrant to end his phone call, so I have the chance to catch my breath. However, he soon moves on and starts walking at his usual brisk pace. The area that he is heading for looks quite rough. I feel a little uncomfortable. I don't know that I want to follow him much further as a female on her own in a place so foreign. I could be anywhere, but it certainly feels like I have entered the wrong part of town. It's so hard to tell what sort of area this is. It could be that it's super trendy. This is New York after all. The graffiti with the bad language and crude drawings could be some kind of art installation, who knows?

Finally, Patrick heads up another alleyway and heads for a graffiti-decorated door. He keys in a code and disappears through the entrance. He is definitely not going to work, unless this is some kind of trendy media-type place. He said he covered Wall Street. I assumed his office would be close by.

I am still catching my breath when Patrick walks back out, but now he is in jogging bottoms and a sweatshirt. He has removed the smart clothes that he was wearing and replaced them with workout gear. I thought he had a busy day with a deadline. Nothing makes sense. I want to call out to him, but he will think I am so odd to follow him all this way. Anyway, he immediately starts jogging, so there is no way I can grab his attention or keep up with him, for that matter. I can only either wait until he comes back or return in the direction I came and head to the shops, even though I am in no mood for the souvenir hunting I had planned. I decide it best to turn back, as I don't know how long he will be and I certainly don't want to hang around here alone.

I have so many unanswered questions. Is this his home? Is that why he didn't want me to see it, because he lives in a run-down area? I can accept that. I don't mind if he doesn't have money for a fancy place. That doesn't explain how he can afford his membership to the exclusive polo club, or the dinner that he paid for last night and everything else he seems to afford though. Perhaps he lives beyond his means and spends everything on socialising and not on his home. I try to make sense of his lifestyle, but it is all one big mystery. I decide to message him to see what he says. Will he say he is in work if I ask him? Perhaps he won't even return my message.

I still haven't heard back from him by the time I reach the shops and my mood is worsening. To top it all off, there is an elf in one of the toy shops that is really irritating me. I don't want to buy an Elf on the Shelf. It is only October.

'No, really, I'm fine. I already have one,' I lie to the overgrown elf, trying not to look at his silly green tights. I only came in for some last-minute gifts for the boys.

How I can't wait to see them. They are going to be so full of tales, especially after the claw machine escapade. Although I still have to give them both a good talking to the minute we all get back.

I am picking up matching T-shirts and putting them in my basket when the elf comes up to me once again.

'Oh, give me two bloody Elves on the Shelf then,' I snap.

I suppose they will make a nice pre-Christmas present, although I detest buying gifts early. When you have boys like mine, their tastes change all the time. One minute they are into Thomas the Tank, then it is Fireman Sam and nowadays it is something totally different each week. I caught them watching *Family Guy* the other day and totally freaked out. What is wrong with *Shaun the Sheep*?

'Thanks, ma'am,' says the elf. The temptation to stick the elves back on the shelf when he is not looking is very strong, but I suppose he must work on commission so I must not be mean. Maybe he has a family and a litter of stray dogs to feed. The thought of all those puppies looking up for food makes me keep it in my basket.

There is not much else in the shop, so I head towards Battery Park for my boat trip to the Statue of Liberty. I absolutely cannot get on that flight without two Statue of Liberty foam crowns for the boys. Jamie mentioned that you can find them in some of the nearby souvenir shops, but I figured it would be more authentic if I went to Liberty Island itself and bought them there. How funny to think that the last time I was in New York I was buying a teeny-tiny thong that wouldn't fit over my big toe today. At least a foam crown would fit my head, maybe I will treat myself to one too, then we can all wear one when I get back.

Looking up at the statue, I can't believe quite how big it is. Although I came here the last time I visited, I forgot how impressive it was. Seeing it again lifts my spirits and I forget the questions I have about Patrick for a moment.

Onboard the ferry on the way back to Manhattan I send Dick lots of photos to show the boys. Now that my secret is out it has become easier to share my movements with them all.

I can't wait to give them the biggest hugs. This time tomorrow I will almost be at home with them. As I am reading their excited responses, a message finally pings from Patrick.

> Honey, sorry for the delay. I am so sick
> after the milk xxx

My mind goes into overdrive again. So, he admits that he was sick; perhaps that explains why he didn't go to work. Surely he wouldn't be able to run like that with stomach cramps though. I decide to message him back later; he can wait.

Following a full day of snooping, shopping and sight-seeing, it's time to meet up with Jamie for our last dinner before we leave this wonderful city. I consider telling him about today and all the questions I have. I think better of it, though, as he might start on again about taking things slowly. He would definitely give me that advice after what I have seen today and rightly so.

'You look fabulous, Amelia,' Jamie says as soon as he sees me.

'Thank you, Jamie!' I say. He doesn't usually compliment me on how I look. It must be all the sex I have been having, or the effects of the Botox are starting to kick in.

'It looks like this holiday has done you the world of good despite the little hiccups.' He laughs.

'Certainly hasn't been without its dramas… But, yes, it's been good.'

Despite my new reservations about Patrick, I have a flashback to last night and my body quivers. There is definitely something amiss, but I have also had the time of my life when we have been together. Just as Patrick promised we would.

Jamie chose a steakhouse to dine in tonight that had been recommended by his boss. He says he has saved the best restaurant until last. I don't know that anything can top the lovely Italian we went to though.

He also said that he has a little something for me. It seems Jamie is more relaxed now that the conference is all done.

A smiling server, with a name badge that says 'Jess', approaches us as we discuss what time we need to leave for the airport tomorrow.

'Hey, you guys, here's the menu,' she says.

'Thank you, anything in particular you'd recommend?' asks Jamie.

'Well, of course, all our steaks are fantastic,' she says. 'I love the rare Angus, personally.'

'Ooh, I don't think I could eat a rare steak,' I say.

'Wow! Are you guys British?' She is so excited that she doesn't wait for the answer. 'I went to London last year. Loved it. Saw Buckingham Palace, Trafalgar Square… I love England.'

'We're from Wales. It's quite far from London,' says Jamie.

'Ooh, Wales, I know. Like Ireland and Scotland. Cool.' The table next to us calls her over bringing her education of the British Isles to an abrupt halt.

'Well, you guys take a look at the menu and let me know what you fancy. I suggest the Angus though,' she says before rushing off.

We eventually decide on two medium Angus steaks. Jess seems quite shocked and I worry that the chef won't be best pleased with us, but it is how we both like our steaks done.

Whilst we wait, we chat about the end of Jamie's conference and what a wonderful time we have had in New York. It is almost like a debriefing of our trip, except that I exclude all the hot and steamy parts.

'So, what will you do now it's time to go home?' asks Jamie. 'Will you see Patrick again soon?'

'He's hoping to come to Wales,' I explain. 'I've had a great time with him, but it's bound to be fun on holiday. It would be good to see him in Wales, and he wouldn't have to rush off to work either. Talking of work, I'm not looking forward to getting back to that bit,' I say.

The time off has made me think about my future. Lisa will never leave the bookshop; she's worked there from school; there won't ever be any opportunity of a promotion for me. I do love being around books, but the dream of helping people like Mum with dementia is never far from my mind.

'I agree, you should get Patrick to come over. I'd like to meet him. Make sure he's good enough for you,' Jamie says, laughing. 'You having problems with Lisa again?' he adds.

Patrick is the only one who knows about my dream of becoming a dementia nurse, and he dismissed it. As he is still the only person I have been brave enough to tell, I hesitate informing Jamie about what he might think is something I could never accomplish.

'No, she's fine at the moment. Just, when the boys were smaller and I was married, it was enough. Now my circumstances have changed. I'd like to retrain at something,' I explain.

'That sounds good to me. Work is always looking for new staff if you want a future in IT? I can put a word in for you,' says Jamie.

'No, I was thinking of a different career. It would involve going to uni and so much work, I'm sure I could never manage it. Just a silly thing I can't get out of my head,' I say.

'What is it? You can be determined when you want to be. I'm sure you could do it. Maths isn't your strongest point, so as long as you don't want to become a mathematician, I'm sure you can do it.' He laughs.

'No, definitely not a mathematician,' I say.

'Well, what then?'

I take a sip of my pina colada before plucking up the courage to tell him.

'A dementia nurse. I know… It would take far too long to train and I'm too old to start now,' I say.

Jamie jumps forward in his chair.

'That is the most wonderful idea I've ever heard. You're so caring and kind. Remember when that old lady fell, you took her to hospital and stayed with her until her daughter arrived. You rang every day to see if she was okay. If it wasn't for you, she may have had hypothermia and died.'

'I know, but anyone would have done the same,' I plead.

'No, not necessarily. They may have helped call an ambulance, but you were dedicated to her recovery. Oh, Amelia, you were born to be a dementia nurse,' he says.

'Well, it was after Mum and… I want to give that help back to other people's mums… and dads, of course,' I explain.

'What do you have to do to get a job like that? I presume you have to go to uni?'

'I haven't looked into it that much yet. I wasn't sure I could give up work to retrain. I couldn't afford that,' I say.

'When we get back, you have to find out. There are grants and all sorts of things. You can study part-time, anything. If this is your dream then you must do it. Imagine the difference you would make in people's lives,' says Jamie excitedly.

I take another sip of my cocktail. He is right. I will look into it when I get back.

'To a great future,' says Jamie, clinking his cocktail against mine.

'Absolutely,' I say, feeling more positive than I have ever felt in my life.

The sizzling steaks arrive, which end our conversation. They are every bit as delicious as I expected. By the time I have devoured it, I consider the possibility that I may never eat again in my life. That is until Jamie asks what we should have for dessert.

'How about New York cheesecake?'

'Oooh, yes. I'm desperate to try some New York cheesecake before we leave,' I say.

The cheesecake quickly arrives by the lovely Jess. I can see why Jamie's boss suggested this place. The food and service are excellent.

'Enjoy, guys,' says Jess, putting it down.

'Mmmmm, so delicious,' says Jamie between mouthfuls. 'I'd say it could even be a touch better than your apple pie and that was nice.' He smiles.

'Even I can't argue with that,' I agree.

Once we finish desserts we ask Jess for some Irish coffees to finish our night off. She delivers them with her friendly smile.

'Hope you guys had a nice evening. Did you enjoy everything?' says Jess.

'Oh, just perfect,' I say.

'And if you don't mind me saying, you guys are just perfect too.' I look at her with a shocked expression.

'I love watching couples. You can always tell who's headed for the divorce court, who's not going to last… You two are definitely going to last. I bet you've been together a long time, haven't you? I can tell because you like your steaks done the same way.' Jess laughs and I laugh too. However, mine is a nervous laugh, because

I'm mortified and don't know how to tell her we are just friends. Fortunately, Jamie responds with a curt reply.

'Oh, thanks, Jess,' he says.

'So, am I right? You've been together years, yeah?' Does she have to probe further? I don't know where to look. Jess is lovely, but I really wish she would go away and stop asking so many questions.

'I think someone's trying to get your attention,' I say, pointing across to the open kitchen where a meal is waiting to be served.

'Well, that was awkward,' I say, as Jess leaves the table.

'She does have a point though; we are good together. To best friends,' says Jamie, as he clinks his glass with mine.

'To best friends,' I say, smiling at Jamie. I have really enjoyed his company during this wonderful break. Sian and Jamie were right, it was exactly what I needed.

'As I said to Jess, this really has been perfect, Jamie. Thank you for arranging dinner, the air miles and everything else you've done this trip,' I say.

'Not at all, thank you for coming and for your amazing company. Ooh, which reminds me. You know I said I have something for you?' says Jamie. 'I wanted to give you this.'

I look down to see a small Tiffany bag.

'What's this?'

'You're always looking for gifts for the boys. I thought perhaps you hadn't thought about something for yourself. I know how much you love this shop, plus I had some travel allowance left over… It's just a token to remember our New York trip,' Jamie says, quickly justifying his purchase.

I open the bag to find a little Tiffany blue box inside. Quickly throwing the bag aside I look into the box. Inside is the most stunning silver heart locket I have ever laid eyes on.

'Oh Jamie, it's so beautiful.'

'I thought you could put a photo of the boys in there. Then they can be with you wherever you are, even if you're away from them,' Jamie explains.

'Jamie, you are unbelievable.' I smile.

I run to the other side of the table to give him a big hug.

'What did I ever do to deserve such amazing friends?' I say.

'Well, you're an amazing friend too, you know?' he answers.

'I don't know that I am really. I've been so preoccupied with everything.'

'Why do you always bring yourself down, Amelia? Whenever anyone compliments you, you always contradict them.'

I look down at the table, feeling as though I have been told off.

'I don't mean that horribly. I just mean that I don't think you realise what a wonderful person you are. You're such a lovely person. Dick was a fool. He was such an idiot to leave you,' says Jamie.

'Aw, thank you, Jamie. Well, Megan was a fool too... For leaving you. You're the most special, amazingly wonderful friend anyone could ever have. You are kind and thoughtful and... You should be snapped up. Any woman would be very lucky to have you.'

'Ha, if only.' Jamie smiles.

'Now look who won't accept a compliment.' I laugh.

We both sip at our coffees awkwardly. This all feels a bit strange, Jamie and I giving each other compliments. We usually tease each other as best friends do.

'Well, we'd better head back. We have a long day tomorrow,' I announce.

We make our way back to the hotel in silence as the sights whirr past the taxi. This is our final night in New York. It will soon be time to face all the washing and ironing that holidays create. I want to enjoy the last moment gazing at the skyline before heading back to the real world.

Chapter 34

The airport – time to leave

'What do you mean there are no seats left in business class?' I ask, not quite taking in what the check-in agent is trying to tell me.

'I'm sorry, miss, but we've overbooked the flight. It's a holiday weekend; it's a busy time of year,' she explains.

I am so excited at the prospect of seeing Rupert and Jasper again that no matter how many times she repeats the same thing, I can't take it in. I am going to be on that flight no matter what. I don't want to believe what I am hearing. Once I acknowledge that I am not on the flight then it means that I will have to accept the awful truth that I won't be home anytime soon.

'Can you not downgrade us to economy? We don't need the upgrade. I don't care where I sit. I'm happy to sit on the wing if I have to,' I say desperately.

The lady looks at me unamused.

'The whole flight is overbooked. We can arrange a hotel room for you near the airport. You're definitely confirmed on our flight tomorrow morning,' she reiterates.

'You don't understand,' I plead. 'I have two boys who want to see their mum. I HAVE to get on that flight. I have to be there for them when they get home.'

'YOU don't seem to understand, miss. There are absolutely no seats on the flight. We've been more than fair and given you a meal voucher as well as the hotel,' she says, handing me the voucher. She looks over my shoulder and beckons a family with lots of children, and an even larger amount of luggage, to come forward.

'It's pointless arguing with her, Amelia. It seems like we're not going anywhere today,' says Jamie, dragging me away. 'Let's accept that we're here for one more night and make the most of it.'

He is right, as usual, I suppose. I have tried to persuade her to let us on that flight for at least fifteen minutes and got absolutely nowhere. There is nothing left to do but explain my predicament to the boys.

The minute I hear Jasper's voice on the phone I am overcome with emotion; all I want right now is to be home with them. However, Jasper is his usual sweet self and tells me that it is not my fault and for me to try not to worry. Meanwhile, Rupert shouts in the background that, as I will now be away for an extra day, they should both get one more present.

I decide that I should message Patrick in the hope that we can have some time together; at least that would make the situation a little more tolerable. It may also shed some light on his mysterious behaviour the other day. If I can only get to talk to him face to face, somewhere neutral and not in the bedroom.

> Hi, guess what? My flight got delayed until tomorrow. Xxxx

He picks up immediately as he was already online. Perhaps he was about to message me.

235

> Oh, honey, your boys will be sad not to see their mom when they get back home. XX

> I think they're dealing with it better than I am. I've spoken to them and explained, but I'm super upset. xxx

> Oh, baby, Don't be sad. What will you do now? Xx

> Well, I was wondering if you were free? Xx

> I have an hour before a meeting. You want me to meet you at the airport? I'm not far away. Xx

> That would be great. You can meet Jamie before we head to our hotel. xx

Jamie will like Patrick when he meets him.

How lucky that he is not too far away. Maybe this is why my flight is meant to be overbooked. Fate is stepping in.

> Cool. See you in 5. Xx

I explain to Jamie that Patrick is on his way over.

'I'm looking forward to meeting this mysterious Patrick,' he says. His tone hits me with a hint of sarcasm.

–

Yet again Patrick is punctual: four minutes and fifty-eight seconds after his message I spot him, dressed quite casually, hurrying through the airport terminal. Patrick gives me one of his beautiful hugs and kisses me passionately on the lips. I am immediately transported to that happy place once again. I finally let go of Patrick to notice Jamie scowling over my shoulder.

I realise that I forgot to introduce them. How ill-mannered of me. I hurriedly get the introductions out of the way, but I notice that Jamie refuses to shake Patrick's hand. Instead, he keeps his hands in his pockets and shrugs a hello at him. I hope Patrick doesn't find him rude; I want them to get along if we are to have any future.

Nobody is speaking and the thought of them becoming friends doesn't look promising right now.

'Wanna grab a coffee?' asks Patrick, breaking the silence.

'Yes, we'd love to, wouldn't we, Jamie?' I answer on behalf of both of us.

'No, you're all right,' answers Jamie miserably. 'I'll run ahead to the hotel and check out the room. Don't be too long.' He turns around, dragging his wheelie bag behind him.

'I thought people in Wales were supposed to be friendly?' Patrick says, laughing. 'He's a bag of fun, isn't he?'

'Oh, don't worry about him,' I say. 'I've known him all my life, he's wonderful. It's just that his girlfriend left him and his dad died recently, maybe he's a bit up and down at the moment.'

–

It is nice to see Patrick in a different environment. The last time we were together was in my hotel room, so it feels good to have a chance to meet him somewhere more neutral.

'Amelia, it's great to see you again,' Patrick says over his lactose-free coffee. 'What a surprise to enjoy some extra time with you. I'm going to miss you when you're back in Britain.'

'That's nice to hear that you'll miss me. I'll miss you too, but you know... You promised I'd get to know you while I was here, meet your friends and things. Your home. Why didn't you take me to your home?' I ask, even though I don't necessarily want to hear the answer.

'I told you, baby. It's been busy and I didn't expect a business trip in the middle of you being here. My cleaner hasn't been and... Gee, you know what single guys are like. Pants everywhere.' He laughs.

Does that mean he throws his dirty underpants all over the floor? Or does he mean his trousers? Ew, no wonder he never married.

'Did I see a flash then? Did someone take my photo? Huh?' Patrick says.

Before I can make any sense of what he is saying, his phone vibrates along the table.

'Oh jeez. I'm going to have to run. My boss is searching for me.'

As he gets up to leave, I spot the check-in agent looking towards me. She is probably wondering why I am in such a rush to get out of New York when I am sitting here with this handsome creature. Why can't life be simple? Why do we have to live so far away from each other? I am genuinely going to miss him, but I am also confused. I want to love him, I really do, but, truthfully, I don't know. His weird behaviour is stopping me.

'So, baby, I'm not sure I can see you later as I made plans now, but I'll try. I wasn't expecting you to be here another day. But, anyhow, before I head off I want to tell you something,' says Patrick, touching my hand.

'What is it, Patrick?' Maybe now is the moment I will learn exactly what is going on. However, before he can open his mouth the check-in agent approaches.

'What now? You'd better not tell me that tomorrow's flight is overbooked too.'

'No. It's good news. A flight to London Heathrow just opened up and has two spare seats. I am a mom too so I understand you want to get home. Where's your friend? You need to check-in immediately if you want to be on it.'

'Oh my word, you are so kind. Thank you, thank you, thank you. We'll take them. I'll get my friend back now,' I say. 'Can I give you a hug?'

'Um, no, it's against company policy,' she says, looking at me a little shocked.

She turns on her heel, and I get my phone out to call Jamie. I only hope he can make it back it in time.

'Sorry, what was it that you wanted to say, Patrick?'

'Oh, just that I love you! Wow, so you got your flight.'

We give each other a hug and say goodbye. He blows kisses as he walks away, but I notice that he is heading to the arrival area and not out of the airport as he should if he were to leave and head back to work. He was quick to

Chapter 35

On an aircraft – time to go home

Sitting in business class is very different to the economy flight on the way out. Instead of a tray table smacked into my face, I have a wide TV screen with countless channels. I have also swapped a plastic cup for a champagne glass and a bag of horrible cheesy pretzels for cashew nuts. This is a much better way to travel, although I do have to walk further to get to the toilets – that is the only downside.

Stretching my feet out onto my foot rest, I am so grateful to be on this flight and that Jamie shared his air miles with me. Hopefully, I don't need to worry so much about getting some type of thrombosis in my cankles either. I still make sure I rotate them from time to time, though, because you never can be too sure.

I always look forward to the captain's announcement when I get onboard any flight, as I love that calm, reassuring voice that they have, something which they must be born with I assume. So, as I hear the announcement begin, I sit upright and listen carefully as Captain Michelson starts to speak.

'Ladies and gentlemen, this is your captain speaking. Welcome onboard your flight to London Heathrow today. I'm afraid that I will be asking you to remain seated and keep your seat belts on for much of this flight as we are expecting some turbulence. We will try and avoid it as much as possible…'

'Shit. I hate turbulence,' Jamie says as he downs his glass of pre-flight champagne in two gigantic glugs.

'How can turbulence be so bad when you're in these humungous seats?' I ask, plumping up my soft cushion behind my back.

All these years I have known him and I had no idea that he wasn't a confident flyer, in spite of all the air miles he racks up. I admit that I was a bit apprehensive on the way out, but that was because I was travelling on my own for the first time in years. Also, I wasn't sure what to expect with Patrick.

'I had a bad flight from Cyprus once and the plane dropped quite a few feet, so I haven't liked turbulence since then,' explains Jamie. 'I don't mind flying, just not turbulence. I know it's stupid. Ignore me.'

I smile sympathetically and tap his hand to reassure him. I pull out the *Duty Free* magazine and start flicking through to distract him.

'Shall I get something for Sian?' I ask.

Jamie doesn't reply but looks around a little anxiously.

There was a nice Lego plane I saw on the flight out, so I think I will get the boys one each, since I didn't manage to get the extra present that was requested by Rupert. I decide on a bottle of perfume for Sian and a make-up kit which has all the types of colours that she uses.

There is no sign of any turbulence as we take off, so I hope that Jamie is feeling a little more reassured now. However, he still declines the food that is offered to him.

'Will you be having the beef Wellington, or the sea bass with couscous, madam?' one of the crew asks me. So different to the limp vegetarian pasta I had on the way over.

'Ooh, definitely the beef Wellington,' I say, my mouth watering at the thought.

'Any wine, or champagne with your meal?' she continues.

'I'll have champagne, please.' I might as well make the most of it.

'You okay?' I ask Jamie. 'You want some of my bread?'

'No, I'm not hungry,' he says. 'Can I get another beer?' he asks the crew.

'There's a nice selection of desserts. Don't you want some Camembert, or something? I'm going to have the chocolate tart,' I say. I wonder if I can take photos of my food to put on Instagram, or would that be too uncouth of me?

'No, I'm fine. I think I ate something, my stomach's a bit dodgy,' Jamie says. He does look like he wants to be sick.

My next glass of champagne and Jamie's beer arrive just as an announcement is made by the flight purser. The seat belt sign, which had momentarily gone off, pings back on at the same time.

'As we will be passing through an area of turbulence, our cabin crew will be coming around to collect your trays. You will not be able to use the washrooms during this time.'

Jamie opens the window blind and nervously peers out.

'I don't like this,' he says, looking at me as if I can save him from the forthcoming turbulence.

'Oh, they always say that and then the turbulence is never as bad as you think. You watch.'

We sit calmly for five minutes as the crew hurry around the cabin, clearing trays and securing the passengers. The plane bumps around slightly.

'You see, this is nothing. Anyway, if the turbulence was that bad the crew wouldn't be allowed on their feet,' I say reassuringly.

'Yeah, you're right,' says Jamie. He seems to be calming down a little bit now.

The cabin crew finish clearing everything away when there is another announcement. This time it comes from the captain.

'Cabin crew, please take your seats.'

Jamie looks at me, his eyes wide.

'He's doing that as a precaution. You know what people are like nowadays; the crew will sue if they sprain an ankle or something. He's probably got to do that so that they can't blame him,' I say.

I look at the passengers around us. 'Do you see anyone else worried?'

Ten minutes later almost every passenger is screaming. A lady to my left is crying, and a man behind us has started praying. Jamie is almost green and looks like he is about to vomit all over me.

'We weren't even supposed to be on this flight, Amelia,' he says almost crying. 'We were going to be on tomorrow's flight, and now we're all going to die.'

Someone in the row in front hears him say the word 'die' and starts sobbing.

I am finding it difficult to remain composed, as I want to get off this flight alive as much as anyone, but I have every confidence in the captain. He sounded very authoritative and, if anyone can get us out of this, someone with a voice like that most definitely will.

'I'm sure the captain knows what he's doing, okay,' I say, grabbing hold of Jamie's clammy hand.

I can't believe how rational I am being. I am normally the first one to crumble in a crisis, but it might also be something to do with the amount of champagne I have been drinking. Business class is definitely the best place to be in an emergency situation like this.

Jamie holds my hand tight. I stroke his arm with my other hand to calm him down.

'It will be over soon,' I say. 'It will be over…'

'What if it is over? What if our lives are going to end now?' he says. I can see his legs are shaking he is so scared.

'I meant the turbulence will be over. Life's not going to be over,' I say. 'The captain will get us out of it.'

'What if it was though? What if we are about to die? I never even told you how much I love you,' Jamie says.

'I love you too, Jamie. You know that, and I know you love me. We've been friends forever and ever,' I say.

'No, I mean I truly love you, Amelia. You don't get it, do you? I've loved you since the first time I saw you. I remember it like yesterday. You were wearing orange leopard print socks, with one of those rah-rah skirt things. You looked like one of those girls in the crowd on *Top of the Pops*. Stunning you were. I never got that sight out of my head. I loved you from that moment onwards.'

'What did you say?' I ask, shocked. I quickly remove my hand from his. I had hoped that nobody would ever remember that skirt and definitely not those socks. If we are going to die, then I don't want that to be his lasting memory of me.

'I've always loved you, Amelia. Always. There is nobody I've ever loved as much as you, and now we are going to die in a plane crash and I have left it too late,' he says. 'All because I was too chicken to tell you how I felt and didn't want to spoil what we have together.'

I am taken by complete surprise by this. Not for a moment did I ever expect Jamie to feel this way. He certainly hid his feelings very well. But then, I suppose, so did I. The thought of him and Megan together made me so envious, but I hid it from everyone and didn't tell a soul. I would never have been courageous enough to tell Jamie how I felt about him.

I lean over and kiss Jamie gently on the lips. As I consider Patrick, I realise that this is so incredibly naughty of me but, if I am truly honest, I thoroughly enjoy it.

Chapter 36

Heathrow airport – back with my boys

The upside of the flight from hell is that due to a delay, and an attempt to land three times, the boys have landed at practically the same time as us. Just as well Dick now knows about my transatlantic adventure.

Tanja Tart is looking a little dishevelled in the arrivals hall, and it gives me great pleasure to witness that she is almost human after all. She has a huge red wine stain down the inside leg of her white linen trousers and, if I am not mistaken, there is a blob of mash on her newly purchased Donald Duck T-shirt. This gives me an enormous feeling of satisfaction.

I stop smirking to myself to give Rupert and Jasper the most enormous, humungous hugs anyone could ever give another human. I hold them so hard that I am almost stopping the circulation to their chubby little cheeks.

'Oooh, come here you two,' I say, grabbing them tight for an extra hug. I feel pretty sure that Jasper has grown since I last saw him.

I am absolutely thrilled that Dick agrees they can come on the drive home with me and Sian. Despite the long drive, Sian was adamant she would come and collect me from the airport. She said that she couldn't wait a moment longer for the gossip (the Welsh term *clecks* was what she actually used). Although I have a lot of her exciting news to catch up on too, by the looks of things.

'Let's see the ring,' I squeal. 'Oooh, it's even more gorgeous in real life.' I hug Sian.

Jamie says his goodbyes, as he has to go straight over to his head office in London. He has to give the staff a talk about what he learnt at the conference, which is understandable after having been given such a wonderful trip on the company expenses. I'm glad we don't have to share a car journey home; I don't know what I would say to him. It's all so embarrassing. His confession and me kissing him, how do we manage to sort this out? It is odd the things that occur at high altitude. You often hear of complete strangers joining the mile-high club: this must be what happens. There should be a warning on flights – *Too much champagne and lowered oxygen levels may cause reckless behaviour.*

After so many years of being best friends, I am terrified this will ruin things between us. Do relationships with your best friend ever work out? There's no denying we know each other inside out, it would be lovely to be with someone who knows everything about you, warts and all. There would be no pretences between us. But what if we were to date and then split up and hate each other? I couldn't stand not having Jamie in my life. This thought is terrifying and why, as much as Jamie has romantic feelings for me, I cannot reciprocate. I am too confused with my emotions right now. I think we both probably got very carried away in a moment of fear. We must remain friends and not spoil that.

'Soooo what's the *clecks*,' says Sian as we turn onto the M4 with our car windows bursting with stuffed Disney characters. 'Spill the beans then,' she continues.

It is difficult to talk in front of the boys, plus I have a Mickey Mouse arm practically stuck up my nostril as I try to balance him on my lap. This is a chat that is required with my arms flailing all over the place over a bottle of Prosecco and a couple of tapas. I tell her that I will fill her in later, although I do begin to divulge what happened with Jamie.

'I thought there was something strange when you both came through arrivals,' Sian says. 'He was looking a bit sheepish. You were looking awkward too, my love.'

'Well, we didn't have a very good flight and then he said how much he loved me,' I whisper. I limit the details as I don't want the boys to know that I kissed their favourite uncle Jamie.

We were both embarrassed when we got out of the turbulence. Then again, so were most of the passengers after all the screaming, crying and praying for their lives.

At least the other passengers never have to see each other again though. Jamie, on the other hand, has to come back to Laugharne. So it is a relief that he is staying in London over the next few days.

'Hmm, well, I have always wondered about Jamie's feelings for you,' says Sian, taking me by complete surprise.

'He never stops talking about you, and he likes almost every photo of you on Facebook. For a guy, that's a sign, don't you think?'

'I don't know. He's one of my best friends, that's why he likes my photos. I've never seen it like that at all,' I disagree.

'Does Uncle Jamie love you, Mummy?' says Rupert from the back seat.

'I thought you were busy with your Lego,' I say. 'No, we are besties, like you and Lucas are.'

'But Lucas doesn't like all my photos on Facebook,' Rupert says.

'You're not even on Facebook, you silly sausage.' I laugh. 'And how do you know so much about Facebook anyhow?'

'Chardonnay's on Facebook. Her mum lets her; she tells us about it,' he explains.

'Okay, well, Chardonnay also wears a lot of make-up for a nine-year-old so…'

'I like Uncle Jamie,' chirps in Jasper.

'Yes, we all do, sweetie,' I reply.

Rupert and Jasper start giggling in the back. All I can hear is, 'No, you ask her. No, you.'

'Ask me what?' I question them.

'Can Uncle Jamie be our stepdad? Like Tanja is our stepmother?' says Jasper.

I've never heard of Tanja Tart being called that before even though she technically is. It feels like a knife went straight through my heart. The boys now have a step-mother. This revelation is another reminder that my family unit will never be the same again. As usual, I put on a brave face and cast away the statement that stings so much.

'Hey now, just because Jamie is good at making things with you, it doesn't mean he should live with us,' I say.

I ponder for a moment and wonder whether now might be the right time to mention Patrick. He insisted that he would visit in a few weeks' time, and this will surely give me the opportunity I need to find out more about him and get some clarity on our relationship. He won't be rushing off all the time if he is in Laugharne with me, so I am bound to get to the bottom of everything.

I take a deep breath.

'Actually, I have something to tell you two…' I stop and wonder if I am doing the right thing. My gut feeling tells me this is a mistake, but I am going to have to say something soon if Patrick is to visit. 'When Mummy was in New York I met up with an old friend of mine,' I begin.

'Yes, Uncle Jamie,' says Jasper. 'We know he was there looking after you.'

'No, baby. Not Uncle Jamie. I have a friend in New York, who I met a long, long time ago before you were born. I met him there, and he said that he'd like to meet you. He may visit us here in Wales.'

'I don't like strangers,' says Rupert.

'He's not a stranger. I've known him a long time,' I say.

'Jasper and me don't know him, so he is a stranger.'

I feel like saying Tanja Tart was a stranger, too, but now you are going on holiday with her and calling her your stepmother. Of course, I bite my tongue.

'What's his name?' asks Jasper politely.

'Patrick,' I say.

'Patrick?' says Rupert. 'Don't like it. I prefer the name Jamie.'

'Yeah, the name Jamie is nice, Mummy,' adds Jasper. 'Where is he from?'

'New York,' I say. 'He's lived there all his life.'

'Does he have a funny accent? Like you see on TV?' asks Rupert.

'It's not a funny accent,' I explain. 'It's a very nice accent.'

The boys start putting on an American accent; like the one on their favourite police programme.

'Ya… all… see this Leygo herrre,' says Jasper, holding up a Lego airplane wing.

'Okay, that sounds nothing like Patrick. That sounds more like a Texas accent.' I laugh. 'You'll see when you meet him what he sounds like.'

'When will we meet him?' interrupts Sian.

'I don't know. He was going to check his work schedule and see when he can get over. You know how hard he works… Well, apparently…' My words linger in the air. 'Apparently.' Sian seems oblivious of my uncertainty.

'Oh, I can't wait to meet him. Will he be able to come to the wedding, Amelia? It would be so great if he could make it to coincide.'

'We'll see, I can't promise,' I say.

For a moment I consider whether I should invite Patrick to the wedding, then I can show him Scotland as well as Wales. Although I won't have much time off work to gallivant around the British Isles. Do I even want to gallivant with him? Will something change drastically on his trip and we will suddenly decide to get married, and the fortune teller's words will ring true. I don't see that happening somehow. She was obviously a charlatan.

'I hope you're not too jet-lagged. We have to be in the bridal shop by ten tomorrow. The tailor will be there. We may need some alterations to be done, so I want to get it sorted quickly,' says Sian.

'Of course, this is so exciting. I'm so happy for you, Sian. You deserve this happiness more than anyone after… what happened,' I say.

It is so wonderful to be back with my beautiful boys and my best friend. The happiness encases my whole body and a warm, cosy feeling rushes over me as I indulge in the comfort of us all being back together again and the excitement of Sian's imminent wedding. It makes me realise that I could never move to New York if things were to develop further with Patrick. This is my home and I don't ever want to leave it. If Patrick does want to be with me, then he would certainly have to think about quitting that job he hates so much and moving here instead. Then again, if he is dying, maybe he could move here and I would be able to help care for him.

We are about to stop in the service station, as the boys need a wee and I quite fancy a KitKat, when I notice that Patrick has sent me a few messages.

> Amelia, please let me know, did you land okay? Xxx

> I'm so worried. I didn't hear from you yet. Where are you?

> I keep getting flashbacks to the wonderful night we spent together. I can't wait to come and visit you. I want to see you desperately. I don't think I can live with us apart! Love you Xxxx

His messages confuse my feelings further. He says he loves me and even worries about me when I don't answer his messages. All I ever wanted was for someone to care about me like that. Why, then, do I have so many doubts?

Chapter 37

Bashful Brides – I hate my dress

Standing in the fitting room of Bashful Brides, I notice yet another message from Patrick. He hasn't stopped messaging since I returned. It is not even twenty-four hours since I stepped off the flight, so his incessant texting certainly makes me feel wanted.

> What you up to? I want to see you. I miss you. XX

I send Patrick a photo of me in my bridesmaid dress. I daren't say it to Sian, but why on earth would you choose lime green bridesmaid dresses?

> WTAF! Who chose that color? Xx

I notice his American spelling and the cultural difference strikes me again. I would probably tell the boys off if they spelt like that.

> I know, hideous colour, but she's my best friend. Xx

I say, adding an emoji with rolling eyes.

> Well, I guess you'd look good in a garbage bag, so you'll be okay ☺

'Bin bag,' I say out loud to myself.

'You what? You look like a bin bag? Amelia, are you coming out of there soon?'

I forgot that Sian was waiting outside with the dress-maker.

Sian is ecstatic as I step out of the changing room.

'Oh, you look so amazing, Amelia. Patrick will love you in it.'

Patrick has seen it and he doesn't love it one bit, I think.

The dressmaker looks me up and down, and everyone decides that, after all, there is no need for alterations even though I have had to take a dress a size larger than normal. It was probably that New York cheesecake that did it. I had at least hoped that all the sex would have worked a few calories off, but obviously not. The wire bodice is already cutting into me as I remove the dress. I am going to have to be careful I don't eat too much over the next few weeks or I will be needing another size up again.

My phone bleeps as I am struggling to get the lime ensemble over my head. I wonder if I should check my phone with this dress halfway over my head, or get the dress off first?

I am eager to see what Patrick has to say. He has mentioned something about Jamie taking a photo of him in the airport and he does not seem very happy. I do remember him complaining about that, but thought Jamie was on his way out of the airport at that time. I'm sure he is wrong. Curiosity gets the better of me, so I find myself standing in the fitting room with one arm in and one arm out of this duchesse satin dress whilst checking my phone. My dress is now hoisted up to my waist, showing the not-so-attractive flesh-coloured tights that I am wearing underneath. They were the only ones I could find in my rush to get here this morning, and I instantly regret it. Thank goodness Patrick cannot see me right now. I have the strange feeling that if he could it would probably be the end of us.

> So why would your friend take my pic, hey? What does he want?

There are no kisses this time.

> I don't know. He didn't say anything to me. Xx

> He has it in for me. I don't know what his problem is. I hope he's going to stay away from me when I come over.

> Umm, okay. When are you coming over? Any news yet? XX

I don't want to get drawn into the reasons why Jamie doesn't seem to like him. After what Jamie said on the flight, there is a chance that he is jealous of Patrick. Although quite why he has taken a photo of him, that bit I do not understand. I wonder if Patrick is making this part up.

After putting the phone down on the fitting room chair, I pull at the dress again. Unfortunately, due to my incessant wriggling about, the zip has now got stuck in my hair. I am going to need some assistance.

'Sian!' I shout. I wait for her to answer back, but nothing.

'Sian!' I shout once again.

She must have gone to look at something in the shop. Oh no, typical.

'Help!' I shout.

Still nothing. I peer around the curtain but nobody is close enough to see me.

I try ringing Sian's mobile, but it must be in her bag as she doesn't answer.

In my despair I google Bashful Brides. Desperate times call for desperate measures and so I find the phone number online and ring the shop.

'Hi, I need help in your changing room,' I say the minute someone answers. 'It's not a prank call. I promise. I'm stuck in the fitting room. Please help me,' I beg.

As I put the phone down, Patrick returns my message.

How about I fly over next week? XX

Will I even be out of here by next week?

> Umm, yeah, cool. XX

> Don't sound so excited! LOL! Xx

If he could see me right now, I think he would understand why I am not sounding super ecstatic.

> No, I am excited. I can't wait to see you. XX

> That's great. In that case, any chance you could do me a huge favor? I lost my credit card. Can you pop it on your card and I'll give you the cash next week?

I immediately agree as I am in such a compromising position.

I suddenly hear my name being called out.

'Amelia, how long does it take you to get changed?' Thank goodness, Sian is looking for me.

'I have to put this one on Facebook,' she laughs as soon as she sees me behind the curtain. The moment she stops laughing, Sian tugs and pulls and, after quite a bit of hair loss and a broken zip, I am eventually set free. The minute I am dressed again I see that Patrick is still texting away; he obviously hasn't got any so-called deadlines to think about today.

> Are you not working today?

I start typing.

> If you're bored, why don't you send me a photo of your office? Send some pics. I'd love to see some. xxx

I notice that, although he has read it, he immediately goes offline. I always ensure that I answer him back straight away and, even though I was in a compromising position, I still responded to him.

I haven't yet confided in Sian about my concerns with Patrick, but finally bring them out in the open as we enjoy a coffee after our wedding shopping spree. I tell her how I followed him.

'Well, I'm sure there's some reason. Maybe he called in sick after his coffee with the milk but then felt better; maybe he had a doctor's appointment later and didn't want to tell you. I mean, if he is sick then there could be a very reasonable explanation.'

'Hmm, yeah. I hadn't thought about it like that.'

'Yup, definitely. I mean, come on, you said yourself he could be dying. He probably doesn't want to scare you off by telling you the truth. I'm sure he's doing it to protect you. It's obvious. Maybe he has even had to quit work because of his terminal illness but doesn't want to tell you the truth. So, then he pretends to go off to work and instead he goes to the hospital for treatment, or something. That's deffo what it will be, lovely. Some guys don't even tell their partners when they've lost their jobs and pretend to go to work every day. Perhaps he's a bit like that and scared to say anything. He could even be trying to protect you from the truth as he's just soooo perfect and dreamy,' says Sian.

My head hurts as I consider the possibility that Perfect Patrick is so lovely that he doesn't want to tell me the truth. That he wants to protect me from all his pain. The poor soul. Nobody can possibly judge someone in this situation. Sian could be right.

'And what about Jamie? Have you heard from him yet?'

'No, we haven't spoken. But that's not surprising when he had to dash straight into work. He's not due back down here until next week,' I say.

I don't tell Sian that I had a sleepless night last night thinking about Jamie and Patrick. I feel as though I need to give Patrick a chance and to finally find out the truth behind him, but I know in my heart that nobody will ever be like Jamie is to me.

However, I just can't risk it with Jamie. I have far too much to lose, so instead I decide to look forward to Patrick's visit and see if we can make it work.

Chapter 38

Laugharne – preparing for Patrick's arrival

I have cleaned the house from top to bottom and even scrubbed the oven in preparation for our visitor. Although Patrick won't be staying with us, I still want to make a good impression in case he pops in. I am beginning to think Sian might be right about Patrick. I have never seen a man more excited to be with me than in our last conversation before he arrives.

'Look at the champagne I bought us.' Patrick smiles over Skype. Now that he has seen me in the flesh I can finally Skype in the bright living room. I guess we all have our secrets. Just as I kept my weight a secret from him, he keeps his health condition a mystery from me. Perhaps I should accept that every relationship needs to have a degree of mystery.

'Ooh, I love champagne,' I squeal. Handsome man, bottle of champagne. How can I not be excited?

'This champagne is very special, a great year. Let's enjoy it in bed together tomorrow.' He laughs.

'Wow, champagne in bed. I've never done that before, but it sounds good. By the way, did you get your new credit card yet? You may need it when you're over here,' I say.

If he can treat us to champagne, I assume he must have it by now. Unless he is so rich that he paid cash. Although I don't imagine that after the look of the place he secretly lives in. He looks a bit vague when a knock on the door interrupts our conversation.

'You expecting anyone?' asks Patrick.

'No, hang on a second.'

I open the door to discover a delivery man holding out the prettiest bunch of long-stemmed pink and white roses, my absolute favourite.

'Hey? Flowers? Did someone send you flowers?' Patrick says as I walk back in still holding them. 'My god, I was so busy with the Sacramento trip I just realised I never did buy you flowers in New York. My dear, Amelia. Please forgive me. I'll make it up to you, I promise I will. I love you so so much. I told you I'd spoil you and I will. Just you wait till I arrive.'

'Oh, so these aren't from you then?' I say. For a moment I thought they could be a present from Patrick.

'Jeez, no. My mind's been all over the place. I guess I shoulda treated my girl to flowers. Sorry, it's the illness…'

I don't say anything as a terrible wave of guilt rushes over me. Whilst he touches on his terminal illness, I realise who the flowers have come from.

'So, if they're not from me. Who are they from?' he asks.

'Oh, Sian, I think. Welcome back pressie,' I lie.

'Oh good, for a moment I thought it might be that creep of a friend of yours. You know, the one you were with in the airport.'

The word *creep* stings and I automatically jump to Jamie's defence.

'Hey, he is definitely not a creep, Patrick. He's my friend.'

'Sorry, sorry, way outta line. I say such stupid things sometimes. Yeah, of course. Nice guy. But I still wanna know why he took my photo. I don't like people doing things like that.'

'I have no idea, Patrick. You must be mistaken. Perhaps he was taking a photo of the airport; maybe there was a plane nearby,' I say.

'Yeah, sure. Well, maybe we'll find out when I'm there, hey?'

'Yes, absolutely. Perhaps you can ask him yourself.'

'Well, I don't wanna see him, but… Anyway, enough of him. So, what shall we do when I come over? Any plans?' asks Patrick. 'Will I see your castle? An Englishman's home is his castle, right?' he continues.

'Absolutely, Patrick. But I told you before, it's not a castle and I am in Wales, not England.'

'Wales, cottage, yada, yada, yada… Yeah, you told me. My bad. Well, I look forward to seeing your cute cottage and taking you to bed with champagne. Perfect, right?'

'Absolutely,' I agree. 'Though obviously, with the boys, you'll be staying in a hotel, right?'

I have told him a thousand times, but I am terrified he thinks he is staying at mine, as he doesn't seem to take things in sometimes. 'I've booked you a nice hotel,' I reiterate.

'Fantastic, let's hope there's room service and a minibar too,' he says with a laugh. 'Well, I'd best pack this bottle and get ready for the flight. See you tomorrow, my darling Amelia. I love you more than anything.' He waves the bottle in front of him. 'Hell, even as much as I love this stuff.' He grins.

With our video chat over I read the card that came with the flowers.

I'm so sorry. I should never have said those things on the flight. I thought we would die and I was scared. I didn't mean any of it ☺
Please forgive me, Jamie xxxxxxxx

I look at the bouquet in front of me and take in its beautiful aroma. As the contents of the message sinks in, I can't help but feel disappointed. Jamie never meant a word of it? I feel like such an idiot. For that moment on the flight, I secretly let my true feelings for Jamie escape. I admitted to myself how jealous I was of Miserable Megan and everything. Thank goodness I talked myself out of it when we got back.

I was right: Jamie was never worth the risk.

Chapter 39

Laugharne – Patrick has arrived

As Patrick has the poem on his WhatsApp and has quoted some verses that I wasn't familiar with once or twice, I considered his fondness of poetry when booking a hotel for him. Obviously, he hasn't answered enough about himself for me to be completely sure that he has a penchant for poetry, but he does have that romantic poet persona at times. I am ashamed to admit that the only poems I truly know are the ones that my mum used to tell me. I don't think they were written by a proper poet or anything, as it was mainly a poem about an apple tart making your bum go rat tat tat, or something. Of course, I won't ever admit this sordid truth to Patrick.

Making up for my lack of poetic knowledge, I have booked Patrick into one of Dylan Thomas's favourite haunts, so I do hope that he will love it. The hotel dates back to the 1700s, but thankfully has been modernised a few times since then. Now the rooms have organic Welsh mattresses and even WI-FI, something that definitely was not around in Dylan Thomas's day. Miraculously, with no WI-FI, it is thought that Dylan Thomas collected inspiration for his poetry through stories overheard in the local bars. Patrick probably doesn't know any of this, so I can't wait to tell him and teach him all about our beguiling little pocket in the Welsh countryside. Americans love history and, of course, Dylan Thomas ended up in New York and so I feel that this is all quite ironic. Girl from Laugharne meets boy from New York – I wonder what Dylan would have thought of it all?

'This is so adorable, Amelia. I love it here,' Patrick says as we greet each other in the small reception. I feel smug with my appropriate choice of hotel; I knew he would adore it.

'Oh, my darling Amelia… I've missed you so much.' He holds me tight and any reservations I have about our relationship vanishes.

'Excuse me, excuse me,' says a passer-by, trying to squeeze past.

'I'm so sorry.' I blush. I am once again oblivious to everything around me. Patrick has that charm about him. I don't know how he does it, but he makes everything else disappear when you're with him.

Even though I have lived in the township all these years, I never tire of the sights of Laugharne. I want to show Patrick as much of it as possible. We walk hand in hand down to Dylan Thomas's Boathouse first. Perhaps Patrick will like it so much that he will fall in love with it, just like I always have.

Patrick thinks the Boathouse is fantastic, and loves the nearby writing shed, which is perched on a cliff commandeering the most breathtaking views.

'I dream of having something like this,' says Patrick. 'A place where you could come and get inspiration and work in solitude. I love this place!'

'I knew you'd like it,' I say, secretly pleased.

You can't go inside the shed, which is a shame as I am sure Patrick would love to get in there, but as we look through the window, you can picture Dylan Thomas working in there. With its desk, scrunched-up pieces of paper and litany of cigarette ends it is a true writers' paradise. Although, personally, I would swap the cigarettes for chocolate biscuits and cups of strong tea if I were a writer finishing a masterpiece.

He wants to look at the castle next, but there is plenty of time for that. I want to take him somewhere truly special. I want to show him where I grew up. Mum's old house. I haven't been past for months, so it takes some courage to see it once again. With Patrick by my side, I finally feel that I can confront the fears I have. It still doesn't stop the nerves about seeing the changes that the new people have made though.

Pulling up outside, I notice the new residents have knocked down the front wall and removed our beautiful gates. They have even made the drive bigger, and jet-skis and two trailers are in place of my mum's small Toyota. Even though she was not well enough to drive for a long time, I still expect to see that car when I look at the driveway. It doesn't seem to be the same house at all.

'Oh, looks very bijou,' says Patrick. 'I thought you just sold a big house.'

Bijou? What is wrong with this lovely house? It is perfection in my eyes. It was certainly perfection when we had it.

'So, any other famous places around here? Any more castles? Did I tell you I love castles? I think I read in a guidebook that there was also a cathedral not too far away,' he says dismissively.

I might be oversensitive but I can't help but feel hurt. To me, my mum's house is more important than any cathedral or castle. Though perhaps I was being insensitive, as he was very young when he lost his parents. I was lucky to have a home with my mum for all those years; he didn't even have that.

'Okay, I suppose I can think of somewhere else to show you,' I manage.

He smiles at me, and my heart melts.

I am beginning to drive in the direction of the castle when Patrick moves his hand onto my leg. He squeezes it tight, and I want to jump. Had I known what he was about to do, I would have at least clenched my muscles so my leg wouldn't feel quite so wobbly.

'You know, I changed my mind. Why don't we head back to the hotel?' Patrick says seductively.

One look at him with his soft dark hair, that smile and the way his cashmere jumper is casually slung over his shoulders, stupidly makes me want to agree. However, I have some questions before I jump into bed with him again and now is the right time to bring them up.

'You know, Patrick, there is so much I want to know,' I start. 'I need you to be truthful with me. Why didn't you take me to your home in New York? You never even took me near there.'

Unfortunately, as I ask my first question, he has a sudden pain in his stomach and needs to rush back to the hotel. He thinks he may have food poisoning from the flight and writhes in agony for the rest of the drive. I am concerned that it is something much more sinister. Please don't let him die here.

'Shall I call my doctor?' I ask. 'You definitely need a doctor if you're in that much pain.'

'No, no, I just need to visit the john.'

'The what?'

'The restroom, whatever you call it. I need to use the john and have a sleep. I'll be fine. Let's maybe take a rain check on today, yeah. I have to catch up on emails anyway. I'll see you for paintball tomorrow, and I look forward to finally getting to meet those lovely kids of yours.'

He seems much better once he gets out of the car, and it looks as though he was faking it. He will do anything to get out of any questions I ask. I am now mad that I have arranged tomorrow. I don't want the boys meeting him, but they will be so disappointed if I cancel paintball. I figured I would find out everything by today but, once again, he has managed to wriggle his way out of answering anything about his health and his home whatsoever.

Chapter 40

A paintball field in Pembrokeshire – this is war

Camouflage colours have never suited me and, with my wobbly bum, overalls are another definite no. Sadly, a corporate party of teaching assistants is currently looking straight at me, and I swear they are giggling at the state of me. I hope none of them are at the boys' school. Luckily, I can't say I recognise any of their faces.

Just when I thought that things couldn't get any worse, the macho man who has checked us in hands me a pair of oversized protective goggles. I had put on so much mascara this morning too. Now my lashes are rubbing up and down like windscreen wipers on high speed, smudging my view against the plastic lenses.

'Yay, let's go,' shouts Jasper the second we are fully kitted out.

The boys run ahead, leaving me and Patrick trailing behind. He looks rather uncomfortable. I don't know if it is the groin protector that the staff made him wear, or if he is afraid that I am going to start questioning him again, but he is certainly not happy about something. I am still miffed with him too.

The marshal leads us to a field with trees covered in splats of red, green, yellow and blue paint. There are lots of hiding places and I try to memorise where I can go.

As well as camouflage trousers I don't like pain, and I learnt on one of Dick's corporate bank events that when a paintball hits you it can really sting. I don't intend going home black and blue today.

I also don't want to hurt the boys. I know it is only a game, but how on earth are you supposed to shoot your own child? Of course, I am going to let them both win. I don't want to shoot Patrick either. He might be a little enigmatic, but he is too beautiful to shoot, and I don't know where the terminal illness lives in his body. Thus, I have no idea what the purpose of this game is going to be. I come to the conclusion that the only thing I can do is keep a low profile and hide behind every tree I find.

The marshal tells us the rules and how important it is not to shoot anyone too close to you. I definitely won't be doing that. I only hope the boys are listening, but surely they are not going to want to hurt their mum?

I run and hide in some tyres that are piled up in the woodland, my bum getting slightly stuck as I climb in. I make a mental note to stop buying cookies during next week's supermarket shop.

I can hear the sound of the paint pellets being shot around me and Jasper and Rupert screaming wildly.

As I hide, I am struck by a horrendous thought: what if Patrick gets carried away with the shooting and hurts them? I meant to tell him to go easy on them, surely he will, won't he?

'Ouch,' shouts Rupert. 'You hit me.'

Oh God, I knew I should have said something. Is he okay?

I poke my head up out of the tyres to see what is going on. In fairness, it is actually Jasper who shot him and not

Patrick. Although I can't see Patrick, so he must be hiding somewhere.

'Are you okay?' I shout over.

'I'm okay,' says Rupert. 'I hurt my leg a little though.'

'Shall we stop the game?' I ask hopefully.

'No, we want to carry on,' says Jasper.

The marshal signals the game to restart and off we go again. Now that the boys know I was hiding in the tyres, I have to find another hiding place. I am arriving beside a tree when I spot Patrick.

I shoot the bottom of his leg with a red pellet and hope that it doesn't hurt too much.

'Thanks, Amelia,' he shouts over to me, sounding rather unamused.

We all run around a little more and I find a new hiding place.

I am a total genius; nobody will ever find me behind this makeshift wooden shed. In fact, ten minutes have gone past and still nobody finds me. I must have run further than I thought as I can no longer hear any voices; they seem to have quietened and moved further away. Oh well, at least now nobody will hurt me and I don't have to shoot my two little cherubs.

Eventually I spot the marshal who comes towards me.

'Do you know where everyone is?' he asks.

'No,' I say. 'Have you lost them?' I start to worry.

'I'm sure they're here somewhere, it's a big area. People are always getting lost in these woods,' he says.

This is not exactly reassuring to hear; they have already been lost once in the past few weeks. I certainly hope Patrick is with them somewhere. Then again, what if Patrick is the problem and has taken them? I start panicking.

'Jasper, Rupert. Jasper, Rupert.' I scream so hard I feel like my lungs will explode.

'You go that way, and I'll go this way,' the marshal instructs.

I start to walk through the woods. I have to find them.

'Rupert!' I shout. 'Jasper, where are you?'

Eventually I hear a muffled sound not too far away.

Heading in the direction of the sound, I spot a leg. I think it could be Patrick's, as I notice the red stain near the ankle.

'Patrick!' I shout as I notice the ankle move. There is no response.

As I get closer to the ankle I see two smaller legs nearby. The three of them must be hiding behind the tree. I approach carefully in case they shoot me by mistake, even though I am in the required surrender pose. I hear them talking and reach in closer to listen to what they are saying.

'Do you get it?' I immediately recognise Jasper's voice.

'Okay, dude.' That is definitely Patrick.

'He won't tell you again.' This time I can hear Rupert's tone.

'You stay away from our mum, or I will ram this gun up your nostrils, one by one. Do you hear me... Duuuuuude?' That is most certainly Rupert.

'Rupert, Jasper! Don't be so rude,' I scream.

I finally move around the tree to find Patrick pinned to the tree trunk with Jasper in his face and Rupert standing back slightly. Jasper's gun is practically up Patrick's nose, and Rupert is holding his gun towards his groin shield.

'I can't believe what I'm seeing. Jasper, Rupert, stop pointing those guns. What on earth is wrong with you two?' I scream.

Patrick peels himself off the tree trunk as the boys step back.

'I am so, so sorry, Patrick,' I say. 'I can't believe they would ever do something like this. It's unforgivable.'

I know Patrick isn't in my good books, but there is no need for the boys to be so violent.

'Say sorry to Patrick,' I say to both Jasper and Rupert.

Jasper looks at the floor while Rupert stares at me confrontationally.

'Say sorry now,' I insist.

'NO!' shouts Rupert.

I give them both the warning stare.

'Sorry, Patrick,' mumbles Jasper.

'Now you, Rupert,' I say.

'No, never,' he says.

'Say it now,' I demand.

'Why should I?' he asks. 'I hate him and so does Jasper, but he's too polite to say it. He's horrible.'

'He is a bit slimy, Mum,' says Jasper quietly.

Patrick looks at me as if to say it is okay. However, it is not okay to be so rude and their behaviour has taken me by surprise. They were brought up to be polite to people, not threaten someone's nostrils and say such nasty things to someone's face. They could at least have told me in private what they thought of him.

'We hate you, Patrick,' screams Rupert. 'Get out of our lives. We don't ever want to see you again. Ever, ever, ever.'

Rupert storms off, throwing his paintball gun on the ground as Patrick and I stand there looking at each other. Jasper chases after Rupert just as the marshal spots us.

'Ah, there you are,' he shouts over. 'Everything okay?'

No, everything is definitely not okay, Mr Marshal. Everything is definitely not okay.

Chapter 41

Laugharne – the truth about Patrick

With the boys in school today it means they won't need to see Patrick again, which is definitely for the best. Rupert refused to speak to me in the car this morning, and Jasper was very quiet, which is highly unlike his usual chatterbox self. Patrick was calmer than I thought he might be about the whole hostage situation with the boys. He laughed it off and said that he didn't blame them and it must be hard for them seeing their mum with someone other than their dad. I am not sure that is their problem, though, as they were quite happy for Jamie to be part of their lives. They have obviously not taken to Patrick and see something they despise. It is amazing how children can sometimes be more perceptive than their parents. However, my boys come first and so if they think he is a 'phoney', as Rupert informed me before bed last night, then I will take their word for it.

Patrick is due to leave today, as he wants to spend a few days in London before flying back. Yet he still hasn't paid me back for the flight. He says that his credit card has still not been replaced and has now asked me to pay the hotel bill on my card, as he doesn't want to use his ATM card. He explained that the rate of exchange at the cash point, to withdraw from a dollar account, is extortionate. I don't understand: he was so generous in New York and now wants me to pay for everything. If I was less suspicious of him, I could say that he believes in equality but, after Rupert's comments, I suspect that this is not what it is about at all. I will bet that he doesn't have a small hotel bill and has put all his bar drinks on there too.

I head to the hotel earlier than arranged, so that hopefully we can at least have a chat before he leaves. I am leaning in to knock on Patrick's door when I overhear that unmistakable New York accent. I can hear him clearly.

'I'm leaving the polo meeting now, then going straight for my flight. I'll see you soon. Love you, honey.'

So that is what this is all about. He has someone else. He must be married. That is the reason that he doesn't want to use his credit card to pay for anything. There will be no trace if I pay for it all. Everything suddenly makes sense.

I knock the door ferociously, and he answers right away.

'Were you on the phone?' I ask suspiciously, noting that his phone is still in his hand.

'No, I was in the bathroom.' He smiles.

'I could hear talking,' I insist.

'Oh, yeah, my boss. I forgot. She was on the phone to me.'

'You love your boss now?' I shout.

He ignores me.

'I heard you say you loved someone, Patrick. Don't deny it.'

'Maybe it was the TV,' he says.

'No, the TV isn't on, Patrick. I'm not stupid. Look, I can see something's going on. You have to tell me the truth, finally. You at least owe me that. Nothing adds up. You won't tell me anything about your illness. Nothing about your home life. You know all about me. The divorce, my mum… You're so secretive. I followed you when I was in New York, if you'd like to know. When you left me in the hotel… I saw you go into the place with the key code, which I suspect is your home.'

Patrick's face drains, although he still refuses to speak. He sits down on the bed and puts his hand through that lovely head of hair of his.

'Busted. I guess we do need to talk,' he says calmly.

'Too right we need to talk,' I say. 'Are you with someone else?'

'Don't be mad with me, okay, honey buns,' he says.

'Don't honey buns me!' I shout.

Patrick is about to speak when there is a knock on the door that startles us both.

Perhaps the minibar guy wants to count what Patrick's consumed before he checks out. What timing.

The banging persists, and Patrick looks at me.

'Answer it and get rid of whoever it is,' he says.

As I open the door Jamie barges in, leaving the door wide open behind him.

'Jamie, what on earth do you want?' I ask. 'How did you know where I was?'

'Sian told me… Look here, I've had enough of this lying cheat. He walks around with his designer clothes and those stupid loafers. I bet he even uses a shoehorn. Look at him,' he says with contempt. 'You need to tell Amelia the truth before I do,' continues Jamie. 'I'm giving you ten seconds.'

'Yeah, I do use a shoehorn. Busted again,' says Patrick.

'Tell me what is going on NOW…' I scream. I want to jump up and down like a toddler having a tantrum.

Patrick looks at Jamie, then at me.

'Okay, okay. Take a chill pill, I'm married. No big fucking deal.'

'No… Big… Fucking… Deal?' I spit out each word slowly.

I knew it. Why did I not realise this before? It was glaringly obvious. All the signs were there, including the Sacramento trip. He is a journalist; he is very good at turning questions on someone else. When I would ask him a question, he would tell me to say more about myself. I found it flattering that he was so interested in what I had to say, but now I see why. How on earth could I be so stupid?

'Why did you do this to me, Patrick? After I told you how Dick was unfaithful, why would you do this? What did you want from me?' I ask.

He doesn't answer.

'Bullshit, Patrick,' says Jamie. 'It's time Amelia knew the whole truth about you.'

Jamie's outburst confuses me further.

'He's not married, Amelia. He will never be married. He's not the type,' says Jamie.

'What? Why would he say…? Oh, I have no idea what is going on here… Someone please enlighten me.'

'You know the conference I was at in New York? Well, it was about security and fraud, remember I told you?'

Something tells me that I should have listened properly to Jamie when we were at dinner.

'Umm, okay,' I say. I have no idea where this is heading.

'Right, well, with the advances in technology there are plenty of facial recognition tools around. I took a photo of Patrick in the airport, as I wanted to check him out. Something about him screamed "scammer" from what I had heard about his behaviour. The way he disappeared and then was all over you... He was very inconsistent. So, I used his photo for an exercise at work, to show the team how easily we can check someone out with facial recognition and, well, I won't bore you with the technical details...'

Patrick puts his head in his hands as Jamie continues explaining.

'This man who... who sits in front of you is not who he says he is. He is called Rudolph.'

'Bastard!' shouts Patrick.

'Now, now. Let me finish, Rudolph... Yes, his name is Rudolph and you are not the first woman who he has tried to con.'

'Con?' I ask.

'I bet you paid for his flight, didn't you?'

'Yes, but...'

'This guy is all over the internet, Amelia. He is a well-known gigolo. He preys on women in vulnerable states. Ones who are recently widowed, or divorced and lonely. He seeks them out. It is what is called a romance scam. He appears as though he is the ideal soulmate, woos the women with fancy meals and the like, may even hint that he doesn't have long to live, but it's all an elaborate investment. He looks for rich, lonely women and seduces them to begin with, but then it turns nasty when they don't give him what he wants. He is not a journalist at all. He works as a baggage handler.

'I bet you got a huge discount on your flight but got Amelia to pay the full amount, so you could pocket the difference. Am I right, Rudolph?'

I think I preferred Patrick when I thought he was married. The fact that he works in an airport certainly seems to make sense. There is so much to take in. Strangely, what saddens me most is that 'he thought I was vulnerable'. Those words ring in my ears... I was a vulnerable divorcee who was... rich?

'I'm not rich, so I don't know why he would pick on me.' This part is completely illogical.

'He didn't know that. You told him you'd lost your mother, right? In his eyes he sees the word "inheritance". Then a divorce from a banker. On paper it all looks too good to be true to a scammer like this.'

'But Dick only worked as a cashier in the bank; he wasn't an investment banker, or anything.'

'Like I say, it all looked too good to resist for someone like this. Sian's media campaign was the perfect opportunity for him. I have had words with Sian, she should never have put you up to this.'

'Sian already knows?'

'I'll explain that bit later. But, yes, that's why she told me where you were. We were so worried about you.'

I sit on the edge of the bed as I take everything in. No wonder he was so charming and perfect. I feel such an idiot for falling for a romance scam. I am old enough to know better. I should have known he wasn't real; it was too good to be true from the start. He was so good at his act. I can't even cry, or shout, or, anything, really. I am just in a state of shock. I feel like the most gullible idiot out there.

'I feel so stupid, Jamie. Why didn't I realise?' I ask.

'It's not you, Amelia. He's tricked lots of women into buying things for him, giving him money, etc. These scammers are good nowadays. They spend a little money on a woman and then expect the unsuspecting victim to spend more on them. They seek people out and know what to say. This was the ideal opportunity for him,' explains Jamie.

'So, it wasn't you that I met all those years ago then?' I ask. 'But, you knew about the thong… I never told you about it; you knew about it already so it has to be you. You remember it, don't you?' Please at least tell me it was him I met all those years ago.

'Of course, it wasn't him, his name is Rudolph Pressario,' says Jamie.

'Jeez, she's slow, mate,' says Patrick, looking at Jamie.

'You're on thin ice here and I'm not your MATE,' warns Jamie.

'Oh, you think you're so smart. I bet he suspected something all along, didn't you Jaaamie? I saw that look you gave me in the airport. You sussed me out right away. Why didn't you tell her sooner if she is so special to you? Don't tell me you only just found out about me?'

Jamie looks at me nervously.

'Well, I have known for a while but…'

I look at both of them in disbelief.

'Why didn't you tell me this sooner, Jamie?'

'I wanted to find out more, Amelia. I wanted to know all the facts first, before rushing in and telling you.'

'Thought so. Sneaky shit. I know guys like you, there's always that brother, or some guy hanging around in the background who starts enquiring about me. They poke about into my business and then start putting ideas into the woman's head. Then they stop paying for things for me and… Yeah. Textbook it is. Every. Fucking. Time. Always some nosy guy,' says Patrick. 'You know what I do to men who get in my way?' he adds.

Patrick closes in on Jamie, but Jamie backs away. You can see that Patrick is no stranger to a fight. It comes as no surprise when he manages to get hold of Jamie and throws an almighty punch, hitting him straight in the face.

'Get off him,' I plead.

Patrick grabs Jamie, as if doing a rugby tackle, and pulls him down on the floor, leaving Jamie's head halfway outside the room and spilling into the corridor.

'Stop fighting. Patrick, please, think of your face,' I beg.

Surely that will stop him fighting. I have noticed the selection of male skincare products that he uses, so it is obvious that his looks are important to him.

Alas, it is too late, there is blood spurting everywhere.

'I'm going to kill you, you piece of shit. I'm going to kill you,' Patrick screams uncontrollably between punches.

Although I am incredibly frightened, I know that I must intervene. Whilst Jamie has managed to return a couple of punches, if this continues Patrick could surely kill him. I find my moment to help when Patrick becomes distracted with the noise of someone coming along the corridor. I get close enough to see that it is Jamie's blood that is spouting everywhere and try to pull Patrick off him. Jamie is in bad shape and we need to get to a hospital urgently.

Fortunately, startled by the person approaching the room, Patrick makes a run for it, giving me the opportunity to ring for an ambulance.

Chapter 42

The nearest hospital – poor Jamie

The hospital reminds me of the last time that I was here. It was when Mum was admitted for the final time. I would wait beside her bed, hoping for positive news, refusing to believe that her life was about to end. Even when she was unconscious, I stupidly thought she would pull through. I never thought that it was finally time to say goodbye. In a way I now realise that I have done the same thing all my life. I have always believed what I wanted to believe. Dick would come home late, smelling of scent, but I still put it down to work, assuming that perhaps the new young female recruits were spraying it around the office. I now recognise it as Tanja Tart's signature smell. He must have thought I was so gullible. Perhaps I am, but it is only because I want to think the best of everyone and every situation. I refuse to believe that there are bad people out there who want to hurt someone else.

Now I realise that I have done this with Patrick. I thought the best of him. How could I believe that he was so fabulous? I saw what I wanted to see. A fairy-tale romance at the age of forty-eight; of course it was too good to be true. I should never have believed that stupid fortune teller either. Was she part of his elaborate scam? Surely that would be too intricate, even for him.

As I sit with Jamie beside his hospital bed, I am in self-denial once again. I am convinced that he does not have pleurisy due to his broken ribs. I also convince myself that his nose is definitely not broken, despite the fact that it looks as though it is halfway across his face.

'I'm sure it will be fine, Jamie. Nothing seems broken,' I reassure him in his deep sleep.

He eventually wakes up when the doctor comes around to explain the extent of his injuries.

'It really hurts,' Jamie says, sounding muffled.

'Are you his next of kin?' the doctor enquires. 'I need to put someone down as next of kin in case of emergency. I notice nothing has been filled out yet.'

'No, no, I am just a friend. I'll step outside if you need to talk,' I reply.

'Yes, she's my next of kin. Please stay, Amelia,' says Jamie.

The doctor takes my contact details and then shows me an X-ray.

'Right, well, you can clearly see the break here and here,' says the doctor, pointing to the X-ray. 'We need to run a few more tests, but...'

To me, I don't see anything at all. It looks like some big black and white photo of a skeleton, if I am honest.

'You are one lucky man. Another inch and we would have a very different story. As for your broken nose... I will need to realign that. The good news is that I am able to manually realign it today,' he says with a smile. 'I shall be back to see you later, Mr Lewis,' he adds.

The doctor pauses for a while and looks a little hesitant before stopping in front of me.

'Can you speak with me outside when you're ready, please?'

I suppose he needs to know who has done this to him.

Poor Jamie, he has broken ribs, a broken nose, all because of me. The only thing he doesn't have is pleurisy, thankfully.

'Should we press charges, Jamie?' I whisper. 'We can't have him do this to you. We need to catch him quickly before he leaves the country. Maybe they can stop him if we phone the police.'

'No, let him go. If we press charges, then you will have to say how you met him and it will be all over the papers that you met a scammer online,' says Jamie. He takes a breath, grimacing as he does so. 'I don't want you to have to go through all of that. Promise me that if the doctor asks any questions that you will agree with my version of events.'

As always Jamie is thinking of everyone else, even as he lies here in this state.

'Oh, Jamie,' I say. I lean over and kiss his forehead. Poor Jamie.

–

The kind Indian doctor is looking at a chart when I spot him.

'Good, I wanted a word because we have a patient who has been admitted who also looks as though he's been in a fight. Although not as bad as Mr Lewis. I wondered whether there was any connection? He's an American with no next of kin here. Just a stab in the dark, but in case you knew him.'

'What? Is it Patrick?' I ask.

'Ah, no, different patient. His name is not Patrick.'

'No, of course. It's Rudolph, is that right?'

'Yes, nice, pleasant chap. Very charming.'

'Well, umm, not really, but, yes. I know him. He was visiting me.'

'Do you want to see him? He's just here,' says the doctor.

The doctor pulls a curtain and there is Patrick. His eye is coming up a nice shade of blue. It makes him look rugged and still does nothing to detract from his handsome face. It is what is inside that is ugly.

'Amelia. Thank God. Look, nobody knows I'm here, okay. Can you please say you're my next of kin? I'll pay you back for the flight money if you do, right. It's my stomach; they think there's a blockage. I thought it was my intolerance but I'm in agony. A woman in reception had to call me an ambulance and everything,' says Patrick.

'I want the hotel bill money back too,' I say. 'Serves you right for all the faking that you've been doing. You know what they say about the boy who cried wolf,' I add.

The doctor looks at me, appalled.

'Sorry,' I mouth, looking back at him.

'We're going to take him down to surgery for some exploration, so it would be good to get this all sorted,' says the doctor. 'Can I put you down?'

The doctor stands with the clipboard waiting for my response. I can feel his breath on me, he is so close. He lowers his glasses and looks at me, as if to hurry me along. I don't want to agree but the busy doctor is waiting, just as he had for Jamie's form a few moments earlier. Stupidly, I feel forced to agree, but only to help the doctor. What neither of them realise is that in a few moments time I am going to call the police. I don't care what Jamie says. Patrick is not getting away with doing this to Jamie, or me.

As soon as I have given my details again, I hurry away. I can't bear to look at Patrick after what he has done.

'Look, I have to meet my friend. I'm going to have to go,' I say to the doctor. Sian has already arrived to see Jamie, and I don't want to waste a moment longer with Patrick. I bid the doctor goodbye.

–

'What the hell happened?' asks Sian as she sees me rushing towards Jamie's ward.

I explain everything and ask her exactly what she knew. Her guilty face tells me that I haven't had enough surprises for one day.

'I have a confession to make. Come to the coffee machine with me for a minute,' she says, leading me towards a row of chairs.

'I feel awful…' she starts. 'Before I say anything else, please understand that I did it all for you. When he was in New York, Jamie told me that he had concerns about Patrick. We could have prevented all of this much earlier. I just wanted you to be happy, Amelia. That's why I even put words into Patrick's mouth. Like, when I called him up that time and I told him about the thong and hinted how you two met. I liked him and thought he could be good for you, even if he wasn't the real Patrick,' explains Sian.

'What? You knew he wasn't the real Patrick all along? It was you that told him about how we met and the thong? This is crazy. Sian, I don't believe you could do this to your best friend. What is wrong with you?' I say.

'Look. I never knew it would backfire, did I? Then Jamie started having suspicions. You know when you went out for dinner with Jamie, the night you saw the show? I spoke to him after he met you and he told me something,' says Sian.

'What did he tell you?'

'He told me about the conference and, as you now know, it was all about fraud and scams. So... he called me, he was worried. He said that from everything you had said about Patrick, it was typical scam stuff. He said he was going to try and find out more about him. I told him not to be silly and not to tell you about his stupid suspicions. But this was the reason he took the pic of him in the airport, so he could check him out when he got back to London and put him into some scanner thing at work. Look, let's go back to Jamie. He'll tell you the rest of it.'

Sian and I don't look at each other as we head back to Jamie. I begin to wonder if I really know my lifelong friends at all.

'Jamie. You have to tell me all you know,' I beg. Between Sian and him, I am not very pleased with either of them right now for keeping all this from me.

'It was obvious, Amelia. I knew something was wrong and I should have stopped it earlier. That's why I told you that night to be careful and not rush into anything. Sian made me promise not to say anything because it was all her idea. I didn't know for sure, so I kept quiet. But I figured he was up to something. I didn't tell you and I really should have,' he says.

'Too right you should have told me. Both of you are as bad as each other.'

I don't want this discussion with Jamie in his condition and, as for Sian, I am so angry with her. If they had told me the truth before, then I would never have slept with

Patrick and fallen for his spiel. I would never have even gone to New York. This has all been because of Sian getting carried away. How could she possibly do this to me? Does she think I am so sad and lonely that she felt it necessary to find a complete phoney on the internet and dupe me? This is mortifying. As for Patrick, he must have been laughing at the thought of such an easy target.

I storm out of the hospital into the cold winter air, where I begin to cry. Today has been far too full of nasty surprises.

Chapter 43

WhatsApp – an apology

Monday

> I'm so sorry.

> Will you at least speak to me?

> I need to explain.

> I know you're reading these as it shows me on WhatsApp.

> I'm probably the last person you want to speak to right now, but I need to tell you my side of the story.

> I should have told you in New York.

I was a fool for not telling you earlier.

Like I said, I'm sorry.

Tuesday

Good afternoon :-)

Are you going to speak to me today?

I hope you're going to speak to me. I miss you.

It feels good to message you, even if you won't reply.

Shall I tell you about my day so far?

I spent my day thinking about you.

I had coffee, a croissant and thought of you.

I thought of the time we had in New York together.

Wednesday

Good morning ☺

Are you going to ask me how I am?

Will you speak to me today?

I had toast for breakfast. I know, a very boring fact. It's difficult having a one-way conversation here.

Please message me back.

An hour has gone by, so I guess this means you're still refusing to message me back.

I'm not going to give up on you.

Nothing's changed, I meant what I said.

Give my love to Jasper and Rupert. I miss them and I miss you too.

Thursday

It's been 3 days now. Why won't you at least speak to me?

It wasn't my fault, please understand that.

You do realise that you can't avoid me forever, don't you?

You're going to have to speak to me at Sian's wedding.

I know you're going to look amazing as a bridesmaid ☺

I can't wait to see you there; I only hope you'll finally speak to me.

Goodnight, sleep tight.

Please speak to me in the morning, btw. X

Friday

This morning I had Weetabix for breakfast.

Oh, I had an orange juice too. Variety is the spice of life, so they say.

Okay, I know I'm acting like a stalker now.

That's why I've decided that today is my last day of messaging you.

It breaks my heart that we have known each other so long. Yet you won't even speak to me right now.

I should never have said I loved you and I should have told you sooner that I was suspicious of Patrick.

I value our friendship so much and don't want to lose that.

I can't imagine not seeing you.

I can't imagine not seeing that beautiful smile of yours.

Will you speak to me?

It's been hours since my first message, Amelia. I'm going to sleep now.

I promise not to message tomorrow and move on with my life. I'm sorry for everything. Jamie Xxxxxx

I sit and think about the messages. I am still angry with both him and Sian for not telling me sooner. They say it takes two to tango, but in this instance, it took three of us to create such a mess.

Sian is to blame for starting all of this and making everything worse by putting words in Patrick's mouth. I am to blame for going along with it all and believing that someone like Patrick would fall in love with me over the internet. Meanwhile, Jamie should have aired his suspicions sooner, then I would never have slept with such a dreadful man. I am angry with myself, just as much as I am with Jamie and Sian.

Most of all, I am embarrassed for being such a fool.

I have made a complete mess of things since the divorce and now it is time to put everything right.

Chapter 44

West Wales – news from the hospital

I am already late for work when I see my mobile light up. It says 'private number', so I am afraid to ignore it in case they don't call back. Perhaps it is the police.

Unfortunately, the police have told me that Jamie refused to confirm it was Patrick who caused the injuries to him. He still protected me, even though I begged him not to. I, on the other hand, refuse to give up. I am waiting for the police to call me back. I want my money returned, but Patrick says everything I paid for was a gift. For a moment I was smug when he said that, as I knew I had evidence of him messaging me in the Bridal Shop, asking me to pay for his flight. However, I also instantly realised that I deleted every single message from Patrick during a moment of rage. I am sure Jamie would know how to retrieve deleted messages but he doesn't want to get involved. I know he is trying to protect me from everyone knowing what happened and I respect that; I just don't want Patrick ever doing this to another woman, which I know he will.

'Hello, is this Mrs Amelia… umm, Simpson?' says a voice on the other end of the phone.

'Yes, it is.'

'It's the hospital. You put your name down as next of kin for…'

'Omg, has something happened?'

'Well, it's just to let you know that we're taking him in for surgery. He's come back for some stitches to be removed and we found what we suspect is a cancerous…'

'What? Patrick has cancer?' After all the faking he has done this is what has happened to him.

'Patrick?' asks the voice.

'Sorry, Rudolph.'

'Rudolph? Oh, Rudolph. That lovely charmer. Ha. No, there was a Rudolph in another ward, but he discharged himself. Didn't he tell you? I thought you were on his next of kin notes. When I entered his notes into the system, I remembered it was a bit strange that two patients had an identical next of kin… Anyway, I digress now, I must stop doing that, sorry. I'm talking about Mr Jamie Lewis. Ooh, we do have our wires crossed here, don't we?'

'Jamie has cancer? Patrick has discharged himself, the snake. What are you trying to tell me here?' I say.

No, no, this cannot be happening. Not to Jamie. And why haven't the police arrested that evil man yet. Surely, he can't be allowed to just walk out like that. I suppose it is all about evidence and he is a convincing liar.

'What snake? Who is Patrick?' she asks.

'Oh, never mind. Long story. What about Jamie? What's wrong?'

'Well, it's just as well one of the young doctors spotted the mass when he came back for his check-up. It was difficult to see previously with all the swelling. We almost missed it. He's very lucky that he managed to break his nose or we may not have found it as early on. He has been sedated, but before he had the procedure, he asked us to call you to see if you could pick him up when he's discharged. He could do with someone to help him home tonight. All being well he can be discharged around 5pm. Is that okay? We'll ring you when he's out of theatre.'

I put the phone down and immediately call in sick. I was supposed to help with the display for the newly refitted shop today but will never make work in time. Besides, how am I supposed to do anything knowing that Jamie has some kind of cancer? I didn't understand the terminology. I would google it and learn what I can, but I don't think I could even spell it. Oh, my lovely Jamie.

I pop the kettle on to make tea. My mouth has suddenly gone dry. Poor Jamie who is always there for me.

I promise things will change if only he will be okay. I'm going to tell him how I feel and risk everything. He needs to know the truth. I have to take that chance.

–

The afternoon can't come around fast enough. I manage to arrange for Dick to take the boys after school and head around to the hospital. I see Jamie right away. He looks okay, a bit dazed perhaps, but not as bad as he could be.

'Oh, you poor thing. What on earth has been happening? I feel terrible that I wasn't there.'

'It's okay,' he mumbles through his bandaged nose. 'It was a polyp of some kind. They're sending off the sample, but they think it was okay in the end. Bit of a panic due to an overeager registrar, apparently. Then when they couldn't stop my nose bleeding they had to whisk me straight down to theatre. Hope you don't mind that they called you.'

'Of course, I don't mind, silly. It isn't cancer after all? Oh, thank goodness, Jamie… Come on, I'll take you home,' I say, reaching my arm out to lead him away.

We don't say much as we leave the hospital. I can hardly understand what he tries to say anyhow with his nostrils mummified like this.

'Can you breathe?' I finally ask. It doesn't look very comfortable.

'Yes, I'm fine. I'm breathing through my mouth at the mo. Well, at least I won't snore any longer,' Jamie says, laughing. 'Aww, that hurt.'

'Shh, don't speak, Jamie. Put your head back and relax. Okay.'

He dozes in the car on the way home. When we finally reach his house he insists that he is fine to stay alone. I kiss the top of his head as I drop him off at his front door.

'Take care, you know where I am if you need anything. Call me anytime, okay. I wanted to have a chat with you about something, so whenever you feel up to it,' I say.

'Sure, let's have a chat soon. I'll be fine, don't worry. Megan said she might pop over with a curry later. She makes a very good one, apparently, with turmeric and…'

'Megan? She's back?' I interrupt.

'Oh, she messaged and I told her I was in hospital. So she said she'd come over with a curry tonight,' he says, before wincing in pain.

Has Megan changed her mind? How can she change her mind like that?

Jamie Lewis is meant to be with me; I just need to find a way of telling him.

Chapter 45

Laugharne – healing rifts

It has been over three weeks since I last spoke to Jamie. I assume he has been pre-occupied with Megan. Her return has come as such a shock to me. The only good thing to happen is that Patrick – I still can't get used to the name Rudolph – has been caught. He was stopped at customs when he was attempting to board his flight back to New York. The police took him in for questioning when he tried to leave the country with an impressive jewellery collection and large amounts of cash in his hand luggage. The police think he had wanted to travel to the UK to meet up with the many other women he was in touch with. This would make sense, as he was only ever going to be in Wales for a few days. After discharging himself from hospital, he spent the rest of his visit meeting up with some of the other women who paid for his lifestyle. One of those women was called Harriet. She was, in a way, his boss, as she practically paid him a salary. Harriet is a wealthy widow living in the Cotswolds that he met online. We have now corresponded and she is a lovely lady who just wanted to meet 'someone nice'. After Patrick stayed with her, she noticed that her jewellery was missing. She didn't mention anything to him, but tipped off the airport so that it would be found by an official. She said she loved Patrick, but was not going to be taken for a fool. He should never have under-estimated the power of a woman who has been hurt.

As for the lady in the background when he would have to rush off our phone calls, I found out that this was his sister. He did have family after all. The bereavement, depression and even the illness were all tall tales to make women feel sorry for him. Harriet tells me that he had told her a different story. He told her how close his sister and him were. Astonishingly, Harriet had even seen her when she flew to New York to meet up with Patrick. Strangely, this fact upset me further. Even in a scam, I wasn't treated as well as Harriet.

As for Sian, she has been frantically finalising the dream wedding that she insists on organising all by herself.

During this time, I have been busy working on my dreams too. I've been speaking a lot to April, a fantastic dementia nurse I met online when I was researching what I need to do to change career. She has been so encouraging; my prospectus from Swansea University, to get me the necessary qualifications, should be here any day. I can't wait to tell Jamie that I have taken the first step.

I also discovered something amazing about myself. I love running! It was an app that promised to turn me from a couch potato into a runner that lured me in; the couch potato bit grabbed my attention when I was scrolling through the app store. Plus, the lovely ladies at the running club were so welcoming when I approached them apprehensively.

So, for the past few weeks, instead of turning to food whilst I figured out what to do next with my life, I ran. I ran and ran and ran. Of course, I had to stop every five minutes too. But the feeling of being free and running was so invigorating. It was so satisfying. Not only do I feel fabulous when I run, but I have also managed to lose six pounds already. Admittedly, my jeans aren't loose on me, but if I suck my belly in hard enough, I can pull the zip up. Who would ever have believed I could enjoy any type of exercise that much? The only downside is that I can't chat to the lovely ladies while I am running, as I am forced to choose breathing over talking.

So many times over the last few weeks I have wished I could talk to Jamie. I wanted to tell him about the running club. I wanted to tell him about my feelings for him, but I wouldn't with Miserable Megan around.

As I calm down about the recent calamities, I begin to understand that Sian could never have realised quite how spectacularly her plan could fail. She most certainly couldn't plan for Patrick to be the type of person he is. Nobody could have foretold that, not even the fortune teller with her ridiculous predictions.

With a little time and fresh air to clear my head I finally feel ready to listen to what Sian has to say about the whole escapade, so we agree to meet for lunch. Her treat, she insists, which I think is fair enough after the mess she created.

'Oh my god! Have you lost weight?' Sian says as she greets me at the Chinese restaurant she has chosen. I am not sure whether she is trying to butter me up, or really means it, but I will take it as a compliment.

'You'll be needing a new bridesmaid dress if you carry on. Don't lose any weight before next week, will you? There's no time for any alterations now.'

'I won't,' I promise.

'I've missed you so much, Amelia. I know you've been mad at me, but I want you to know that I love you to

303

bits. I didn't mean for any of this to happen. I just get overexcited sometimes and this was like a dream come true. It was all so exciting and magical. I wanted to help make it happen. How the hell was I to know he was a bloody looney?' says Sian.

'I know, I understand that. It's all been very unfortunate.'

'Do you forgive me?' Sian asks.

'Absolutely,' I agree.

'So, what's news? Anything further on Patrick?'

'Hoping to get some money back, but who knows. He had so many women on the go that I could be at the back of the queue,' I say.

'Well, the main thing is you're rid of him.'

'Definitely. It could have been a whole lot worse. Can you believe that Harriet loaned him ten thousand pounds? And then he had the cheek to steal her jewellery. At least he can't ever do it again. He got his karma,' I say.

'Oh, too right, and about time,' says Sian. 'By the way, have you spoken to Jamie?'

I tell her about the call from the hospital. About Miserable Megan reappearing with her health-busting curry.

'When I had that phone call to say that he may have cancer, I truly panicked. It made me realise how much I had accepted that he would always be there for me. Yes, he was one of my best friends, but I realise that I do truly love him. I don't want to see him with someone else. I can't bear to listen to him talk about her. I think I've lost him.'

'No, you haven't lost Jamie. You know how fond of you he is. He admitted his love for you on the airplane. We know it's you he loves,' says Sian.

'Yes, but then he sent me those flowers, apologising for his remarks.' I take a swig of wine and think back to how he has already made his feelings clear. 'Only I could have someone say something like that to me.' I laugh.

'Oh, he only said that he didn't mean it because he was embarrassed. Leave him to me, I'll sort him out.'

'No, Sian. Absolutely no chance. We all know what happens when I trust you and it doesn't ever end well,' I say.

Sian looks at me, embarrassed.

'Sorry, that was a bit harsh,' I apologise.

'He asked if Megan could come to the wedding. Did he tell you?' Sian says.

A sinking feeling hits my stomach. I have left it too late. I had my chance and I missed it. Why didn't I make more of it on the plane? I was confused about my feelings and didn't want to spoil what we had together, now I have missed out on true love. A wonderful relationship with a lovely man. A man who helps clean out an attic, a man who enjoys walks along a beach, only I never got to do that bit with him. Now he will take Miserable Megan with him on the long walks he enjoys.

'Don't worry, I told him no guests,' giggles Sian. 'Do you really think I'd let Miserable Megan spoil my day?'

We laugh so hard that I forget about all the trouble we have had.

'I missed you. Let's never ever argue again?' I say.

'It's a pact,' says Sian, clinking her glass against mine. 'Just one thing you have to promise,' she says.

'Hmm, I don't know. Depends what it is.'

'Leave Jamie to me. Let me work on him. Give me until the wedding, okay. Miserable Megan will soon be a thing of the past. I hope her cats and her naked yoga trainer are ready to welcome her back.'

'You're so mean, Sian.' I laugh. 'Please don't talk to Jamie about me though. If he's happy with Megan then leave it be. Promise me you won't say a word.'

'Wait for the wedding. That's all I'll say. Wait for my wedding day. Wooohooooo. I'm determined you two are going to get together,' says Sian.

'Sian, stop it. Don't you dare,' I plead.

'Haha, we'll see,' Sian says with a laugh.

'Not "we'll see". Sian, you've pushed it far enough already with Patrick. You have to promise you won't speak to him,' I insist.

'I promise.' Sian grins.

'Sian, put your hands where I can see them. Uncross your fingers.'

But Sian refuses to do so.

Chapter 46

Gretna Green — Sian's wedding day

'You look absolutely stunning,' I say. Sian really does.

I often forget that Sian has encountered her own unhappiness and hides behind the façade of being totally over the top. It is utterly fantastic to see her so happy on her wedding day. As chief bridesmaid, I will ensure that she has the best day of her life.

Sian's wedding dress is ivory and embellished with the most delicate crystals. When I first saw the dress, I was quite surprised as it's demurer than her normal style. However, now that it has been teamed with a matching fur cape, I can see why she chose it. The fake fur makes her look like a beautiful Russian princess and, with her silver Gina shoes, she looks like a doll.

Kitty and I – Kitty's the other bridesmaid; she is a distant relation of Sian's – don't look like a pair of limes as I had feared. We all seem to fit together perfectly. Perhaps I should have more faith in my best friend. Occasionally she does get something right.

The ceremony is in a candlelit olde blacksmith's shop. Sian and Rob are getting married over an olde black-smith's anvil and it is the most beautiful, picturesque scene. Sian chose the setting carefully. When Rob proposed, he gave her a wrought-iron heart that he had made especially for her, so she felt this was the perfect backdrop for the wedding. A wrought-iron heart was an usual choice I thought, when Wales has so many wooden love spoons available. But I suppose you couldn't get married over a giant love spoon.

I have tears in my eyes as I witness Sian's happiness on this delightful day. She is surrounded by all those who love her for her silly ways and outlandish ideas.

Kitty and I stand to one side while the vows are being spoken.

'I, Sian Mary Jones take you, Robert Morgan, to have and to hold from this day forward, for better for worse, for richer, for poorer and for even poorer after I've been shopping, in sickness and in health, to love and to cherish, from this day forward until death do us part.'

The whole congregation burst out laughing. Trust Sian to add in her own vows.

Sian and Rob kiss and the succinct ceremony is over too quickly, leaving the photographs next.

'Stand together, please,' the photographer instructs.

There are the usual photos of the bride and groom first and then with the bridesmaids and best man, Mike. It is obvious that Kitty quite fancies Mike, as she keeps asking him what he is wearing under the kilt that he has been made to wear. As he is one of Rob's co-workers in The Banana Men, I am sure he won't mind showing her at some point over the course of the day.

'Group shot. Can we get all the group together?' shouts the photographer to the whole wedding party.

I see Jamie in the distance talking to someone I don't recognise. I have been working so hard in the demanding role of bridesmaid, ensuring everything is perfectly organised, that I haven't spoken to him yet. This will be the first time we have seen each other since I dropped him at home after his operation. I notice he still has a bandage on his nose.

I also spot Jane; none of us have seen much of her since her separation with Markus. It seems an old flame had been waiting in the wings and she moved on quicker than any of us would have believed. He looks a nice guy and as I look at the two of them, standing near the wedding car, I begin to wonder if everything is meant to be and all planned out in advance for us all. Perhaps she was meant to marry a two-timing rat bag to make her realise what a good person her ex was.

The boys join us for the wedding photos, and it gives me a chance to check that they are not too bored. I do feel that weddings can be tedious for children. Bless them, they are struggling to stay still for the group photos.

'Now bride and groom alone again. Shall we go over here?' the photographer asks, pointing at some trees nearby.

Sian's new mother-in-law, Ivy, is amazingly lovely, and very unlike the mother-in-law I had to endure with Dick. Sian is very fortunate with lovely Ivy. She invites the boys to inspect the blacksmith's shop, as I am told that Ivy adores children and always dreamed of having grandchildren. I can see that she is a natural as she whisks them away.

Unfortunately, now left alone, this means that I am currently a gooseberry, listening to Kitty and Mike flirt. This leaves me with the ideal excuse to find Jamie and say hello. I see he is talking to someone I saw him with earlier, a blonde, attractive woman in her thirties. She must be from Rob's side, as I have never seen her before.

'Jamie, can I have a word, please?' I say, dragging him away from her. 'I am sorry about all that has gone on between us,' I start.

Jamie goes to open his mouth, but I quickly stop him.

'You don't have to speak,' I say.

We keep walking as I continue my apology. Jamie looks ahead; it is difficult to gauge what he is thinking.

'I don't ever want to lose you, Jamie. I know things have been a bit difficult between us since the flight, so I just wanted to say that you will always be my best friend no matter what. I also know you didn't mean what you said about being in love with me; you have made that clear. I wish you well with Megan and hope we will remain friends,' I say.

'Megan? What's she got to do with us?' asks Jamie.

'Well, it's just that if you had meant what you said and if you weren't with Megan... Maybe in another world we would have been soulmates. I just wanted to say that I love you to bits, Jamie Lewis, but I understand you two are now back together,' I say bravely.

'Megan and I aren't together. When did I say we were back together?'

My mouth hangs open as I absorb this news.

'You're not back with Megan?'

'Heavens, no way. She's busy bending about with her naked yogi. She rang me when I was in hospital as she'd left her favourite relaxation CD at mine. When I told her I was in hospital, she said she'd make me a curry so she could post the pictures on Instagram of her helping a sick person. It wasn't even very tasty,' says Jamie.

We both laugh at this.

'But you asked if Megan could come to the wedding,' I say.

'Oh, that was only because when she was over, I told her Sian was getting married. She asked me to text Sian and ask if she could come to the wedding, as you all go back years. I felt so cheeky, but she was quite insistent. She wanted to see who she was marrying more than anything, I think. You know Megan can be a bit inquisitive,' he explains.

'What a cheek. Sian doesn't even like her,' I say. 'Oops, sorry,' I add, covering my mouth with my hand. 'Didn't mean for that to slip out.'

Luckily Jamie finds this funny.

'Well, I can assure you, we are definitely not together,' he says.

'Absolutely not?' I ask.

'Absolutely not.' Jamie grins.

'In that case…' I say. 'I think we should… um.'

I look up and see that we are underneath a sign which says 'The Kissing Gate'.

I point up at it.

Jamie seems to be grinning, and I pray that I haven't misjudged the situation.

'Come here,' I say.

I move towards him, so close that I can smell the soft scent of his aftershave. Getting my face close to his, I feel his breath on my lips. My heart is beating so fast as I pull closer until our lips are practically touching.

At first, I give him a peck on the lips and pull away slightly to check his reaction. He doesn't appear too disconcerted, so I move in once more.

This time his body reacts positively. He meets my lips even though the plaster on his nose is getting in the way slightly.

His mouth opens and so does mine and there it happens. We are finally kissing, a bit like the airplane moment only with much more intensity.

As we kiss, I feel complete, as though he is the missing piece of a jigsaw.

It is something very special.

I have no idea how long we are standing there as the next thing I know I hear clapping. Pulling away from each other, I open my eyes to find Sian and Rob laughing and clapping at us.

'Thank God for that,' shouts Sian.

Jamie grabs my hand tightly and looks at me with his familiar smile.

'Sian told me how you felt. We had a good chat. I was going to ask you on a date myself later, but I wanted to have a few drinks first to give me some Dutch courage,' he says.

'I have been sweating all morning, wondering how I was going to approach you. That Sian! I warned her not to speak to you,' I say.

'You know Sian, always meddling,' Jamie says with a laugh. 'Truthfully though… I love you so much, Amelia. Always have, always will. I didn't mean what I said on the card. I knew exactly what I was saying on the plane. Why has it all taken so long? Why didn't we do this before?'

'Because it wasn't the right time.' I smile. 'Love is all about timing. It has to be the right time,' I explain.

Rupert and Jasper are coming out of the blacksmith's when they see us.

'Mummy and Uncle Jamie are holding hands,' says Rupert.

'See, I knew they'd get married,' says Jasper.

'We're not married,' I quickly pipe up.

'No, but you should be. Why don't you get married today while you're here?' says Rupert.

'Okay, enough, boys,' I say. 'We're definitely not getting married today. We're going to take things very, very slowly.'

'Yes, we've waited over thirty years for this – we don't believe in rushing things.' Jamie laughs.

I look up at Jamie and laugh too. As I do so I notice that his mouth looks like the Joker, as my lipstick is all over his face.

'You look so funny.' I smile. 'You should see your face.'

I go into my little clutch bag to find a tissue.

'Here.' I am moving to wipe his face when I spot some writing on the napkin.

I had forgotten this was in here. I suddenly remember that this was the bag I had used in the Japanese restaurant in New York. I had put the paper napkin in there to show Patrick what the fortune teller had written on it, but I didn't get to tell him.

I stare at the words she wrote.

> *Your future husband is in New York… It took a long time to get together.*

Nine Months Later

Chapter 47

Laugharne – one big happy family

'Who wants pancakes?' I ask.

Rupert and Jasper put their hands up. Jamie does too.

'Okay, three pancakes coming up,' I say.

'Do you want to make some for Sian and Rob? They should be here any second,' says Jamie.

'Good idea, now she's eating for two she doesn't stop,' I reply.

They are due over for breakfast shortly, something that is now a Saturday morning ritual. However, they expect to be a little later today, as Sian had her scan at 9am. At first she assumed she was nauseous because of the oysters at her hotel in Barbados, then, when she missed her period, she thought it must be the menopause. She made me go to the doctor with her as she was so scared.

'What if I get more facial hair and I suffer from hot flushes?' She had quizzed the doctor before he could even examine her.

Fortunately, Dr Johnson wanted to rule out pregnancy before answering any questions and made her pee into a pot. She later had blood tests, which also confirmed that she was very, very pregnant. I am not sure who was more excited, me, Sian or Ivy.

She will make an amazing mother, and Rob will be a great dad. I am so thrilled for them both. She will be the most fun mum ever, provided she doesn't have a ditzy moment and forget her baby somewhere, like she always does with her sunglasses.

'Did you see my last scan on Facebook? I just posted it on the way over,' Sian says as she and Rob sit down.

'No, I've been busy making the pancakes,' I reply.

'Have a look. I already got twenty-five likes on the way from the hospital to here. I wish bump would hurry up, though, that's what I would like.'

I put the pancakes down on the table, along with the Nutella jar – which is half full. Now that Jamie is here, I leave it for the boys to enjoy. I can't resist a tiny teaspoonful though; some habits are hard to break completely. However, thanks to my running and my mostly healthy diet my jeans finally fit and I don't want to jeopardise that.

'Boys, this isn't a good example, okay. I really shouldn't use my phone at the table, but it's a special occasion,' I say. 'I have to look at Sian's little baby in her tummy.'

However, the boys are far too busy eating their pancakes to notice anything I say or do.

Logging onto Facebook, I notice there is a message. I do wonder if I should open the message first but, as there is a baby scan involved, I head to Sian's page and click 'love'.

'There you've got one more reaction now.' I smile.

I check the message while I am logged in. It is in my 'other' folder, so nothing that can't wait. In fact, I am not going to open it as I assume it is spam, but then something makes me look twice.

Hi Amelia,

I don't know where to start…

A lady called Roxanne wrote a newspaper article a while back appealing for me. I was in Guatemala, helping turtles, at the time and only just got back to NY. My cousin showed me the newspaper upon my return. I remember the day we met. The shopping you left in the cab… (I won't embarrass you!) and the moment I saw the most beautiful girl in the world. I hoped that you would call me, but you never did. I took this photo of you as you headed into Tiffany's. I hope it brings back memories.

I no longer work as a calligrapher. I do a lot of volunteer work and spend most of my time overseas, so I never married or met anyone special. Unless you count Henrietta, the cutest Hawksbill turtle you ever did see! Did you know people are harvesting turtles and such species are becoming extinct? It's heartbreaking.

Anyhow, I hope to hear from you soon, Amelia. I am so sorry it has taken you so long to find me. I always hoped we would meet again and felt, in my heart, that fate would one day bring us back together.

Love always,

Patrick x

I look at the photo he has sent. It has a crease in the middle where it has been folded. There is no denying that it is me. I sneakily look at Patrick's profile; his teeth were perfect. So, he was perfect. Then I remind myself; nobody is perfect, Amelia. However, I can't deny that he is very handsome, according to the profile picture of him holding a giant turtle.

He was a calligrapher and not a journalist. It all makes sense. The beautiful writing, his pen…

'Are you okay?' Sian asks.

'Yeah, fine,' I say, touching the heart locket around my neck.

'You don't think there's something wrong with my scan, do you? I'm so worried that I'm an older mum,' says Sian.

'No, not at all,' I say. 'It's nothing. I'm absolutely fine and it's definitely not to do with baby, okay,' I reassure her.

I take a deep breath and look at Jamie across the table. He is ruffling Rupert's hair.

'Not long now until Mum starts school like you guys,' says Jamie.

'Yes, I'm so proud of Mum going to school when she is sooooo old,' teases Rupert.

'Mummy will make a great dementa nurse,' says Jasper.

I can't help but laugh at his pronunciation.

'She will indeed, boys,' agrees Jamie.

'Aww, thanks, you lot, I can't wait to get started in uni as a very mature student.' I laugh. Thank goodness for student loans.

They move the conversation to the yurt trip we have booked next month. They are all so excited.

As they chat amongst themselves, I know immediately what I must do.

I happily press the 'DELETE' button and erase the memory of Patrick once and for all.

Like I have always believed, relationships are all about timing.

A letter from Helga

Wow, what can I say? I am unbelievably thrilled to be writing you this letter. Thank you só much for choosing to read *Twice in a Lifetime*. This is my debut novel that I started writing back in 2015. This book is for women everywhere who have faced difficult times and had no choice but to remain highly tenacious. It is also a book about decisions and how the choices we make shape our lives and the lives of those around us.

It has always been my dream to become a published author, and my dream has finally come true. Thanks to Hera, the reader will now meet Amelia, a mother who desperately tries to hold everything together whilst her life falls apart. Although she juggles school runs with falling apart, Amelia also has some funny moments along the way. The book also features a very handsome New Yorker, a Nutella and creme egg addiction, and Robson Green gets a mention too. I had lots of fun writing this as I laughed at some of the escapades that Amelia and her best friend, Sian, got up to. It also brought back many memories of growing up with my best friend and the perms and shell suits that we dared to wear.

Although I have now written my second romantic comedy, this debut will always remain precious.

I do hope that you will enjoy this book and my zany sense of humour. I would love to hear your thoughts in a review. I am also very responsive on social media, so please don't hesitate to contact me. You can contact me via:

www.twitter.com/HelgaJensenF
www.facebook.com/helgajensenfordeauthor
www.instagram.com/helgajensenauthor

Once again, thank you so much for your support and for reading *Twice in a Lifetime*.

Acknowledgements

An enormous thank you to Keshini and Lindsey at Hera and the wonderful editors involved in bringing this story to the readers. None of this would have been possible without you.

Thank you to Nicolas Forzy and the many informative events held at the Emirates Airline Festival of Literature (EAFL) for teaching me all I know. The first chapter of this book was one of the winning entries in the EAFL Montegrappa First Fiction Competition in 2017, so I also have to say a huge thank you to Luigi Bonomi and the team for such a fantastic opportunity. Also, thank you to the very fabulous agent, Jonathan Lloyd, who I had the privilege of meeting at EAFL. Your words always inspired and motivated me.

A thank you must also be said to the Romantic Novelists' Association (RNA) and the reader who went through my early draft. The RNA is an excellent organisation, full of lovely writers.

Of course, I must say an enormous thank you to JK for being so wonderful when I'm working away in the study; and for the fish fingers that you randomly deliver to ensure I eat a balanced diet!

Thanks to my fantastic cheerleading team, my Gulf Air girls (particularly AB447), we struck lucky the day we all met.

To all my other fabulous friends who relentlessly support me, where would I be without you? Some of my writing inspiration may have come from the antics Sam Jones and I got up to growing up, but the less said about that, the better!

Suzie gets a special mention for being particularly amazing and putting up with my dramatic moments, love you.

To my lovely writing friend Jenny, your turn next.

Thank you to a very kind and generous English teacher, called Mrs Nicholas, for spending her time ensuring I got that English GCSE. I swore I would pay her back somehow. Not sure if this is quite what she would have imagined!

Also, thank you to a very supportive sea lion (long story!) and lucky trolls; everyone should have one!

On a more serious note, this is a special mention to those who sadly didn't make it to see this book published. To my mother, Brian, and my beautiful friend Avril Scourfield, an extraordinary lady who will not be forgotten. Also, remembering Teddy and Tommy, thank you for all the joy you gave me over the years. Always in my heart.

Finally, a humungous thank you to my readers for giving up your valuable time and money to choose to read this book. I do hope you will enjoy it.

Happy reading!

xoxoxo